I knew she was strange. I knew she could get violent. But I hadn't thought she'd come after me here.

I walked over to the stone fireplace to read the plaques mounted above it. As I stood reading, I heard footsteps behind me. Hector's here, I thought, and turned around.

Kirsten stood in the middle of the floor, wearing black sweat pants and a black tank top, her long blonde hair pulled back hard and gathered into a pony tail. Despite the cold, despite her bare arms, she didn't shiver. She put her hands on her hips.

"I warned you to stay away from him," she said. "Twice."

Calm down, I told myself, and looked at her directly. "You don't want to try anything here," I said. "It's a park, for God's sake. It's a public place."

She moved her eyes to the left and the right, smiling a small, tight smile. "It's a public place," she said. "But no one's here. Just you and me."

"Hector's arriving any minute. You don't want him to see you acting crazy."

"Hector's been delayed. He's got car trouble." Again she glanced left and right, not moving her head, not taking her focus off me. "This must've been beautiful once. What a shame vandals kept defacing it. Those damn teenagers. And now a mugging. A fatal mugging. Those damn teenagers."

She's a doctor, I reminded myself. Yes, she's a black belt, and yes, she's got some bizarre obsession with Hector. But she's an intelligent, educated woman. I can reason with her. "Kirsten, stop and think. You've got a successful career, a reputation to protect. Why risk all—"

She screamed and sprang forward.

American Sign Language interpreter Jane Ciardi's life changes when she takes a job from a Cleveland private detective and agrees to keep tabs on a deaf African-American teenager whose odd behavior alarms her wealthy father. Jane also needs to discover the truth behind two murders—including the murder of the first interpreter the detective hired.

To get closer to the teenager, Jane joins a fitness center owned by a family that brings new meaning to the word "dysfunctional." The more Jane learns about the center, the more she suspects some people go there to get more than a workout. Somehow, she realizes, the fitness center's secrets are connected to the two murders and to the deaf teenager's odd behavior. Jane's struggle to unravel all the secrets tests her resourcefulness, her loyalties, and her courage—but will that be enough to save her life?

KUDOS for *Interpretation of Murder*

In *Interpretation of Murder* by B. K. Steven, Jane Ciardi is a ASL (American Sign Language) interpreter who is hired by a private detective to get close to a deaf girl whose father is worried about what she is getting into. Jane quickly gets in over her head. Not only is she concerned about the ethics of an interpreter essentially spying on a deaf person, but people start dying and Jane is afraid she'll be next. The book starts out strong and captures your attention immediately. There are lots of twists and turns in the plot that will keep you turning pages until the end. ~ *Taylor Jones, Reviewer*

Interpretation of Murder by B. K. Stevens revolves around an interpreter for the deaf who is desperate for an interpreter job since no agency will hire after she was a whistle blower on a court case where the interpreter lied to the court about what the deaf person was saying. As a result, she takes a job with a private investigator, even though she is unsure if the job is ethical. Her mission is to befriend a deaf girl and report on her activities, since the girl's father is worried about her and the company she is keeping. In order to get close to the girl, Jane applies to the same upscale health club, only to discover that the deaf girl and her boyfriend are involved in some very dangerous activities that could get them all killed—Jane included. I enjoyed this story very much. It gives you a glimpse into the world of the deaf, a world that most of us can't even imagine. It has to be so hard for deaf people to exist in a world that is so dominated by those of us who can hear. The plot is strong and will keep you riveted, and you'll learn a lot while you're at it. ~ *Regan Murphy, Reviewer*

INTERPRETATION OF MURDER

B. K. Stevens

A Black Opal Books Publication

GENRE: MYSTERY-DETECTIVE/WOMEN'S FICTION/ROMANTIC ELEMENTS

INTERPRETATION OF MURDER

Cover Design by B. K. Stevens

Print ISBN: 978-1-62642-59-2

First Publication: APRIL 2015

Published by Black Opal Books **http://www.blackopalbooks.com**

DEDICATION

In memory of

Cathleen Jordan

Editor, *Alfred Hitchcock's Mystery Magazine*, 1981-2002

Chapter 1

"To be fair," he said, "I should tell you the last person I hired for this job got killed. Probably, it had nothing to do with the job. Probably. So. You interested?"

You can't afford to be picky, I'd told myself, not after the way you've messed up. If a chance for a paycheck comes along, take it. But I didn't like that second "probably."

"You haven't told me what the job involves," I said. "I assume you have a deaf client, and that's why you need a sign-language interpreter."

"Nah, the client's not deaf."

To me, Walt Sadowski didn't look much like a private detective. I don't know what I'd expected, but it hadn't been this—a marginally heavy, unevenly balding man, fifty or so, big black-rimmed glasses parked on a broad, bland face.

He sat forward. "His daughter's deaf. She's nineteen. Nice enough kid, her dad says, but rebellious. Lately, she's been acting weird. He's afraid she's mixed up in things that could hurt her."

Already, I'd started to feel uncomfortable. "So you'd like me to talk to her?" I said, knowing that probably wasn't it. "To sign with her, that is, and find out what's going on?"

He shook his head. "Her dad says the direct approach won't work. So I've been following her on and off, keeping track of where she goes and who she sees. The problem is, I can't tell what she's talking about, because she doesn't speak. Bugs won't work, tape recorders, anything I'd normally use. Now, she's got this boyfriend, and they spend lots of time together, waving their arms around and stuff. If I knew what they're saying—"

"Just a minute," I cut in. "You want me to spy on her? I can't. It's not ethical. Interpreters keep their clients' communications absolutely confidential."

"She's not the client. Her father is. And it's not like he's trying to repossess her car or something. She's a teenager, for Pete's sake, and he's worried sick about her. How is it unethical to help a father protect his kid?"

I thought back to the ethics class I'd taken two years ago. In every situation we'd discussed, the deaf person was the client. If the client's a hearing person, does that make a difference? Would it matter that I'd be trying to help? I lifted my hands. "It doesn't feel right. And is it legal? Don't private detectives have to be licensed?"

"Hell, I'm not asking you to detect anything. I'll handle that. You'd just be—well, providing a service. Like if I was working on a case, and I came across something written in a foreign language, and you translated it. That's all."

Not the world's most convincing analogy. "I don't know. This isn't something interpreters do."

"Look, Miss Ciardi," he said and stopped. "Okay if I call you Jane? Jane, I know it's unusual. That doesn't make it wrong. And the client says I gotta hire an interpreter right away, and the other people who applied are nowhere near right. So don't say no yet. Here, I'll get you more coffee. Plain, right? Two packets of sweetener?"

He ambled off. I wouldn't have expected Walt Sadowski to pick this place for the interview. It felt too trendy for him. Ginger's Pantry is a coffeehouse that caters to people in their twenties and thirties, the kind of place with big fruit-studded muffins, fussy little pastries, and lots of syrups and foams and sprinkles to keep the coffee from tasting like coffee. At 3:30 in the afternoon, the long, narrow room wasn't crowded: a few couples, chatting quietly; two teenaged boys, poking at iced concoctions and looking bored; a young woman, brooding over her laptop; a tall young man sitting at a table near the counter, constantly checking his watch. Well, maybe Walt Sadowski thought this would be a comfortable setting for me, since at twenty-nine I match the place's demographics neatly. And he might've figured I'd rather meet him in Shaker Heights than drive to his office in downtown Cleveland.

He returned to our table and handed me my mug. "I'll tell you about the case. Maybe you'll get interested."

"It's not that I'm not interested, Mr. Sadowski. But I have serious ethical reservations."

"Call me Walt. And I know you got reservations." He stopped stirring his coffee and looked up. "You're not a nun, are you? You look like a nun."

I got that a lot, and no wonder—my long auburn hair pulled back from my face and twisted into a coil at the nape of my neck, my simple black dress with its high neckline and long sleeves, absolute minimum makeup, no jewelry, no buttons.

"This is how we dress for work. It's to reduce distractions, to help clients focus on our hands and faces when we sign. I thought you might want me to interpret today. No, I'm not a nun." Though for the last eight months, I thought, I might as well have been one, considering how flat my social life had been. But he didn't need to know that.

"Good," he said. "Not that I have anything against nuns. Some of my best teachers were nuns. But if you were one, that might add to the ethical reservations. Anyway, like I said, the father's worried. For one thing, he doesn't like this boyfriend she's been hanging around with the last few months."

"What's wrong with the boyfriend?"

Walt lifted a shoulder. "For one thing, he's white."

"Oh. And your client, I take it, isn't?"

"African American—though when you meet him, don't say `African American,' or he'll go on for an hour about how he's not African, he's just American, and `Black' makes him feel plenty proud. It's sort of a thing with him. A word to the wise."

"I'll remember that. If the boyfriend's race is the only problem—"

"It's not. He's also too old for her. He's twenty-seven. And when the girl's that young, an eight-year difference—it makes a difference. Plus he's sorta low class. And the client's high class, a lawyer, really rich, senior partner in a big firm downtown. He doesn't want his daughter dating some loser with tattoos and no regular job. This boyfriend works part-time at a cousin's garage, part-time at a pizzeria. Plus he teaches martial arts at a community center. That's how he and the daughter met."

"Martial arts?" My interest picked up. "Which art?"

"Hell, I don't know. Karate, judo, one of those. Anyhow, the daughter found out he knew sign language—he's not deaf, but he's got a deaf brother, that's how he learned—so she started taking classes. Now, that right there is weird. She's never cared about sports. Her dad's big on sports, always wanted her to go out for one, but she wouldn't. Then suddenly she starts going to these classes twice a week, and a month later she joins a fitness center."

"That's not so weird." A difference in age, a few tattoos—so far, this didn't sound like an emergency. "A martial arts instructor who signs is rare. I can see why she'd get interested. As for the sudden interest in fitness, maybe she wants to lose weight."

"She doesn't need to. She's already thin." He looked up as the door opened behind me, as a shaft of October cold cut through the spicy warmth of the restaurant. "See? There she is."

Two women walked past us. The younger one had cinnamon-colored skin, her dark hair pinned back on one side, falling beneath her shoulders in tight-clustered curls. The other woman, in her mid-twenties, was pale, with short, carefully sculpted blonde hair. Both women were pretty, both on the short side, both flawlessly slim. They joined the man who'd been checking his watch, and the younger woman rubbed her fist against her chest in a circular motion—*sorry*. The man shrugged it off. She pointed to the other woman, and a flurry of signs followed, including some finger spelling. He shook the blonde woman's hand and walked off to get coffee.

I glared at Walt. "That's not fair. You're trying to draw me into taking the job. You didn't say the client would be here."

"She's not the client," he reminded me. "And I didn't know for sure she'd come. Her and the boyfriend sometimes meet here around this time on Mondays—it's near that fitness center—but sometimes, they don't. I thought if they did, it'd be a little audition for you, like. So? What'd they say?"

They hadn't said much. It seemed prissy to refuse to tell him. "She apologized for being late, and she introduced them. She finger spelled the woman's name. It was fast, and too far away to be sure, but I think it was Jenny Linton. And the man's Sam Ryan?"

"That's right." He seemed delighted by this tiny confirmation of my skills. "Say, you'll be great at this."

"I'm not sure. Even if I decide it's all right ethically, I don't know how good I'd be at interpreting from a distance, from odd angles, when the person isn't looking at me. And I don't see how I could watch them closely enough without being obvious. They'd spot me in minute."

"You'd be surprised what people don't notice. Just don't stare, don't crane your neck. Keep a low profile. And from now on, don't wear an interpreter's outfit. Dress like normal people."

The two women didn't communicate much while Sam got the coffee. Evidently, Jenny didn't sign. There were some smiles, some words jotted on a small spiral pad, some nods as they admired each other's manicures. I wasn't sure of the younger woman's name. Sam had greeted her with what could be a name sign for "Rose" or "Rosa" but could also be a private term of endearment.

When Sam returned to the table, I got to work—not craning my neck, not staring, keeping a low profile. I hadn't decided to take the job, and I hadn't forgotten about the interpreter who'd been killed, but I couldn't help enjoying the challenge.

Unfortunately, Sam sat with his back to me. He did most of the speaking, most of the signing. He seemed to be addressing himself primarily to Jenny, signing so the younger woman could follow. I watched for five minutes and then shook my head.

"It's no good. I can't see his hands well enough. I catch a word from time to time, but I can't put anything together. Is the deaf woman's name Rose?"

"Rosa. You can see her hands, can't you?"

"Pretty well, but she's not saying much, just *that's right*, *good*, and *go ahead—ask her*, things like that. She—wait. She just signed *promise*. She turned to Jenny and signed *promise*, in a very emphatic way. But I can't tell what the conversation is about."

"What about Jenny? What's she saying? You can read her lips, right?"

"No, I can't read lips. Lots of deaf people can't, either, at least not well. It's harder than most people think. And I've had no reason to learn, since I can hear."

He frowned. "You work with deaf people. You oughta know how to read lips."

What did he think, that deaf people and interpreters communicated by silently mouthing words at each other? Forcing down my irritation, I tried to focus on the mix of sign and speech at the other table. But the two teenaged boys who'd been fiddling with their drinks kept distracting me. They'd noticed the signing and clearly considered it hilarious: they mimicked it with bizarre, exaggerated gestures, twisting their faces into ugly grimaces. Rosa had her back to them, and Sam was too caught up in the conversation to notice, but I felt ready to walk over and slap their silly faces.

With an effort, I concentrated on Rosa's table again. Sam didn't look so unsavory. He was two or three inches over six feet and obviously built. Even his back looked muscular. The glimpses I'd caught of his face had been enough to let me see the attraction: strong, good-humored features, olive-tinged skin, a sweetly unruly mop of light brown curls. I hadn't spotted any tattoos, so he must have them in reasonably discreet places. True, he wore earrings—large, dark, button-shaped ones. Rosa's father probably didn't like those. Walt Sadowski probably didn't, either.

Sam leaned forward over the table now, his eyes fixed

on Jenny Linton's face. Rosa took her cell phone from her purse and held it toward Jenny, showing her something. A text message, photos, a video? Sam kept his signs low and small. I couldn't make out a single word.

"I don't know what Sam just said to Jenny," I said, "but it upset her. See? She's blushing, shaking her head." Rosa crossed her arms across her chest and tapped her shoulders. "Now Rosa's getting upset, too. She just told Sam to take it easy."

He didn't take the advice. Instead, he grabbed the cell phone, bringing it closer to Jenny. She stared at it, then stood abruptly and headed for the door. Sam looked at Rosa. She swung her arm out and brought her fingers together in a sign even Walt could have interpreted: *Go*. Sam nodded and took off, following Jenny out of the restaurant.

"That didn't go so well," Walt commented. "I wonder what he showed her, what he said to get her so worked up. Jenny Linton, huh? She sure is pretty. Rosa's father gave me the names of some of her friends, but he never mentioned Jenny Linton. You sure you got the name right?"

"Pretty sure." I doubted Jenny was a long-time friend. She hadn't met Rosa's boyfriend before, and she and Rosa hadn't developed an efficient way to communicate. But somehow Rosa had persuaded her to come here, apparently so Sam could ask her questions. *Go ahead—ask her*, Rosa had signed. Ask her what?

Walt's cell phone rang, and he glanced at it, grimacing. "I'd better take it. It's a client. It's confidential. I should step outside."

"I'll wait." I glanced back at Rosa, who was bent over her cell phone, texting furiously. At the next table, one boy slapped his friend on the arm and pointed toward her. He said something, his friend laughed and shook his head, and the first boy spoke again. Then the second boy stood slowly, looking at Rosa. I looked, too, and saw the purse sitting on the floor behind her, ignored as she focused on her message. Bastard, I thought. Sneaking up on a deaf girl, snatching her purse—what could be safer? What a great joke to brag about to his disgusting little friends.

He moved quickly now, reaching her table in a few strides, scooping up the purse, heading for the door. Without thinking, I stood up, putting one hand on the table for balance. When he got within range, I lifted my right leg and pivoted, then snapped the kick out to connect, not gently, with his stomach. He doubled over, the air knocked out of him, with a loud half-gasp, half-curse. People sitting nearby took notice, pointing and exclaiming. Rosa looked over in time to see me grab his wrist and twist it back far enough to make him drop the purse.

"It doesn't go with your outfit," I said. Then I let him go.

He looked at me wildly before running out of the restaurant, his friend seconds behind him.

I picked up the purse and brought it to Rosa. "*I think this is yours*," I signed.

I don't know what surprised her most—the fact that she'd been robbed, the fact that she'd gotten her purse back, or the fact that I'd signed to her. For a second, she looked stunned. Then her face broke into a slow, delighted smile, and both her hands flew to her chin before spreading out and down in a wide, emphatic *thank you.*

A man from behind the counter, probably the manager, hurried over, asking if something was wrong. I explained what had happened, signing as I spoke so Rosa could understand. Several customers called out to confirm what I said. Others lifted their fists to signify approval. This would make a perfect story to tell at the dinner table: A petite woman who looked like a nun kicking an oversized teenaged boy, rescuing a deaf girl's purse. I saw Walt Sadowski watching us, arms folded across his chest, shaking his head. The probable-manager apologized, assuring me the restaurant was usually safe, offering to call the police but looking relieved when I said not to bother. He turned to Rosa with shrugs and smiles that expressed regret with reasonable eloquence.

"Two free lattes!" he shouted, running to the counter. Customers applauded. Rosa and I looked at each other and laughed, both embarrassed but also, I think, a little thrilled by the sliver of action that set this afternoon apart from others.

I smiled. "*I'm glad I could help*," I signed, and held out my hand.

She shook it but looked distressed. "*Please, sit down. I want to thank you again.*" She gestured at my clothes. "*You're an interpreter?*"

"*That's right. I'm Jane Ciardi.*"

"*Rosa Patterson. Are you a black belt*?"

I shook my head. "*The highest belt I have is red, in tae kwon do. But I've taken kickboxing, too, and tai chi.*"

She widened her eyes. "*You must be really good. I'm learning sogu ryu bujutsu.*" She finger spelled it. If there's a sign for *sogu ryu bujutsu*, it's news to me. "*It's a mixed martial art. My boyfriend teaches the class—he can sign. You should come.*"

I lifted my shoulders. "*Mixed martial arts*? *Too rough for me*."

"*No, you'll love it.*" She grabbed her spiral pad and jotted down an address. "*Tomorrow night at 7:00. It's fun. Will you come*?"

I accepted the jagged-edged paper and tried, frantically, to think through the implications of what had happened. I'd be no good to Walt as a spy now. Was that the end of the job? Or would he want me to spy at closer range? I didn't want to deceive Rosa or betray her trust. But what if she really did need help?

I stuffed the paper into my purse. "*Maybe*," I signed, and gave her a business card. She thanked me again and left. The probable-manager, appearing with two lattes heavy with whipped cream and chocolate shavings, seemed disappointed that Rosa had gone. I consoled him and carried the lattes to the table where Walt sat waiting.

"Great job at keeping a low profile," he said, as I'd known he would. "But maybe this is good. That piece of paper—her phone number? She wants to get together?"

"She wants me to come to the martial arts class Sam teaches."

"Good," he said. "You saved her purse, she's grateful, you've got a common interest. That's all good. That's better than trying to decipher signs long-distance and hoping she doesn't notice. It'll be an undercover deal, like. You get close to her, she confides in you about what she's up to, you report to me, I—"

"I'm not sure I can do that. Ethically, it's still problematic. And I need to know more about the other person you hired. He was an interpreter, too?"

Walt's shoulders moved up and down in a hedging, hesitant motion. "Not officially. He wasn't certified, like you. He was a senior at Cleveland State. Journalism, I think. But he knew sign language. He took two semesters, to get out of taking French or Latin or whatever. When I interviewed him, he really knew what he was talking about."

And how could you possibly evaluate his skills? I wondered. How could you possibly tell whether he knew what he was talking about? "Then he got killed. That's the part I want to know about. How did that happen?"

Walt grimaced, picked up a spoon, and skimmed a

layer of cream from a latte. "It happened a couple weeks after I hired him. He was following Rosa on his own, and he said he was making progress. He never had much to report, though. Then, last week, he got killed. Too bad. Nice kid. The cops decided it was a burglary gone bad."

A burglary gone bad. I'd come to hate that phrase. The court case that pretty much ruined my interpreting career had eventually been shrugged off as a burglary gone bad. "What happened?"

Walt grimaced again. "It was a Saturday night. The cops say it looks like he'd been out, and someone was burglarizing his apartment. Then Gary came home and surprised the burglar. And the guy basically beat him to death."

Dear God. "Was Gary rich? Did he have a lot of things worth stealing?"

"Some things." Walt had worked his way down to the actual latte. He took a skeptical sip and set down his mug. "The burglar took his laptop, his roommate's laptop, some cash, like that. And he made a mess, ripped things apart. So the cops had good reasons for saying it was burglary. And you got no reason to worry."

I probably didn't. A drug addict desperate for a fix might break into a student's apartment, might get panicky enough to kill if the student walked in. I shouldn't let that scare me away from a paycheck. I took the job.

I felt pretty good about the decision as I drove to Little Italy, waitressed for five hours, and drove back to Richmond Heights through the slow, sleet-like rain, a double order of chicken marsala in a Styrofoam container seat-belted into the passenger seat. I continued to feel pretty good as my roommate and I split the chicken and watched Conan O'Brien, as I signed for her when the closed captions didn't do justice to a joke. Abby thought the job sounded exciting. "*Another freelance client,*" she signed. So what if the stupid agencies wouldn't place me? I could be my own agency. I could set my rates lower than theirs and drive them out of business. She'd design a website for me, and business cards, and letterhead. She already had some great ideas.

That got me excited, too. My own business, I thought. I'll be an entrepreneur. I'll show those damn agencies. I'll damn well make them damn sorry. I pictured the agency directors cursing themselves, and felt more excited than ever.

I didn't stop feeling excited until I got up the next morning and turned on the local news—until I finished making coffee and looked up to pay closer attention to the report about the dental hygienist who had drowned last night. That's when I saw the picture of the slim, pretty young woman with short, carefully sculpted blonde hair. She'd been found in the Cuyahoga River, the report said, downstream from the entertainment area called The Flats. I didn't have to wait for the closed captions to confirm the victim's name. It was the woman who came to Ginger's Pantry with Rosa yesterday, the woman who rushed off when Sam asked her a question she didn't want to answer and showed her something she didn't want to see. Jennifer Linton.

Chapter 2

I sat on my haunches, arms crossed against my chest, feeling my mouth go dry, feeling the sweat start on my forehead. This is not going to happen, I thought. It's impossible.

Sam stood next to me, bending over slightly, his hands resting just above his knees. "Now, tuck your chin," he said. "And close your mouth, so you don't bite your tongue. Then relax and let it happen."

I kept my chin tucked but shook my head. "I can't. It's counter-intuitive."

"You'll be fine," he assured me. "You're so close to the floor that you can't hurt yourself, even if you do something wrong. But don't stick out a hand or elbow. Don't try to break the fall. You don't need to break it—it won't hurt. And try to distribute your weight over your whole body when you hit the mat. Now. Take a deep breath and let yourself roll back."

All around me, people were falling—falling straight forward, falling straight back, falling on their sides. A few other cowards were starting from their haunches, but most were starting from a standing position, throwing themselves down without hesitation, slapping the mat with their hands as they landed, jumping up, and falling again. Eight-year-old children were doing it. A heavily overweight woman in her sixties was doing it. I seemed to be the only person in the room who realized it was impossible.

"Come on, Jane," Sam urged. "Learning how to fall is important. Someday, it could save your life."

Not very likely, I thought. Squeezing my eyes shut, I swayed back maybe an inch before straightening up again.

"Almost," Sam said. "Next time, just let go. Be the fall."

Be the fall? Had he actually said that? Good grief. If I'd wanted that kind of New Age crap, I'd have stuck with tai chi. But my legs were getting cramped, and I felt ridiculous staying in this position for so long. I clenched my teeth, tried to throw myself back, made it less than halfway, and stuck a hand out to stop myself, landing on my behind, not my back.

Sam sighed. "Pretty good. We'll try again Thursday. Want to join the group practicing kicks?"

"Fine," I said. Anything I can do on my feet, I thought.

Rosa stood nearby, hiding a smile behind her hand. "*Nice job*," she signed, and I winced. I can spot an insincere sign when I see one.

Kicking went much better. I was more advanced than the other students in my group, and the instructor gave me ego-soothing compliments. Sam moved from group to group, dispensing advice and encouragement. There were seven or eight deaf students, the youngest around ten, the oldest around forty. Word of Sam's special expertise must have spread through the deaf community. Probably, some of these people had been interested in martial arts for years but never had a chance to learn. Not that Sam's signing was pure American Sign Language. He had a large ASL vocabulary, but his grammar was a freewheeling mix of ASL and English, with improvised gestures and facial expressions thrown in. That wasn't surprising, if he'd picked signs up from a deaf brother but never studied ASL formally. The students had no trouble understanding him.

When class ended, the three instructors led us in the bowing-out ritual, with Sam signing the commands the others shouted. He was a good instructor, I'd decided, even though he hadn't gotten me to fall. Probably, not even a private lesson with Chuck Norris could inspire me to do that.

As students filed out, I thanked Rosa for recommending the class, and Sam joined us. We both signed as we spoke so Rosa could understand.

"I hope you weren't discouraged," he said. "It *is* counter-intuitive to let yourself fall. But once you get past the mental part, the physical part's easy."

I nodded, not convinced, and turned to Rosa. "*Was it hard for* you *at first*?"

"*Not really*." She seemed sorry to admit it. "*I always thought it was fun. You won't give up, will you*? *You'll keep coming*?"

I turned both hands palm up, moving them up and down slightly as if weighing something in a balance, making my facial expression mildly doubtful. It was somewhere between *probably* and *maybe*. Walt Sadowski had told me to take every opportunity to spend time with Rosa and find out about what was going on, and he'd promised to pay for the class. True, when I'd heard the news this morning, I'd thought about walking away. Jenny Linton met with Rosa and Sam yesterday, they had a disagreement, she ran off, and she died hours later. I'd worked hard to convince myself the other interpreter's death was a coincidence. I didn't have much energy left for convincing myself this second death linked to Rosa and Sam was a coincidence, too.

I'd called Walt. He'd seen the report, he'd said He'd look into it and talk to me tonight. That gave me enough confidence to show up for class, not enough to make a long-term commitment.

"I hope you *do* keep coming," Sam said. "You've got a flair for martial arts. Your kicks had real power, real focus."

"Thanks. Not as high as they used to be, though. I'm out of shape."

"You know what's great for limbering up?" he said. "A stretching machine. Do you have access to one?"

I shook my head. "I've seen pictures. They look like fun."

Rosa's face brightened. "*You should join my club, the Elise Reed Fitness Center. It's got all kinds of machines, pools, even an ice-skating rink.*"

I'd never been to the Elise Reed center, but I'd heard of it. It was named after a Cleveland celebrity, a figure skater who won both gold and silver Olympic medals in the sixties, then came home to marry a local high-school football coach and raise a family. I remembered the commercials I'd seen as a child: Ray and Elise Reed Connolly and their three flagrantly fit children holding hands as they strode through the gleaming center, the immense fountain near the main entrance graced with a marble statue of Elise Reed at her moment of greatest Olympic glory—body bent back impossibly far, one leg poised in the air, arms stretching up joyously. It'd been years since I'd seen those commercials, but the image stayed sharp in my mind. I shook my head. "I can't afford a place like that," I said and signed.

Rosa pushed the objection aside with a scrunched-up nose and a wave of her hand. "*There's a really cheap one-month trial membership. You apply online and then come in for an interview. You can always drop out at the end of the month. Or maybe you'll find a way to keep coming.*"

One month of working out at a first-class fitness center—that could do me a lot of good. It seemed dishonest to accept a trial membership if I couldn't afford to join when the month ended, but who knew? Maybe, by then, my business would take off. And joining would give me a chance to get closer to Rosa, to get her to open up. Whatever the trial membership cost, Walt would pay. If I stick with the job, I reminded myself. And if I do, this membership will be one hell of a fringe benefit.

"*Maybe.*" I made my sign less doubtful this time.

Back at the apartment, Abby asked how class had gone. I gave her a quick summary, promising details later. Right now, I had to call Walt.

"I looked into it," he said. "I talked to a friend on the force and asked about Jenny Linton."

"Do the police feel sure it was an accident?"

"Pretty sure. Or suicide, but they didn't find a note. And she went to The Flats a lot. According to her roommate, for the last six months or so, Jenny went out two or three nights a week, usually to the Flats—got all dressed up, stayed out late. She didn't have a boyfriend, the roommate said. She'd taken to hitting the clubs alone."

The lack of a boyfriend could explain the increased interest in clubbing. When Abby and I go clubbing, we say it's because we feel like dancing. That's more dignified than saying we're scouting for boyfriends. But when we meet men who looked like prospects, we don't complain. I wouldn't go clubbing alone, though, and I seldom go to The Flats. I always go with Abby or another friend, and I generally stick to the suburbs. Jenny must've been braver than I am. She probably could've fallen backward in a martial arts class, too. "That's what she did last night?"

"Yeah, the cops found her car parked outside an east bank bar. So it looks like she had a few too many, maybe went outside because she felt sick to her stomach, ended up in the river. It's happened before, you know."

Yes, I knew. When I was in high school, whenever my mother lectured me about boys and drinking, and anything else that sounded like fun, she'd speak darkly about the drownings at The Flats. In the eighties and nineties, The Flats, a low-lying area on both the east and west banks of the Cuyahoga, had been the center of Cleveland nightlife, packed with thriving bars and restaurants, with comedy clubs and theaters and micro-breweries. Then, in 2000, in just one month, three people drowned in separate incidents. Politicians demanded investigations; places got shut down for safety and health violations; reports of violent crimes increased; people stopped coming. Since then, repeated attempts at revitalization keep nudging this spot and that spot back to life. But the Warehouse District has taken over as the most popular entertainment destination, and the memory of those drownings still shades conversations about The Flats.

"I know about the other drownings," I said. "On the noon news, they were the focus of attention. Thirty seconds about Jenny Linton, five minutes of background about the drownings and speculation about whether bad times are coming back for The Flats. So Jenny had been drinking?"

"I got that impression, yeah. My friend didn't say so flat-out."

"You didn't ask him flat-out? Why not?"

Walt sighed. "Because I didn't want to seem too interested. Then he'd ask why I cared, and who knows where that might lead? I sure as hell didn't want to drag Rosa's name into this, get cops hounding her because she had a blow-up with Jenny the day she died. So I accidentally ran into my friend at this place he goes for lunch, bought him a burger, steered him toward gossiping about Jenny, backed off when he changed the subject. In this business, you gotta protect the client. That's priority number one, always."

But someone had died. Shouldn't finding out the truth about that be priority number one? Walt obviously had his own code of ethics.

"Are the police considering the possibility that someone pushed Jenny into the river?" I asked. "Did your friend say anything about that?"

"Not a word. But I'm sure they're questioning people who were at that bar. My friend seemed to assume it was an accident, though. Like those other drownings."

Yes, that was the natural assumption. The police, the media, the public—all were bound to see Jenny's death as just another tragic drowning at The Flats. If this *had* been murder, the killer had found a clever way to mask it. I chewed my lip in frustration. "What else did you learn about Jenny? She was a dental hygienist, right?"

"Yeah, in Beachwood. I went there this afternoon, said I had a monster toothache, begged an emergency appointment, and chatted up the receptionist while I waited for the dentist to fit me in."

"That was smart," I said.

"Smarter than I thought. Turns out I had an abscess ready to burst, didn't even know it. Novocain's still wearing off."

"Did you find out how Jenny knew Rosa?"

"Only connection I found was she went to the same fitness center Rosa does. The Elise Reed Center. She started going there last spring. I said that sounded like a pricey place for a dental hygienist, and the receptionist said Jenny got a cheap trial membership."

Blood doesn't literally run cold. I know that. But I felt a definite chill spread through me. "That's for only one month. After that, she would've had to pay full price. I know, because Rosa suggested I get the same kind of membership."

"Hey, that's great. She must really like you. So you can get this trial membership, hang out with her, find out—"

"Hold on," I said. "Jenny Linton got a trial membership and probably hung out with Rosa at this center. Now you want me to do the same thing?"

"Hell, what're you thinking? That someone pushed Jenny in the river because she hung out with Rosa? Or are you thinking Rosa pushed her in? That's nuts."

It *did* sound nuts. "So you're convinced there's no connection between Jenny's death and Rosa—or Sam?"

"I got absolutely no reason to think so. And I don't think there's anything dangerous about you joining that center."

I didn't really think so, either. Neither Sam nor Rosa struck me as a homicidal maniac with a bizarre fetish for luring women into joining a fitness center and then pushing them into the Cuyahoga. And if I wanted to start a business, I had to build a client base. I couldn't walk away whenever problems came up. "All right. I'll apply."

He signed off. Abby had made tea. I took a mug gratefully and filled her in on the details.

She frowned. "*He's not telling you everything he knows about Rosa and Sam.*"

"*Probably not,*" I agreed. "*Walt doesn't know me from Adam, and I keep going back and forth about taking the job. For all he knows, I'll quit tomorrow and spread gossip about his client's daughter. I bet he's telling me just as much as I need to know to do my job.*"

"*He didn't tell you much about the interpreter who got*

killed, either," Abby pointed out. "*Not even his last name*?"

"*Only his first name. Gary.*"

Abby headed for her computer and started typing key words: "Gary," "Cleveland State," "burglary." She got plenty of hits. While she skimmed and printed articles, I went to the kitchen to search cupboards and refrigerator. I'd worked for Cathy's Cleaning Crew today, salvaging an apartment vacated by tenants who skipped out after not paying rent for two months. It'd been a smelly, grungy catastrophe, and I hadn't had time for more than an apple on my way to martial arts. Now, it was time for serious food. I didn't find much to work with, only odds and ends, but reached for the wok.

By the time I returned to the living room, carrying a serving bowl and two plates, Abby sat curled up on the couch, going through articles with a yellow highlighter and a red pen, her usual tools for marking up everything she read. Abby's very visual. I don't know if that's connected to her deafness, or if it's another side of the artistic nature that makes her such a good graphic designer. She looked at the bowl warily.

"*Now what*?" she asked.

I handed her chopsticks. "*Salami stir-fry. Just smell it. How can you resist that smell*?"

She looked at the steaming heap of salami and shallots, of grape tomatoes, green beans, water chestnuts, and raisins on a bed of couscous. "*Do I have to*?"

"*One taste. I want your opinion.*"

Her first bite was tactlessly reluctant. By the third, she'd lifted an eyebrow in mild approval. "*I didn't know we have sweet-and-sour sauce.*"

"*We don't. That's marmalade, with a little lemon juice and brown sugar. Plus cornstarch and red pepper flakes. What do you think*?"

"*Don't patent it,*" she advised. "*But it doesn't taste as bad as it looks.*"

As we ate, I read. Gary Nichols had been twenty-one, a Toledo native, a journalism and promotional communication major. He'd been beaten to death by a burglar just over a week ago, on Saturday, October fifteenth. His roommate, out of town for the weekend, found the body on Sunday. The police had determined that the burglar had picked the lock to the third-floor apartment, but they had no definite suspects.

I turned to articles that appeared a few days later, in the *Cleveland Plain Dealer* and the *Toledo Blade*. Gary's roommate said what a great guy Gary was. A professor spoke of his enthusiasm, of his dreams of becoming an investigative reporter for a big-city newspaper. High-school teachers and friends told stories about his work on the school paper, his sense of humor, his community service. Abby had printed several pictures. They were blurry, as pictures produced by computer printers usually are, but still gave me a distinct sense of a slight, lively-looking young man with reddish-brown hair curling over his collar, eyes dark and eager behind his wire rims. Such a shame, I thought, surprised to realize I'd misted up. The Toledo paper had published an interview with his parents, but I couldn't stand to read that, not yet.

I looked at Abby, who was re-reading the professor's interview, and touched her arm to get her attention. "*What do you think?*"

She gazed at the article. "*He wanted to be an investigative reporter. I bet he was excited about working for a private detective. I bet he thought it'd be good experience.*"

"*True.*" Probably, I thought, private detectives do some of the things reporters do: asking questions, gathering information, drawing conclusions. But Gary's job had been limited to following Rosa and observing her communications. "*Walt said Gary never had much to report.*"

"*Maybe Gary didn't report everything he'd seen. Maybe he held some things back.*"

That made me laugh. "*I never realized you're so suspicious. You think Walt's holding something back, too. Do you think everyone's holding something back?*"

Abby shrugged. "*It's usually true.*"

Good point. When I'd answered Walt's ad, I'd listed the agency I used to work for on my resume, letting him think I'm still an interpreter in good standing. "*Do you think Gary discovered something damaging about Rosa? Or Sam? Why wouldn't he tell Walt?*"

Abby shrugged again. "*Maybe he was keeping it for himself, for a story. If it was really juicy, it'd be a great way to introduce himself to the* Plain Dealer."

I stared at her. "*You* are *suspicious.*"

"*I'd make a good private detective. Maybe you should be* more *suspicious.*" She glanced at her watch. "*I'm going to video-relay my mother. You should call your mother, too. It's been over a week.*"

"*Soon,*" I signed, not sure I meant it.

After Abby left the room, I leafed through the articles again and then picked up the least-blurry picture of Gary Nichols. It seemed silly to think this slightly goofy-looking college kid had discovered anything significant while squeezing part-time detecting in between classes. It seemed downright absurd to imagine he'd discovered something potent enough to get him killed. And Rosa and Sam seemed so friendly and open. Could they have a secret they'd kill to protect? I pictured Sam working patiently with the deaf students and then tried to picture him beating Gary Nichols to death. No. Sam had the physical strength to do it, but the act didn't fit with anything I'd seen or sensed. Rosa was probably strong enough, too, but that image was so ridiculous I didn't even try to conjure it up.

I started gathering articles together, then paused, got a piece of paper from the printer, and jotted down Gary Nichols's address, the names of his roommate and the professor who'd been interviewed. I should be more suspicious, Abby said. Maybe I'd see if I could find out more about what Gary Nichols had learned while following Rosa and Sam. Walt wasn't likely to tell me. If I wanted that information, I'd have to go after it myself. And, for reasons I couldn't put into words, I did want it, very much.

Chapter 3

The Elise Reed Fitness Center worked fast. It had to be 10:00 at night when I clicked "Submit" on the online application for a trial membership. At 10:00 the next morning, the phone rang. The associate director had read my application, a woman said. Could I come for an interview this afternoon? Would 1:00 work?

Since I didn't have any jobs lined up all day, it worked fine. At 12:45, I sat in a reception area leading to three private offices, flipping through a fitness magazine, trying not to feel intimidated by the perfectly toned arms and thighs flexing across its pages. I supposed the furniture was stylish. It was definitely stark. The reception desk looked like a command center, rounded and metallic and huge, enclosing the receptionist on three sides. She looked up briefly when I came in and then got back to slicing through envelopes with a brass-bladed letter opener that looked like a dagger—just as long, just as sharp.

Four narrow metal-framed chairs lined one wall, hard black plastic seats shooting back and down at a sharp angle, hard black plastic backs too low to support anything more than a few inches above the waist. There were no arm rests. No one could slouch in these chairs. These were chairs designed for people who never slouched, who sat only when absolutely necessary, who perched restlessly for a few moments before speeding off to the next calorie-burning, muscle-building activity. The room had nothing cushioned, nothing soothing, no wood, no fabric, no plants, no nonsense. One piece of art hung above the desk, a large unframed square on which thin black triangles spiked upward against a gray background. For some reason, it made me feel like doing pushups.

The outer door opened, and a woman entered, around thirty, comfortably plump, thick blonde curls framing a sweet, round face. Squeezing into a chair, she introduced herself as Emily Davis. Like me, she was applying for a trial membership. She was a high-school guidance counselor, she said, and was up for promotion to assistant principal. When I commented on her diamond ring, she said she was getting married in April. I described my shaky constellation of jobs and talked about the martial arts class, about not having the nerve to fall, and she laughed just enough to show she appreciated the humor, not enough to make me feel like an idiot. She asked intelligent questions about interpreting, and I asked about the frustrations of working with teenagers. It was three or four notches above pleasant chat. I liked her immediately.

Shortly before one, another woman walked in, tall and broad-shouldered and tanned, everything flat that should be flat, everything rounded that should be rounded. Her sleeveless black top revealed deltoids and biceps and triceps that must have been sculpted during long, vigorous hours in the gym. I couldn't call her pretty—her features were too blunt and unyielding—but she was striking, her ice-blue eyes large and penetrating. Her hair, pale blonde and absolutely straight, fell halfway to her waist. It might not have been the best choice for a woman who seemed to be in her late thirties—it did nothing to soften her features—but it added to the total Amazon effect. The receptionist looked at her with what might be awe.

"He's on the phone, Dr. Carlson," she said, "and he has appointments."

The woman gave her a quick, confident smile. "It's okay," she said, and walked into the associate director's office without knocking.

Ten minutes later, she came out and gave Emily and me an appraising look. She shook my hand. "I'm Kirsten Carlson. I'm a member here. And you're…"

"Jane Ciardi. I'm applying for a trial membership."

"I know. That's great. This is an incredible facility. It's open twenty-four hours. Did you know that? And the people are fantastic. We're like one big, happy family. Good luck, Jane. Hector can see you now." She glanced at Emily. "Hi," she said, and left.

The associate director's office, like the outer office, featured sleek metallic furniture, including, I was sorry to see, more of those nasty chairs. There were personal touches, too—family pictures, a glass case packed with trophies. Not that I paid much attention to the décor. I paid more attention to the associate director.

He seemed to be in his early thirties, slim and quietly muscular, just over six feet, with short sandy brown hair, a broad forehead, and a chin that was probably too narrow for perfect symmetry but brought his face to a definite, intriguing climax. His eyes held me most—large, blue-gray, intelligent and intense but brightened by humor. I'd love to see what those eyes look like when he laughs, I thought.

He stood up. "Welcome to the Elise Reed Fitness Center. I'm Hector Connolly. Please, call me Hector."

I shook his hand. "Connolly—that's the name of Elise Reed's husband, isn't it?"

"Right. I'm one of their sons." He pointed to a large

photograph on the wall, showing a family in winter gear, holding skis, backed by snowy slopes. Big, handsome Ray Connolly stood at the center, flanked by petite, lovely Elise Reed Connolly and two beautiful little boys. A petulant, plain preteen girl stood off to the side. "That's my favorite picture of our family. It was taken in Montana. We spent a week there every winter, until Dad died."

"I'm sorry. I didn't know he'd passed away."

"Yeah, it didn't get much press." He gazed at the photograph before turning to me with a determined smile. "It was a car accident, eighteen years ago. We still feel his influence here every day, though. We're a total fitness center, Jane, and that means more than exercise. It means whole-hearted commitment to a healthy way of life. Commitment—that's one of the three principles my father instilled in the teams he coached, and one of the three core principles of our program."

He handed me a red-and-white brochure with *Commitment, Competition, Character* emblazoned in gold. "I see," I said, not knowing what else to say. It'd feel silly to agree commitment, competition, and character are good.

"Dad believed it all starts with commitment—to a team, a goal, a way of life. That's strengthened through competition. You compete with yourself, sure, to achieve your personal best, but you also compete with others. It's the only way to motivate yourself to achieve still more. And that combination of commitment and competition creates character."

This time, I simply nodded. It seemed to me that building character involves more than just commitment and competition. I had to wonder, too, if Ray Connolly's core principles might've been different if he'd been less intent on alliteration.

But I didn't say so. I wanted that trial membership.

"So, that, in a nutshell, is the Elise Reed Fitness Center philosophy." Hector smiled again. "Let's talk about you. I see from your application you've studied martial arts since college, and you're taking *sogu ryu bujutsu* now. That's the kind of long-term commitment to fitness we want to see. How do you like *sogu ryu*?"

"I like the combination of techniques—the emphasis on joint locks and pressure points, for example, as well as kicking and punching. I think that's a more realistic approach to self-defense." I smiled self-consciously. "There's also an emphasis on knowing how to fall. I don't like that so much."

He grinned. "That might take some getting used to. It's great you're trying." He looked at the print-out of my application. "And you say you like to cook and experiment with recipes, and you also enjoy dancing. Ballet? Jazz?"

"No lessons since middle school. Now, it's social dancing. Club dancing."

"Great way to work off tension. And calories. Now, about your employment situation. You say you're an ASL interpreter and list an agency as your employer. But the agency says that while technically you're still on the roster, it hasn't given you an assignment in several months. Something about an ethics dispute?"

Damn. I'd hoped he wouldn't bother calling, not for a one-month membership. "Yes, but I didn't do anything unethical. I filed—"

"That's okay." He held up a hand. "None of my business. But we do have an interest in whether you can afford the trial membership and whether there's a chance you can handle a regular membership when the month is over."

"The trial membership's no problem. I have three part-time jobs and often work over forty hours a week. Also, I'm actively looking for a full-time job, and I do free-lance interpreting. I'd like to start my own business."

"Great. Of course, to start a business, you'd need to put together some capital. In this economy, that's tough. But maybe you'll find a way. Or maybe you'll find a job that lets you combine all your interests."

Does such a job exist? "Maybe," I said, "I could cater dance parties for deaf martial artists."

He laughed, and it did wonderful things, not only for his eyes but also for his mouth, his chin, his whole face. "Perfect. Now, the center has several special memberships: Home-Away-from-Home memberships for people who come to Cleveland on business, Take-a-Look one-day memberships for people who want to check out the facility. The one-month trial membership is *really* special, only twenty percent of the regular price. You even get a free Try-It-Out tote bag." He grinned, acknowledging the silliness of the sales pitch. "In return, we expect a commitment to total fitness. That means no tobacco, no street drugs. And alcohol and caffeine in moderation, if at all."

"Tobacco and street drugs are no problem. I've never been tempted by either. As for alcohol and caffeine, I strive for moderation." And with caffeine, I thought, I fail, every day.

"Fine." He made a note. "If you get the membership, we'd like you to schedule an appointment with our nutritionist and sign up for a team activity. Since competition's a core value, we have lots of team sports. That sets us apart from most centers." He paused, evidently thinking it over. "Our mixed volleyball club's a favorite with lots of members. I participate myself. Do you think you'd enjoy that?"

If I'll get to see you in shorts and a sweaty tee-shirt, I

thought, I'll enjoy it a lot. "That sounds like fun."

"Great. I should tell you it meets Sunday mornings. Is that a problem? What I mean is, are you a regular churchgoer?"

"Not regular enough to satisfy my mother."

He chuckled. "So when you go, it's only to please your mother."

"Not really. I enjoy the music, and the memories. But right now, spiritually—I guess I'm drifting." The same way I'm drifting with work, I thought, and relationships, and everything else. The conversation had taken an odd turn. I decided to lighten it. "Actually, these days, most services I go to are Jewish. My roommate got me a job interpreting at her synagogue. She's the only deaf person in her congregation, though, so if she doesn't go, there's no work for me. Poor thing—she used to go once or twice a month, but now she goes every week. She says she's not going just so I'll get paid, but I bet she is."

"She sounds like a good friend. So, your application says you're single. Will your boyfriend mind if you spend lots of time at the center?"

That was clumsy, I thought, and felt that tightening in my stomach I get whenever I think a man might be interested in me. He wants to know if I have a boyfriend, I thought. Does he want to know if I'm available? "Actually, I don't have a boyfriend right now."

"That's hard to believe." He looked up, and the warmth in his eyes made my stomach tighten again. Possibly, I thought. Definitely, possibly interested.

"I was engaged for almost three years," I said. "But that ended months ago, and there's been nobody special since."

He nodded sympathetically. "Guy turned out to be a loser, huh?"

"Not at all. But we finally realized there must be a reason we both kept finding ways to put off the wedding, and it was probably a good one."

He seemed pleased. "Yeah, there's a lot to be said for freedom. Let's talk about your fitness goals."

He went on to recommend machines I should try. Poor Emily, I thought. She's been waiting in that wretched chair a long time. I felt sure I'd get a trial membership. Hector wouldn't go into so much detail if he didn't plan to give me one.

As we were finishing, the office door opened, and a man walked in. He hadn't knocked, hadn't waited for the receptionist to announce him. Same build as Hector, same forehead, same chin—disloyal as I felt to think it, he might've been even better looking. But his eyes were angry, not amused. He gave us a brief, technical smile. "Sorry to interrupt, Hector, but I need to speak to you about these proposed accounting changes."

Hector's mouth twitched. That was the only sign of displeasure. "Fine," he said. "As you can see, though, I'm busy right now. I'll be with you soon. Jane, this is my brother, Jason. Jason, this is Jane Ciardi. She's applying for a trial membership."

Jason looked me over, giving me another smile—a smile with a smirk in it, a smile that made me feel as if he knew something unsavory about me. "Yes, I heard. Nice to meet you, Jane. I'm sure you'll get that membership, and I'm sure you won't mind if I barge in. Our sister, Diana, is right outside in the reception area. She'll show you around the facility and answer any questions you might have. How does that sound?"

I looked from one Connolly to the other. They're bookends, I realized—one standing, one sitting, but a matched set, each furious at the other and trying not to show it. Jason's smile had broadened but not warmed. His arms stayed at his sides, tensed, elbows at sharp angles, fists clenched. As for Hector, the relaxed, confident man I'd been chatting with moments ago had vanished. His back had gone stiff, his face had gone blank, and both his hands pressed down hard against his desk, fingers spread and arched. After years of interpreting, I've come to listen to what isn't said, to pay attention to hands and faces. These brothers don't like each other much, I thought. Time to get the hell out of here.

I forced a light tone. "It sounds fine," I said, "unless Hector has more questions for me."

Hector smiled, aiming his words at me but still staring at his brother. "That's all right. I have all the information I need. You'll hear from me soon, Jane. Thanks for coming in."

He walked me into the reception area and introduced me to his sister. I looked at him as he walked back into his office, shutting the door behind him. Poor baby, I thought. He's got some sort of hold on you, doesn't he? You're probably in for a rough time.

Diana Connolly shook my hand with three measured, powerful up-and-down movements. Everything about her seemed rigid—rough-hewn face, big-boned build, short straw-colored hair, severe black pantsuit "It's a pleasure to meet you, Jane," she said. "Let me show you the facility. This way." She took off without ever meeting my eyes directly, each stride equal to at least two of mine.

I shot a sympathetic glance at Emily, who was shifting an inch this way and an inch that way, flexing her shoulders, trying to adjust her bottom, not having an easy time with the chair. I hope I see you again soon, Emily, I thought, when we both get our trial memberships. Then I hurried after Diana.

She walked down the hallway briskly, pointing things out as we passed them. "Rock wall to your left, racquetball court to your right. And this is where the spinning classes meet. As you can see, it's outfitted with large-screen plasma televisions, so you won't get bored if you work out on your own."

Twenty stationary bicycles were ranged in neat rows, but I saw only one woman pedaling away. Well, on a weekday afternoon, most people would be at work. "Everything looks new," I commented.

"Yes, we update constantly. Every piece of equipment is state of the art. Let's move on."

She pointed out other exercise rooms and offices. Twice, staff members came to her with questions. Diana was the chief financial officer, she'd said, but she seemed to know everything about every facet of the center, to be the person everyone sought out for advice about everything.

"There's someone I want you to meet," she said, pushing open the door to another reception area. "Let's see if she's in."

A man of sixty or so stood by the desk, holding a ledger. Like everyone else at the center, he seemed in perfect shape. Even in a suit and tie he looked solidly athletic, his gray hair trim, his face calm and intelligent.

"This is Paul Kent," Diana said, "my mother's senior advisor. Paul, this is Jane Ciardi. She's applying for a trial membership."

He lifted an eyebrow. "How do you do? And I'm sorry, Diana, but if you're hoping to introduce her to your mother, it's not possible. She felt weak, so I drove her home. By the way, I was about to call you. Jason heard about the accounting changes you and Hector want to make. He has some concerns."

"I believe he's expressing those concerns to Hector now," Diana said, dryly. "I told him we'd all meet in my office at four to discuss them. I'd like you there."

His brow creased. “Or we could wait until tomorrow, so your mother can come.”

“There’s no need to bother Mother with this. We’ll settle it.”

“All right.” Shaking my hand, he looked at me more closely. The corners of his mouth lifted slightly. “A pleasure, Miss Ciardi. I imagine I’ll see you again.”

Diana and I walked back into the hallway. The upper floor of the Reed Center is a mezzanine, allowing the building’s central core to shoot straight up from ground level to skylights, allowing the cold October sunlight to pour down uninterrupted. Pausing, we gazed at the main level as Diana pointed things out—the fountain with its statue of Elise Reed, gyms, pool, daycare center, café, double doors leading to the ice rink. I spotted Jason Connolly standing by the reception desk, conferring with a petite gray-haired woman.

“That’s Greta, our main receptionist,” Diana said. “She’s a treasure, but don’t start a conversation with her if you need to get somewhere. She does tend to talk. There’s the elevator, going up to this level, down to the parking garage. It’s for members with disabilities or injuries. Hector wanted to make it a rule that able-bodied members must use the stairs at all times, but Jason and I thought that’d be going too far.”

“Jason, Hector, and Diana. You all have names from classical mythology.”

Diana smiled, barely. “Yes, our father loved the old myths. He didn’t read much, but he loved reading about the old myths. He didn’t read actual epics or plays, only collections of stories probably intended for middle-school students. He wanted us all to have strong myth names—Jason, heroic leader of the Argonauts; Hector, Troy’s most valiant defender; Diana, goddess of the hunt.”

She didn’t seem to regard her father with the same

reverence Hector had shown. "Those *are* strong names," I said stupidly.

"So it seems." Again, her thin lips twisted into a joyless smile. "But Jason betrayed his wife, and she paid him back by killing their sons, cooking them up in a stew, and serving them to him for dinner. Hector got killed in single combat, and his body was dragged seven times around the city he couldn't save. And Diana? Diana was a virgin goddess. No husband, no children, nothing of her own. Maybe, if Father had read actual epics and plays all the way to the end, he'd have chosen different names."

This time, even a trite reply seemed risky. So I kept gazing down. I saw Rosa walk in, gym bag slung over her shoulder. Jason took notice immediately. Planting himself in her path, he placed his open hand on his right cheek, bringing it up and out in an awkward but enthusiastic *hello*. Smiling, Rosa returned the greeting. Then Jason stepped back, moving his head up and down in an exaggerated way, making it clear he was looking her over. He spread his fingers in front of his face and brought them together under his chin. "*Pretty.*" Rosa laughed, put one hand to her chin, and brought it out and down an inch—a rather reserved "*Thank you.*"

Probably, that exhausted Jason's ASL vocabulary. He reached into his shirt pocket, took out a folded sheet of paper, and handed it to Rosa. She read it, hesitated, then nodded. Smiling broadly, Jason put his arm around her shoulder, and they walked toward the café. Even from the mezzanine, I could see the broad gold glint of the wedding ring on his left hand.

I heard a sharp intake of breath and looked at Diana. She was scowling. She'd seen the interaction, too, obviously, and she obviously didn't like it.

Neither did I.

Chapter 4

This is the most shameless thing I've ever done, I thought. But I knocked on the door anyway. A gangly young man opened it, yawning. He had chin-length curly brown hair, with bangs so long they half-hid his eyes. His white tee-shirt looked two sizes too big, and his loose, knee-length blue shorts bagged and wrinkled.

I smiled. "Good afternoon. I'm Jane Ciardi. Are you Brian Plummer? Gary Nichols's roommate?"

"Yeah." He pushed the hair out of his eyes. "Damn. Are you, like, a friend of Gary's? Do you know what happened to him?"

"Yes. I'm sorry about the loss of your friend. I'm also sorry to trouble you about something that may sound trivial." Here comes the lie, I thought. "I met Gary three weeks ago. I'm an American Sign Language interpreter, and he came to an event where I was interpreting—a talk by a visiting journalist, at John Carroll University?"

I raised my voice at the end, making the statement into a question, and paused, as if waiting for Brian to say Gary had mentioned the talk. Brian shrugged, the best response I could hope for. At least he hadn't declared that Gary never attended such an event, that there had never been such an event. In fact, there hadn't.

I took a deep breath. "After the talk, Gary introduced himself and said he did some interpreting, too. We talked awhile, and I lent him a dictionary of ASL idioms. Did he mention it?"

"No." Brian took a moment. "Damn—a book. And he never returned it, and you want it back?"

"I'm sorry. It must seem petty, considering what happened. But I used that book in my certification classes. My notes are in it. It's a thick blue paperback. Have you noticed it?"

"Nope. But I'm packing up his stuff for his parents. You can take a look."

I stepped into a tiny, dark living room, curtains pulled tight against the afternoon sun, no lights turned on. Clothes were draped on chairs, on the television, on objects too shrouded by stuff to be identifiable. Shoes and pizza boxes littered the floor. The only neat spot was a nearly empty bookcase. "My goodness," I said. "The burglar really ripped this place apart."

"What?" Brian looked up from a box he'd been opening. "Oh. No, the burglar didn't do much in here. This is how it always looks. Anyhow, I put Gary's books in this box. Maybe you can find yours."

He dumped about twenty books onto the floor—not, of course, including my dictionary, which sat safely on a bookshelf in our apartment. I crouched and made a show of searching.

Brian stepped back. "You know, Gary had sort of a crush on you. He was bummed about you not returning his messages."

That made me drop a book. "He never left me messages."

"Sure he did. I heard him." Brian raised his pitch in what I assume was an imitation of Gary's voice. "'Jane, please call back. I want to talk.' 'Jane, I just need five minutes.' He called you like six, seven times."

What was this—*The Twilight Zone*? "You've got me confused with someone else."

"No way." He shook his head. "He kept it up every night, the whole week before he got killed. He was, I don't know, mysterious about it, wouldn't tell me who this Jane was. I kept giving him a hard time about his new girlfriend, and finally he laughed and said, 'She's not my girlfriend. She's too old for me. But she *is* hot.'" Brian leered. "That's gotta be you, right?"

"No. We spoke only once, after the talk at John Carroll." It was hard to sound convincing when the whole thing was a lie.

"Look," Brian said, tolerant but insistent, "I understand you being embarrassed about not calling back, now that he's dead and all. But don't tell me he didn't call you." He yanked a calendar—I think it featured cats and dogs in sado-masochistic poses—from the wall, flipped to the last page, and handed it to me. "There. Is that your phone number?"

I stared at the page, labeled "Very Important Puppies." Across the columns for names, addresses, and telephone numbers, someone had scrawled with green felt-tipped pen: a small heart enclosing "RP" and "SR," a thick triangle with "Jenny—292-3635" in the center. My God, I realized. Rosa Patterson and Sam Ryan. And Jenny—Jenny Linton, the woman who drowned. It had to be. This linked the two dead people to each other, linked them both to Rosa and Sam. I memorized the phone number before handing the calendar to Brian. "It's not my phone number. And it's not my name. I'm Jane, not Jenny."

Brian stared at the calendar, stared at me, stared at the calendar again. "My bad. Who'd have thought Gary met two hot older women with names beginning with *J* right before he got killed? Sorry. Find your book?"

"I'm afraid not." I re-packed the box, pausing to smile ruefully at a dog-eared copy of *All the President's Men*. Naturally. If Gary dreamed of being an investigative reporter, that book would be a favorite. It looked like he'd been rereading it—he'd stuck a bookmark in it. Idly, I looked at the bookmark. A broad, laminated, red strip. *Elise Reed Fitness Center*, it said in bold white letters. *Take a Look!* And there was Gary's name printed on a label plastered to the strip, and there was the date. Saturday, October eighth. So Gary had bought a one-day pass for the center, one week before he died.

"Too bad," Brian said. "But I haven't gone through Gary's closet yet. I'll watch for your book, call you if I find it."

I made myself smile. "Thanks. I'm sorry about Gary. He seemed nice. He talked about wanting to be a reporter and said something about working on a big story. He talked so fast that I couldn't follow him. Do you know what the story was?"

"Nope. But he *was* working on something special, so special he wouldn't talk about it. Usually, Gary couldn't shut up about stuff he was working on. This was different. When I'd ask him about it, he'd say, 'Wait and see.' It probably wasn't a big deal. Gary could get all worked up, think he was uncovering some international conspiracy or something. But it always ended up being nothing."

Maybe not this time. I sighed. "Then he got killed by a burglar. Did the burglar steal much?"

"Yeah. My laptop, Gary's laptop, my high-school class ring, Gary's IPod, this gold watch Gary inherited and kept in his sock drawer. Plus I had almost two hundred in cash in an empty juice can in the freezer. He even found that. But some stuff he took was weird. He cleared out Gary's desk—notebooks for his classes, essays, everything. He went through my desk, too, took some used flash drives. How much are *those* worth? Is that weird, or what?"

"It's weird." I struggled to keep the theories under control. Had Gary discovered something while watching Rosa? Had the burglar tried to scoop up whatever evidence Gary found? How might Rosa be involved, and Sam, Jenny Linton, the Reed Center? I gave Brian my card. "Thanks for offering to call if you find my book."

He looked at the card, looked at me, and grinned. "Maybe I'll call, anyway. Gary wasn't the only one who could appreciate hot older women. I mean, it's quicker with older women, right? No bothering with all the where-are-you-from, what's-your-major crap, because you've already done that, like, a thousand times."

Oh, God. I looked at him—messy hair drooping over lazy eyes, baggy tee-shirt, wrinkled shorts, vacant leer. True, I was desperate for some social life. But there were limits. "I'm a nun," I said. "Bless you, my child." I made the sign of the cross and left.

I found Professor Craig Morris in his office and steeled myself for more lies. This time, I didn't claim I'd met Gary, only that I'd read about his death, I knew he did some ASL interpreting, and I wanted to write a profile of him for an interpreters' online newsletter. This way, if I felt too guilty about the lies, I could actually write the profile and submit it. Not that the newsletter would print it, since it never prints profiles of interpreters. But Professor Morris didn't know that, and I figured a journalism professor would want to help someone working on an article. I was right.

"Gary was special." Professor Morris sat back, crossing his legs. "A solid writer—not outstanding, but he'd made progress since his freshman year. A good researcher, too, though he got impatient with research sometimes, rushed to confrontation before he had enough information. But his writing and research didn't set him apart. His enthusiasm did. So many students are cynical in an easy, thoughtless way. They want to be cool, so they never take anything seriously. Not Gary."

I took notes furiously. In all the movies I'd seen, reporters took notes. "Some people I've spoken to said Gary was working on an article he was especially excited about. But nobody knew what the article was about. Do you?"

He chuckled. "Yes and no. He was doing an independent study with me, writing an investigative piece about irregularities at the local veterans' administration office. But I don't for one minute believe that's what he was really working on."

I looked up from my notes. "Why not?"

"Because I suggested it." He smiled a sad, affectionate smile. "In the three years I knew him, Gary never liked any topic I suggested. He always wanted something bigger, something sexier. When we started this independent study, it was the same thing. I suggested the veterans' administration piece. Gary hated it. It was boring, he said. He'd find something better. Weeks went by, he hadn't settled on a topic, and I said he had to make up his mind. Then, suddenly, he said he loved the veterans' administration idea. After that, every time we met, he said he was making progress. But he never showed me anything. He didn't seem anxious, though. He seemed as happy and excited as I'd ever seen him, and with Gary, that's saying a lot. I felt sure he was working on some other project, something he didn't want to tell me about yet. And any day he'd come bounding into my office, plunk some article he saw as ground-breaking on my desk, and tell me to notify the Pulitzer committee."

He tried to look amused, but his eyes were too soft,

and he'd picked up a pencil and was turning it over and over in his hand. Poor man, I thought. He's really grieving. "I'm sorry," I said.

He nodded, still smiling. "Thanks. As I said, Gary was special. Make sure that comes across in your profile. I'll miss him." He tried to broaden his smile but didn't make it. "And now I'll never know what the real article was about. That damn kid."

I drove to the apartment, feeling horrible. In two hours, I'd told at least two dozen lies. I almost never tell that many lies, not even when I talk to my mother. And I'd stirred up painful memories for Professor Morris, and I'd asked Brian to keep searching for a book that'd never come near his apartment. I didn't have to feel too bad about that one—now that Brian thought I was a nun, he had no motive to search. I felt awful about the rest, though.

And now I had Jenny Linton's phone number. No big deal. Chances were, I could've gotten it from the phone book. But since I'd come across it in such an unusual way, I felt obliged to use it. What should I do—call her roommate, tell more lies? I couldn't even think of lies to tell. Table it, I decided. Use the phone number later, if you can find a way to use it intelligently.

Inside the apartment, two voice-mail messages waited. In the first, Hector Connelly said I'd been approved for a trial membership, and he'd set a "Try It Out!" tote bag aside for me. He hoped I'd come to the volleyball game Sunday, he said, and joked about hoping my mother wouldn't bully me into going to church instead. It wasn't funny, but his tone was so charmingly self-deprecating that I laughed out loud. I'd have to raid my tiny savings account and shop for volleyball outfits.

In the other message, Walt Sadowski said he hoped my interview at the Reed Center went well and urged me to call if I had anything to report. And I should come to his office at 3:00 sharp tomorrow to fill out tax forms.

Irritated, I hung up. I was all for filling out tax forms if it helped me get paid, but why 3:00 sharp? His secretary would just hand me the forms.

She could do that any time. In fact, 3:00 fit neatly between two jobs, but I didn't like being bossed around. Then there was the question of whether I should report anything that happened today. Probably, yes—Walt was the one qualified to decide if information was significant. But he was keeping secrets from me, doling out information on a need-to-know basis.

Why should I be in a hurry to tell him everything? And he probably wouldn't like it that I'd done some investigating on my own. No need to report anything now, I decided.

Now, I wanted to shake the day off, to put the lies and doubts behind me, and to think about nothing. I looked down at my dress and frowned. Today, I'd worn a slightly modified version of my interpreter outfit—hair pulled back, dark colors, high neckline. I'd wanted to look steady and fiscally responsible when I'd interviewed for the trial membership. When I'd talked to people who might still be mourning Gary, I'd wanted to look respectful. But enough was enough.

Shaking off the day meant shedding the uniform. I plucked out the imprisoning pins, tossed my head back, and brushed until my hair fell beneath my shoulders in full, loose curls. My most flattering jeans, my most daring red silk top, dangly red earrings—I examined myself in the mirror and felt liberated. No more Sister Jane.

When Abby got home, she turned toward the kitchen and sniffed. "*No garlic. I thought Wednesday's pasta night.*"

"*The pasta's at Geraci's,*" I signed. "*Get changed.*

I've got to get out. Then let's go someplace where we can dance."

"*Fine with me. I had doubts about tuna ravioli anyhow.*"

Minutes later, she came out of her room, wearing a short black skirt and a silvery top, possibly more daring than mine. A friend had told her about this place in The Flats, she said, called Lemmings. The house band turned the bass up so high the walls shook. You could really feel the vibrations in your legs, your chest, everywhere. How about going there after dinner?

The Flats—not the ideal destination if I wanted to shake off the day. "*And who's this friend who told you about Lemmings*?" I asked. "*The mysterious Nate*?"

Abby smiled. "*Maybe.*"

She'd met him two weeks ago. And he was about the right age, he was a professional, he was Jewish, he was deaf—for Abby, that was a potent combination. If he had even half the personality of a doorknob, she'd marry him in a heartbeat. Obviously, we were going to Lemmings. I opened my hand and touched my thumb to my chest. "*Fine.*"

By the time we got there, the crowd had reached a decent size, and the walls were in fact shaking—not surprising, since they looked as sturdy as your average sheet of card stock. The club consisted of one large room, predictably dark, with low ceilings, neon outlines of guitars on the walls, a raised platform for the band, a tiny dance floor, a long bar along one wall, and plenty of battered wooden tables scattered about. In back, a deck stretched out over the river, each table with a hurricane lamp in the center, each candle flickering enticingly. It had a high railing. These days, every deck at The Flats had a high railing. But no one had ventured out, maybe because people preferred the crowded warmth of the bar to the bracing cool of the deck. Or maybe, after what happened two nights ago, people wanted to keep their distance from the river.

Minutes after we found a table, a man came over—Nate, of course. Abby introduced us, shrugged apologetically, and headed for the dance floor. I watched them move and laugh in easy harmony. Seems like a nice guy, I thought. I wished Abby well and ordered a drink.

The need to dance no longer felt as sharp. I'd get to it, but for now listening and watching felt like enough. I spied on couples, enjoying glimpses of courtships—some frantic, some slow and awkward, some comfortable and happy. I shifted my attention to the bar. That blonde woman looks angry, I thought. Did someone stand her up? The girl in the aqua tank top looks too young. Did anyone check her ID? And that man looks familiar.

He was an inch or so over six feet, with olive-tinged skin. His light brown hair was slicked back, and his gray sports coat looked expensive. Gold wire-rim glasses, a gold watch—

Damn, I thought. He looks just like someone I know, or almost just like someone I know. But the hair is wrong. I stared at him again. The ears, I realized. The ears are wrong, too. He should be wearing large, dark, button-shaped earrings. Good grief. It's Sam.

Why wasn't he with Rosa? Well, she was nineteen. If Sam wanted to go to a bar, he'd have to go alone. And the slicked-back hair, the expensive clothes and watch—not his usual look, but lots of people dress up to go clubbing. The glasses confused me, though, and the lack of earrings. And he didn't seem to be having much fun, sitting by himself, ignoring his drink, constantly checking his phone, only occasionally looking up and glimpsing to his right.

Should I go say hello? Without understanding why, I

decided against it. And when Abby came back, flushed with exercise and happiness and eager to tell me things, I put my hand over hers and shook my head. Signing might draw Sam's attention, and for some reason I didn't want to do that.

She stared at me, bewildered; I shook my head again and waited. Minutes later, Sam stood up abruptly, threw a few bills on the bar, and left. I watched him walk out into the night, lifted my hand from Abby's, and rubbed my fist against my chest.

"*Sorry,*" I signed. "*The man who just left is Sam, Rosa's boyfriend. I didn't want him to notice us. Something odd is going on.*"

Abby stared at the door, stared back at me. "*What?*" she asked.

"*I don't know,*" I signed. "*But something.*"

Chapter 5

On Thursday, I met Rosa's father and brother. I hadn't expected to. But when I went to Walt Sadowski's office to fill out tax forms, there they were.

So that's why Walt wanted me here at 3:00 sharp, I thought, fuming—because Ulysses and Frederick Patterson wanted to meet me, and their time is valuable. I was getting fed up with Walt's stinginess with information. Maybe some of it was necessary, but why not tell me about this? At least I could've dressed appropriately.

Walt dragged out the introductions, listing Ulysses Patterson's many accomplishments, damn near fawning—natural, I guess, since an important lawyer might provide future business. Frederick, Walt said, was also a lawyer, an associate at his father's firm. Ulysses Patterson cut in then, to amend "lawyer" to "attorney" and say Frederick made law review at Princeton. I get it, I thought. Frederick's the good kid. Rosa's the problem child. I thought of my sister, with her husband and her baby and her steady, respectable job—everything my mother values, everything I can never seem to manage. My sympathy for Rosa shot up, and I took an immediate dislike to Frederick.

"You three will want to get acquainted," Walt said. He wasn't actually drooling, but I pictured saliva dripping down his chin in thick, long globs. The image made me smile. "Use my private office. Take all the time you like."

"We'll take five minutes," Ulysses Patterson said, his tone making it clear that devoting six minutes to me would be a waste of his time.

Inside Walt's office—decorated, I was surprised to see, with hazy pastel posters declaring that everything happens for a reason, that luck equals opportunity plus preparation, and that if we believe it, we can achieve it—Ulysses Patterson claimed the swivel chair behind George's desk, I sat in a flimsy wooden chair facing him, and his son stood by the window, gazing out. Both father and son had Rosa's cinnamon skin, her wide-set eyes, her strong, straight nose.

Ulysses Patterson had the sort of build Grandma Ciardi calls "portly"—not fat, really, definitely not flab-by, but you couldn't exactly miss him. He looked about sixty and was two-thirds bald. His son, thirty or so, was tall and slender and kept his hair very short; it barely formed a shadow. Both wore three-piece blue suits, crisp white shirts, and solid-colored ties.

While I looked them over, Ulysses Patterson did the same to me. Finally, he pointed to my tee-shirt. "'Top Skorz,'" he read. "What is that? A band?"

I blushed. "It's a place where I work. We help students prepare for the SAT."

"Oh," he said. "Top scores. Well, it's fortunate spelling isn't covered on the SAT. So, Miss Ciardi. Mr. Sadowski says you may spend a fair amount of time with my daughter in the days and, perhaps, weeks to come. Your primary duty is to inform him about what she does and the people with whom she associates. Have you, at this point, made significant observations or drawn tentative conclusions?"

I thought of Jason putting his arm around Rosa; of Rosa's and Sam's initials enclosed in a heart on a dead man's calendar, next to a dead woman's name; of Sam sitting alone in a bar in The Flats, wearing what might almost be called a disguise. Were those observations significant? I definitely couldn't draw conclusions about them. "Not really. But Rosa's very friendly, very pleasant." I cursed my cowardice.

The corners of his mouth twitched downward. "How kind of you. Naturally, as her father, I consider her a wonderful young woman. But I'm also, as you know, concerned. And I hope, in addition to observing her, you might be a good influence. Your skills enable you to communicate with her, and you're close to her age but old enough to be a mentor. That puts you in an ideal position to advise her about certain matters—for example, about how unsuitable her association with this Sam Ryan is."

Poor man, I thought. You don't understand the first thing about your daughter. "I'm not really qualified to advise Rosa about her relationships."

"You're probably not really qualified to help students prepare for the SAT, either," he said sharply. "But you're paid to do it, so you try your best. I ask you to do the same on *this* job, to try to wean her from this potentially dangerous relationship. Another matter. You're an interpreter, so I assume you're biased in favor of sign language, as opposed to oral approaches?"

Here we go, I thought. "I'm not an expert on deaf education. That's a separate field. But judging from what I've seen and read, I think, for most deaf people, sign language is the most effective way to communicate."

"The *easiest*, perhaps," he said. "That doesn't make it

the most effective. And I'm sorry to see my daughter relying on a method of communication that isolates her from most of the world. At first, my wife and I sent her to schools that used speaking and lip-reading exclusively. She made progress—not as much as we'd hoped, and she sometimes got frustrated, there were some behavior problems, but that would have passed. Then, when my daughter was eight, my wife lost faith in the oral approach and insisted on sending her to a school that used sign language."

I'd heard this story so many times. It always made me ache with sympathy, even though it almost always had a happy ending. "Did Rosa pick sign language up quickly and show a strong preference for it? Did she lose interest in speaking and reading lips?"

He looked uncomfortable. Maybe he hadn't realized how predictable his story was. "Yes. But my daughter's very bright. There's no reason she can't learn to speak and read lips. I'm sure if she'd made a full effort, she'd have had a breakthrough, and by now she'd be functioning more independently. But she's stubborn, so very stubborn. She refuses even to try any more. So I hope you'll use whatever influence you have to persuade her to try again. May I rely on you?"

"It wouldn't do any good. I'm sorry, Mr. Patterson, but I can't honestly advise Rosa to try something that usually ends in failure and frustration. Have you learned sign language? How do you communicate with her?"

His eyes filled with pain, and he looked away. "My wife learned. She took classes. My daughter and I communicated through her. Since my wife passed away, four years ago, we've communicated primarily through notes."

For the first time, his son spoke up. "I know a little sign. I have some books and DVDs, and I took a class.

But I don't have a knack for it. I have to finger spell almost everything, and that's so slow. It *would* be better if Rosa would learn to speak and read lips, Miss Ciardi."

I lifted my shoulders. "If I find a natural way to bring it up, I'll try to help her see the arguments on both sides. But I don't think I should force that conversation."

"I agree," Ulysses Patterson said. "Don't say anything that might make her suspicious. If the opportunity arises, however, there's another topic you might discuss. After my daughter graduated from high school, I naturally hoped she'd go to college. She refused. Instead, she went to beauty school for a few months. May I assume you'd have no reservations about encouraging her to enroll in college? May I assume you agree young people benefit from higher education?"

Not if they're not ready for it, I thought. Not if they're not interested. Then it's a waste of time and money for everyone involved. But I shouldn't try debating that with him. "I agree higher education can be very beneficial."

"Then try to point her in the right direction. I don't want her to be a manicurist for the rest of her life. She's capable of much more."

I hadn't known Rosa had a job—another fact Walt hadn't shared. My respect for her grew. I'd thought she was a rich girl living in Daddy's house while breaking Daddy's rules, spending all her time amusing herself. No, she was working. And there's nothing wrong with being a manicurist, if that's what she wants to do. But that was another subject I shouldn't debate with Ulysses Patterson. "I understand."

"Good." He sat back. "Let's review. Your primary duty is to observe my daughter and report to Mr. Sadowski. Second, help her see how unsuitable Mr. Ryan is. If you can accomplish anything beyond that, good. I suppose you should get to your tutoring job."

That sounded like a dismissal. "It was a pleasure to meet you both." I stood up.

"I'll walk you to your car," Frederick said.

His father gave him a surprised look. So did I. Walk me to my car? But I nodded, and Frederick followed me out of the office.

"Look," he said when we got to the parking garage, "I'm sorry if you were offended by my father's manner, or by what he said. He tends to be—imperious. It's his way. And he's really worried about Rosa. I think that made him even more imperious than usual."

"It's all right." Another surprise. I wouldn't have expected Ulysses Patterson's son to give a damn about my feelings. "I could see he's worried. And not being able to communicate with Rosa must make everything harder."

Frederick half-nodded. "It does. But I don't know how well he and Rosa would communicate even if she *could* read lips." He paused, as if unsure about whether to go on. "Don't get me wrong. He loves Rosa, very much. But she was a late-in-life child. Judging from something my mother said, I gather having another child was her idea. He was forty-four when Rosa was born. I was already twelve. I think starting all over again with a new baby threw him. And when we realized Rosa was deaf, I think he felt overwhelmed. My father isn't used to having problems he can't solve."

Frederick's thought about this a lot, I realized, and wondered how often he'd been able to talk about Rosa. It probably helped that I was a professional, that he could use that as an excuse for opening up. Maybe that was why he'd walked me to my car. "It sounds as if your mother was the one who found it easiest to communicate with Rosa."

"Oh, yeah. Those two were incredibly close. I felt almost jealous, seeing them curled up on the couch with their Nancy Drew books, signing and laughing, using this secret language I could never seem to crack. My mother kept us connected to Rosa, kept us functioning as a family. When she died—it was cancer—we all fell apart. My father couldn't show it, but I think he felt lost. And Rosa was so damn angry. Not that it was anyone's fault, but she was so miserable she got mad at everyone. She insisted on transferring to this boarding school in New England. She used to speak and read lips a little, but after one semester there, she stopped. And my father refuses to learn sign." He flashed a grim smile. "He says Rosa's stubborn. He's right. Guess where she got it."

I smiled, too. "And you got forced into the role of peacemaker?"

"The Patterson Family United Nations, that's me. And about as successful at making peace as the United Nations has ever been. Anyway, maybe it'll help you to know all that. That's why I told you."

That's not why, I thought. "Thank you."

"No problem." He grinned awkwardly, as if he'd said what he'd wanted to say and didn't know how to end the conversation. "So, what made you decide to become an interpreter?"

Sooner or later, everybody asked. "I wish I had a better answer. Sometimes, when people ask me, I'm tempted to say it's because I have a deaf parent, a deaf aunt, at least a deaf neighbor. But I don't. I've just always been fascinated by sign language, the way some kids are fascinated by dinosaurs or butterflies. I've always found it beautiful, and fun, and, well, elegant. Concise. So I learned the ASL alphabet when I was a little girl, watched *Children of a Lesser God* a thousand times, started taking community college classes in high school. And it feels good to help people communicate, and I enjoy the challenge of making the transition from one language to another, especially since the two languages are so different."

"Then I guess you've found your calling," he said. "As for me, when I was a kid, I was fascinated by dump trucks. But no way was Ulysses Patterson's son going to be a dump truck driver. Law school was the only possible destination." He grinned again, more comfortably this time. "Probably, that's for the best. Probably, dump trucks aren't really as infinitely exciting as they seem."

"Probably not." Naturally, Ulysses Patterson would want his children to aspire to greatness. It must frustrate him to have Rosa work as a manicurist. Something struck me for the first time. "Frederick and Rosa—Frederick Douglass? Rosa Parks?"

He laughed. "Yes, my father's big on Black American history. It could be worse. My mother said he'd wanted to name me Booker. And he was all set on naming my sister Sojourner, but Mom put her foot down. It kills him that he's named after a white man, even a general who fought on the right side." He held out his hand. "Maybe we could keep in touch. My father can be off-putting. It might be hard for you to ask him questions that might help you help Rosa. Would it be all right if I call from time to time, Jane?"

I shook his hand. It was a nice hand—strong but not overpowering, cool but not cold, smooth but firm. Honey, I thought, you can call me any time. In principle, I don't like good kids. My sympathies naturally gravitate toward screw-ups. But I decided, just this once, I might be able to stomach someone who'd made law review at Princeton. "I'd like that, Frederick," I said, and gave him my card.

As I drove to Top Skorz—Ulysses Patterson had a point about that. The cutesy spelling bothers me, too—I turned up the radio and sang along lustily to "Angel of the Morning," even though it was only the Juice Newton version.

Two interesting men in two days. Frederick wasn't as dazzling as Hector, but he wasn't bad. If he'd let his hair grow a bit, he wouldn't be bad at all. True, both Hector and Frederick had families that seemed a tad dysfunctional, but my own family hadn't exactly stepped out of a 1950s sitcom. And both Hector and Frederick had fathers with odd ways of choosing names for their children. I almost envied them that. Once, I'd asked my father why he and my mother named me "Jane," why they named my brother and sister "Mark" and "Ann." My father had shrugged. "Short," he'd said. "Easy to spell."

I put in my hours at Top Skorz, nudging drowsy teenagers into maintaining consciousness while we worked through reading comprehension questions. On the drive to the community center, I ate the second tuna sandwich I'd packed that morning; the first had been lunch. Class will feel good, I thought. After a long, sedentary day, physical activity is just what I need. Maybe I can relax enough to let myself fall.

I couldn't. Again, for what felt like hours, I crouched on the mat, arms crossed over my chest, while Sam ran through every motivational cliché he knew. He wanted me to fall forward this time, and eventually I faked a tumble, semi-purposely sabotaging it by bending at the waist, slowing down, and leaning to the left. Gradually, ever so gently, I eased myself onto the mat with no trace of a thud.

Sam sighed. "Good try," he said, fake-hearty. "Charlie's demonstrating joint-locking techniques. Why don't you try those?"

Those went much better. Charlie paired me with a teenager named Robert, who had curly blond hair and a smooth, blank face. He also had a football player's build, but I had no trouble bringing him down to the mat when I twisted his wrist or forearm. When Charlie complimented me on picking techniques up quickly, I smiled. Robert scowled. He couldn't get the moves straight, or remember techniques well enough to repeat them seconds after they'd been demonstrated. When Charlie had to keep reviewing with him after the rest of us had everything down, I saw Robert's face flushing bright pink. Poor kid, I thought. He's probably an athlete. It must be embarrassing to have such a tough time mastering something physical.

Sam joined our group. "When most people think about pressure points," he said, "they think about going for the groin. But men instinctively protect their groins. Some women do, too. You have a better chance of catching people off guard if you go for places they aren't expecting. Pair up."

"Yes, sir," we shouted, and I found myself facing Robert again.

We'd try a kick, Sam said, and aim for a spot on the outer leg, about six inches below the waist. We'd be surprised by how painful a kick to that spot could be. To demonstrate, he delivered a slow, gentle roundhouse kick to Charlie's upper leg.

Charlie laughed. "Oh, yeah. I felt that."

Sam turned to us. "Now you try. Face each other, take a fighting stance, and take turns. Just a tap, or you could hurt someone."

Robert lifted an eyebrow. "Ladies first."

Fine. I lifted my right leg, swung it out slowly, tapped Robert in the designated spot, and brought my leg down. "Did you feel that?"

He shrugged. "Not really. Ready?"

I nodded, and he grinned. He breathed in, tightened his fists, yelled, and let loose with a kick—a full-force kick, hard and fast, to my outer upper leg. The pain stunned me. Dizziness hit first, then nausea. I staggered back and bent over, bracing my hands against my knees. I will not throw up, I vowed. I will not give that brat the satisfaction.

Sam had heard the yell, had seen the kick. He hurried over and put an arm around my shoulders. "You okay, Jane?"

Already, the nausea had subsided, the dizziness had started to clear. I straightened up. "Fine," I said.

Rosa had come over, too, and watched with sympathetic eyes. Other people murmured in disapproval.

Sam glared at Robert. "What the hell? I told you, just a tap."

Robert spread his hands. "That's all I did. I tapped. She couldn't take it." He smirked. "Time to toughen up, huh, Jane?"

"That's enough," Sam said. "It'd serve you right if I threw you out of class. Jane, want me to send him home?"

"No, it's okay," I said. "Let's go on."

Sam hesitated. "We usually spar now. Maybe you should sit that out."

"I'm fine." I looked at Robert. "How about you?"

"No," Sam said. "I'll find you another partner."

I faced Robert and lifted my fists. "Not necessary."

Sam didn't like it. "Okay. But, Robert, I'm watching you. No rough stuff."

You're warning the wrong person, Sam, I thought, and waited for the command to start sparring.

I let Robert take the lead. He advanced, grinning, and threw a few punches to my head. But I'm good at blocking—that's always been my strength—and deflected them easily. Then I feinted, jabbing at his face with my left hand. While he blocked that with his arm, I threw a punch with my right hand and tapped him on the cheek lightly, just to show I could.

Before, he'd been showing off. Now, he was mad. He snarled, stepped back, then lunged forward with a yell, trying to repeat his earlier success by aiming a roundhouse kick at my upper left leg. I'd expected that. Bringing my left hand down in a swift circular motion, I hooked it around to grab his leg. He looked at me, startled, and I took two steps backward, forcing him to hop forward awkwardly, his arms flailing. People started to notice, to point, to laugh. I waited a long moment, still holding his leg, while he swallowed and stared and tried uselessly to get his balance. Then I hooked my right leg around his left leg, sweeping it, simultaneously striking his chest with the heel of my right palm. He fell to the floor, too hard. It winded him. Still holding his leg, I looked at him as he lay there spread-eagled. Then I let out a yell and brought my right fist down for a punch.

I stopped an inch short of his groin. He was too terrified to scream, too winded to move. Finally, I let his leg drop, stepped back, and daintily straightened my shirt. "Time to toughen up, huh, Robert?" I said.

Several people applauded. Many laughed. I saw Sam grinning, saw Rosa clapping and bouncing. I stepped forward to help Robert up. "You okay?"

"Yeah." He sounded dazed. "Sure." He blinked, took three short breaths, and looked at me uncertainly. Then, slowly, he grinned. "That was cool. Can you show me how to do that?"

"You bet." I held out my hand. "No hard feelings?"

"Hell, no," he said. "You neither, right? I mean, it was nothing personal."

I smiled. "It was never personal. Just business."

It took a moment, but he got it. Grinning, he gave my hand a quick, firm shake. "Yeah, right. Business, not personal. That's good. See you next week, Jane."

Not such a bad kid, I reflected, watching him amble off. Any teenager who can recognize a reference to *The Godfather* deserves a second chance.

After class, Rosa and Sam and I went to a restaurant to drink Cokes, eat nachos, and retell the story of my triumph until even I got sick of it. "*I don't like bullies,*" I signed. It felt cozy, sitting in a restaurant full of people but being completely private. I thought of what Frederick had said about feeling jealous while watching his mother and sister communicate in their secret language. I understood that. Sharing that secret language with Rosa and Sam made me feel closer to them, more distant from everyone else. I noticed a woman at the next table casting glances at us. But she can't understand us, I thought. Somehow, it made me feel special.

"*Maybe now Robert will think twice before bullying someone else,*" Sam signed. He grinned. "*And maybe he'll pay more attention when I try to teach him how to fall. That's why he got winded when you swept his leg. He fell wrong, so he couldn't bounce back and defend himself.*"

Rosa frowned. "*No sermons. Leave Jane alone. Let her enjoy it.*"

"*Thank you,*" I signed. Robert couldn't bounce back, I thought, because I was holding his leg. And if he *had* bounced back, I would've knocked him down again.

The woman at the next table touched her companion's hand. "Look," she said, nodding toward us. "They're talking with their hands. They must be deaf. Isn't that cute?"

Sam heard her, too, and got a wicked gleam in his eyes. "*Let's play deaf,*" he signed, looking at me. "*It's fun. People say stupid things. We can translate for Rosa.*"

Playing deaf—I hadn't done that since college, when

friends and I had gone to a restaurant or mall after ASL class and put on little shows for passersby. It isn't fair. You're tricking people, tempting them into saying tactless things. And there's always the risk you'll hear something you'd rather not. But Sam's right—it can be fun. And it was my job to get close to Rosa and Sam, so I could try to figure out what, if anything, they were up to. I looked at Rosa, who nodded eagerly.

"OK," I finger-spelled, bringing my hand forward slightly.

The woman's companion—her husband, probably—looked us over. "Can they really communicate like that? It looks spastic."

"Oh, no," she said. "It's graceful. And of course they can communicate. Sign language is so expressive. It's a universal language."

Smiling, I signed the exchange for Rosa. She had to frown to keep a straight face. "*Not so universal,*" she signed. "*I met a deaf person from England and couldn't understand him at all. Even the alphabet is different.*"

"A universal language, huh?" the man said. "You mean if a deaf person from China walked in, he could understand what they're saying?"

The woman nodded. "Absolutely. Sign language is very symbolic. Those signs are symbols, and the symbols stand for things."

"*And how does that make sign language different from other languages*?" I asked after signing the exchange for Rosa. "*How does that make it universal*?"

"If it's universal," the man said, "shouldn't *you* be able to understand what they're saying?"

The woman peered at us, knitting her eyebrows. "I think I almost can. They're talking about their feelings. The Black girl's sad, and the others are comforting her. Did you see how she scrunched up her face and brought her hand down in front of it? She's saying she feels down, depressed."

In fact, Rosa had signed "strange," commenting on the bizarre ideas some hearing people have about sign language. We all worked at not laughing that time. With a dramatic sweep, Rosa put the back of her hand to her forehead and mimed a tragic expression. That should keep the woman going awhile.

"See?" the woman said. "She's definitely sad. Maybe someone she cared about died recently. Maybe she feels as if she caused it somehow, or didn't do enough to help."

When I signed that, Rosa looked stricken. Abruptly, she brushed her right palm against her left fist, twice. "*Enough.*"

"Seems primitive," the man commented. "I don't see how you could express *ideas* that way. But they probably can't think the way we do. I mean, basic stuff, sure, like what to have for breakfast, but not much beyond that. If they could really *think*, couldn't they learn to talk?"

At this point, I agreed with Rosa. Enough. Luckily, the waitress came over. "Want refills on your Cokes?" she asked.

"No, thank you," I said, loudly, making each word distinct, signing simultaneously. "We're ready to leave." I stood up, nodding to the couple at the next table. "Have a pleasant evening."

Sam also stood, also turned to the couple. "E equals MC squared," he said. "That primitive enough for you?"

Rosa gave them a parting message, too, an "F" handshape morphing into a "K." Sign really isn't a universal language. But I think they grasped her meaning.

Outside the restaurant, we lingered. Clearly, the last few minutes had upset Rosa, but she collected herself and said, again, that she was happy about my trial membership at the Reed Center. We tried to find a time to meet there. Friday wouldn't work for me, and Saturday was Rosa's busiest day at the salon. I asked if she went to the Sunday volleyball games, but she said no, her father insisted she go to church. Then she shrugged and admitted she liked going to church, too. I bet she's never told her father that, I said to myself, but kept my face blank, as if I had no hint of the tensions between them. She could meet me at noon, Rosa said. We could work out and then have lunch at the center's café.

"*Great*," I signed. Dinner at Geraci's had obliterated my eating-out budget for the next month, but this would be a business lunch. I'd make Walt pay. We said goodnight, and Rosa and Sam walked toward his car, arms around each other's shoulders.

They're so sweet together, I thought as I started my car. Too bad Ulysses Patterson can't be glad Rosa's found someone she cares about.

Someone she cares about. The hearing woman's words came back, the words that shattered Rosa's joking mood. "Maybe someone she cared about died recently," the woman said. "Maybe she feels guilty, as if she caused it somehow, or didn't do enough to help."

Jenny Linton died three nights ago. She and Rosa must've been friends, since they'd come to Ginger's Pantry together. Rosa probably cared about her, at least a little. Did she feel guilty about Jenny's death, "as if she caused it somehow, or didn't do enough to help"? If she didn't feel that way, why had she reacted so strongly to the woman's words?

The need to find out what was going on felt more urgent than ever. Among other things, I felt pretty sure Rosa cared about me, too, at least a little.

Chapter 6

When I got to the gym on Sunday, I felt glad I hadn't yielded to temptation. Yesterday, I'd tried on shamelessly skimpy shorts and sleeveless, low-scooped tops designed to cling, more than cover. In the end, I'd bought black sweat pants that fit more precisely than my baggy old gray things, with a matching jacket and a lavender tee-shirt that hovered between demure and friendly. Sometimes, I'd decided, subtler is smarter.

It was the right decision. Most other women were also wearing sweatpants. The few in outfits more suited to beach volleyball looked silly.

At least, most did. Not Dr. Kirsten Carlson, the Amazonian type who'd been so friendly while I waited for my interview. She wore a bright turquoise sports bra and shiny black shorts. On her, they looked natural. Hell, if I had a body like that, I'd wear shorts and sports bras to funerals. If she'd looked like an Amazon before, she looked like a goddess now. She spotted me and strode over.

"Hey, Jane!" she said. "Hector told me you got the trial membership. Fantastic! You're on my team, okay? Don't let Hector steal you away."

"Fine," I said, flustered but flattered. "I haven't played volleyball since high school, though. I'm not sure I even remember the rules."

"You'll be great. Come on—I'll introduce you to the other girls."

Seven or eight women stood in a cluster, chatting. All seemed to be in their twenties or early thirties, all looked slender and fit, and all were pretty, even with hair pulled back and faces scrubbed clean of makeup. They'd make an attractive backdrop for Kirsten. I remembered my sister's explanation of how she'd picked her bridesmaids. She'd wanted them to be pretty, she'd said, but not too pretty. She wanted the pictures to look good, but she didn't want anyone outshining her. Maybe Kirsten felt that way about volleyball. Maybe that's why she wanted me on her team. Fine. If she thought I looked good enough to fit in with these other women, that was compliment enough. I had no illusions about rivaling Kirsten.

I couldn't keep track of all the names, and the jobs went by in a blur, too. Daycare teacher, bakery clerk, bank teller—I'd sort it out later.

"You're on Kirsten's team, aren't you?" one said. "Great—we're teammates. Kirsten's a fantastic captain."

"You want to start?" another said. "I'm usually on Kirsten's starting six, but you can have my spot."

"Thanks," I said, "but I'm rusty. I'd better watch for a while first."

"Good idea," a third one said. "Let's hang out together."

I couldn't imagine a friendlier bunch. Kirsten had described the center as one big, happy family. I saw what she meant.

And the heart of that big, happy family, clearly, was the Connolly family. Hector and Diana arrived together. She nodded to people as she passed, headed straight for the other side of the net, and began an elaborate stretching routine. Hector took his time, greeting everyone, trading jokes. When he came to me, he smiled, looking into my eyes with gasp-inducing intensity.

"Glad to see you, Jane," he said. "These Sunday morning volleyball games are a tradition with my family. We've done this every week since I was eight. Now you're part of all that." He grinned. "Of course, I'll still spike every ball you get across the net."

"Just you try," I said. Not that I felt confident about getting a ball across the net at all. But given the mood building in the gym, a jaunty response seemed appropriate.

Laughing, Hector slapped me gently on the back, giving me another melt-my-heart grin before heading for his side of the net to join Diana in her stretching routine. She smiled at him, he smiled back, and I sensed a powerful brother-sister bond. Had my own brother ever given me a smile that unreserved and affectionate? Maybe once or twice, but not in the last decade. As for my sister—no. Not once, not ever. I didn't even have to think about that.

Kirsten clapped her hands, shouting it was time to warm up. One woman spoke tentatively.

"Should we have a moment of silence for Jenny first?" she asked. "I mean, she was part of the team, and—"

Kirsten cut her off. "Jenny would want us to win. No stalling."

She led us in a swift series of jumping jacks, squat-thrusts, and toe-touches that left me winded and sweat-soaked. Kirsten looked cool, eager for more. The men on our team, perfectly nice-looking men, watched the women with interest. They might reasonably expect to draw some interest in return, but Kirsten didn't pay much attention to them, and neither did the other women. Clearly, this was a women's team—the men were there only so we'd have the required male-female mix. For some reason, that felt like fun. Sisterhood is powerful, I thought, and didn't fake my next toe-touch, twisting my waist more than it wanted to twist and slapping my fingertips against the floor.

As we finished our warm-up, Jason Connolly walked in. His muscles bulged nicely under his tee-shirt, but his face looked ashen, his eyes blank. Was he hung over? Had he dosed his orange juice with vodka this morning? Both explanations seemed possible. "I'm on your team today, Kirsten," he said.

She stopped mid-jumping jack. "That's stupid. Of course you're on Hector's team. You're co-captain."

"I'm on your team. And I'm serving first."

He picked up a ball and got into position. Kirsten glanced across the net at Hector, who gazed at his brother, then shrugged.

Kirsten shrugged, too. "Okay. And if you want to serve first, fine. But after this, if you're on my team, you serve when I say."

Kirsten and Hector got their starting players into position, and the rest of us sat against the wall. There were maybe three dozen people in all. Hector had said these games were a favorite with members, so I'd thought the gym would be packed. Damn, I thought. With so few people, I'll actually have to play.

I expected the game to begin, but everyone seemed to be waiting for something. Finally, a door opened at the far end of the gym, and a man and a woman entered, the woman leaning heavily on the man's arm. It was Paul Kent, the man Diana introduced me to when she showed me around the center. And the woman—I drew my breath in. The woman was Elise Reed.

She still looked like the flawless marble statue in the center of the fountain. Cleveland's Ice Princess, the newspapers called her in her days of Olympic glory. Now, almost half a century later, she was a princess still—not a regal princess, but a friendly, fragile princess, a Disney princess, a gently aging Snow White. She was tiny and thin, so thin she looked brittle. Her coal-black hair seemed an appropriate assertion of her right to remain a symbol of youth and beauty forever. She was just so exquisitely lovely.

But she's ill, I realized. So pale—no one should be that pale. And she winced with every step. Both my grandmothers are in their eighties, and both have arthritis and other ills. But they're both still vigorous, still ornery. Grandma Ciardi still tells me not to be a damn interfering idiot when I insist on shoveling her snow. Elise Reed's problems must go deeper than age. Was it cancer, a weak heart? Her brave, pained smile spoke of terrible ailments.

She and Paul made their slow progress across the gym. Did the pain in her eyes grow more intense when she saw Jason on the other side of the net? Hector and Diana came to her, conferring in whispers. Finally, she nodded—a slow, sad nod. Paul guided her to the server's position, and Hector handed her the ball. Elise Reed looked at us and smiled.

"Welcome, everyone," she said. Her voice was high-pitched, making me think of a bird's chirp. But it was surprisingly loud. "It's always good to spend these Sunday mornings together. Let's get started."

She paused, the ball poised in her left hand. Then, with more force than I would've thought possible, she tossed the ball in the air and smacked it, sending it clear across the net. No one on our side tried to touch the ball, and it landed in the center of our court with a graceful bounce.

"Your point, Elise," Kirsten declared, and everyone cheered and clapped.

Elise Reed smiled, took Paul's arm again, and walked to the back of her side of the gym, where two chairs waited.

Now, things started. This wasn't like gym class, when we stood in two ragged lines, waiting to see if a ball happened to drift toward us. This was fast, hard, and noisy, people racing to the net and back, grunting and swearing and shouting, hurling themselves into the air with such force they often fell down after hitting the ball. I remembered what Hector said about competition being one of the center's core values. I definitely saw that in action now.

The primary competitors were the three Connolly siblings and Kirsten. Hector's easy grin vanished. He ran everywhere, throwing himself at the ball, not pausing even when he wiped sweat from his face. He and Diana seemed to be competing with each other, as much as with the players on our team. Neither hesitated to jump in front of the other to get at the ball. Diana stayed silent throughout the match, her face set and joyless. She seemed driven—when she missed a chance to score, her body went rigid. On our side of the net, Jason seemed even more determined to prove himself. He was an angry, aggressive player, incredibly fast and strong, cursing when his teammates faulted and even when they passed to someone else. Kirsten played exuberantly, as energetic and fierce as the others but still able to smile, to cheer on her teammates, to whoop with delight whenever we scored. Of the four, she seemed to be the only one actually having a good time.

Those four players stayed on the floor the whole time, game after game, but the captains rotated the rest of us regularly. Eventually, I got my turn and managed not to disgrace myself. I didn't score but didn't fault, and several times I got close enough to pass the ball to a better player. Even so, it was a relief to sit down again. In fifteen minutes, I'd gotten exhausted, drenched with sweat. I looked at my hands—the tension had left them clenched and shaking. Maybe next Sunday, I thought, I'll let my mother talk me into going to church.

It seemed to go on forever. I didn't know how those four kept going so long, at that level of intensity. Finally, our team won, and Kirsten led us in a cheer. Jason didn't join in, but he looked grimly satisfied, his anger lifting for the first time. Hector, grin already back in place, came over to congratulate us. Diana stayed on her side of the net, scowling, then walked back to talk to her mother.

But I didn't pay much attention to Diana. Instead, I watched out of the corner of my eye as Hector walked over to Kirsten. He'd been gracious to everyone on our team—I'd gotten my high-five, like everyone else—but Kirsten held his attention. He stood a few inches from her and said some mocking thing. She laughed, throwing her sweaty arms around his sweaty neck. He grabbed her and kissed her on the lips, and she drew her head back and then leapt forward, wrapping her powerful legs around his waist. He held her there, kissing her twice more before letting her go. They put their arms around each other and walked off the court, laughing.

What an idiot I'd been, thinking Hector was interested in me. How could he be, with Kirsten around? He'd been nice, but only because he was a good salesman. He wanted me to get hooked on the center and find a way to pay full price. I remembered how Kirsten strode past the receptionist and entered his office without knocking. She had special privileges. What man in his right mind would deny her special privileges? And she was a doctor—a doctor of what I didn't know, but no matter what it was, she outclassed me. Well, maybe Frederick Patterson would call.

I glanced at my watch. Half an hour until I'd meet Rosa. Sweaty as I was, it'd be silly to shower, since I'd be working out again soon. Maybe I'd look for those stretching machines.

Jason walked over. "Jane, right? We met the other day. Hey, nice job this morning. Too bad you didn't get more time to play."

"Fifteen minutes was plenty. I'm out of my league here."

"Not at all. So, did Hector tell you about our special programs? That's my area."

"He gave me a brochure. I haven't had time to look at it yet."

"Then I'll fill you in." He put an arm around my shoulder—smoothly, confidently, so smoothly and confidently it happened before I realized he was aiming for me. "We'll go to the café, I'll buy you a lemonade, and I'll give you all the details. We've got a singles' night coming up next week. I bet you'd enjoy that."

Already, he'd started walking me toward the door. "Thanks, but I'm meeting a friend soon. I'd better shower first." Right now, the women's locker room felt like the safest spot.

He tightened his grip on my shoulder and quickened his pace. I couldn't get away without wrenching myself free and making a small scene. "You played for fifteen minutes. You don't need a shower. And you smell great to me. So, about the singles' nights. We have them every other Monday."

There didn't seem to be any graceful way to avoid this. And, I remembered, I'm a private detective now, or at least working for one. The whole point of coming here is to find out what Rosa's up to, and Jason could be involved in whatever that is. Maybe I should welcome a chance to spend time with him.

It didn't happen. As we neared the door to the gym, Paul Kent stepped into our path. "Nice to see you, Jane," he said. "Jason, your mother wants to speak to you."

Jason's grip on my shoulder tightened again. "Tell Mom I'll come by this afternoon. I promised Jane I'd buy her a lemonade."

"Your mother wants speak to you *now*." Paul didn't frown, but his smile stiffened. "I'm sure Jane will excuse you."

This felt like a good time to duck free of Jason's arm. "Of course. I should take a shower anyway. I'll see you around, Jason."

I walked away quickly, but not so quickly I missed the angry whisper Jason aimed at Paul: "For Christ's sake. What'd Mom think I was gonna do, screw her in the café?"

Now I *did* feel like a shower. I scrubbed hard. Tomorrow, I decided as I rinsed my hair. Tomorrow, without fail, I'd tell Walt about Jason. If his own mother didn't trust him to drink lemonade with a woman who was clearly of legal age and then some, he shouldn't be anywhere near Rosa.

I met up with her as she walked into the center. She took me to the stretching machines and showed me how to use them. They weren't exactly fun—Amnesty International would probably condemn any country that used them to interrogate terrorists—but I could tell the agony would improve my kicks. After fifteen minutes of cycling and fifteen more on treadmills, we decided it was time for lunch and headed to the locker room to towel off.

I noticed a suede jacket hanging in her locker—beautifully fitted, a rich chocolate color, with dull brass buttons and black sleeves, wide bands of chocolate suede at the wrists. "*That's a pretty jacket,*" I signed.

Her eyes grew heavy. "*It's not mine. A friend lent it to*

me last week. I'd forgotten to bring a jacket, and it got cold all of a sudden. She said she'd wear her sweatshirt, and I should wear the jacket. And now I can't return it to her."

I perked up. Could it be? "*Why not?*"

Rosa seemed to wilt. "*She was partying at The Flats, and she drowned. It's awful. She was so nice. I'd like to return the jacket to her roommate—she could give it to Jenny's parents—but it's awkward. You know?*"

I did know. There are services Rosa could use to get in touch with a hearing person she'd never met—video-relay services, for example—or she could show up at the roommate's door with a note. But I understood why a teenager might find that awkward. And I'd been looking for an excuse to talk to Jenny's roommate.

"*I could return the jacket,*" I offered. "*Give me your friend's telephone number, and I'll do it today.*"

Rosa was so grateful she made me feel like scum. She thought I was helping, but I was using her to try to get information her father might turn against her. It's for her own good, I told myself. And it's my job. That didn't make me feel much better.

Even so, my pulse quickened as Rosa jotted down the phone number I'd already memorized. Right after lunch, I'd call. Maybe I'd discover the connection between Gary Nichols and Jenny Linton. Maybe I'd figure out whether that connection had anything to do with why they'd both ended up dead.

Chapter 7

Lisa Brewer opened the door to her apartment. She was close to six feet tall, big-boned but lean, a ruddy complexion and large, blunt features, sparse blonde hair held back with a cloth headband and twisted into a casual knot. In college, we'd called that "the jockette look." Lots of women on teams favored it, maybe to prove they were too intent on sports to fuss with hair. "Jane, right?" she said. "The one with the jacket?"

"That's right." I held it out. "As I said on the phone, your roommate lent it to Rosa Patterson, and Rosa didn't know how to return it herself, because she's deaf."

"Yeah, the deaf Black girl. Jenny mentioned her. Thanks. You wanna come in?"

Yes, I did. "Thanks. Rosa thought Jenny's parents should have the jacket."

"That's sweet." Lisa looked at the jacket sadly, probably remembering times she'd seen Jenny wear it. "But they won't want it. They don't want any of her clothes. They came to Cleveland to—well, take Jenny home. They packed her pictures and old yearbooks, but when her mom opened her closet, she started crying, and finally her dad said I could keep the clothes or give them to Goodwill."

"That's so sad." I pictured the scene, felt tears starting, and willed them back.

"It was rough." Lisa wiped away a tear of her own. "I mean, Jenny and I weren't super-close. We were both looking for roommates, a friend introduced us last year, and that's how we ended up sharing an apartment. We mostly lived separate lives, just said hello, split pizzas sometimes, like that. But she was nice. I liked her. And now I've gotta decide what to do about her clothes. She had *so* many."

"Why not keep them?" I said, knowing the answer. I'd seen Jenny.

"They wouldn't fit me. I could give them away, but it might take months to find another roommate, and meanwhile I've gotta handle the rent and utilities on my own. I thought I'd sell them." She looked at me closely. "I bet they'd fit you. Wanna take a look? She had some pretty things."

Acting interested would give me a way to stay longer, to possibly learn more about Jenny. "I couldn't afford much, but sure. I'll take a look."

She led the way to Jenny's bedroom. It's a typical apartment bedroom, a small white-walled box. Probably, Jenny had warmed it up with pictures, knickknacks, a colorful bedspread. But those were gone now, the room stripped down to a bed-frame and mattress, a cheap wooden armoire, a sagging bureau with only a tissue box on top. I had a sharp sense of Jenny's death—not as something to figure out, but as the loss of a human being. One week ago, a woman lived in this room. Now she was gone, and the room held almost no trace of her. Yellow flowered curtains hung in the windows. Jenny had probably picked those out, pictured them hanging here, wondered how they'd go with her other things, debated about the price. All those little thoughts and choices, all part of a person who no longer existed. It made me feel how cruel and sudden death can be, made me feel wrong about looking at her clothes and trying to uncover her secrets.

Lisa opened the armoire doors. "Most of her dressy stuff's in here."

I found the armoire crowded with skimpy, shiny things and pulled out a strapless pink silk dress. "'Dressy' is right. She must've gone out a lot."

"Lately she did, yeah. When we started rooming together, she'd usually come home from work, microwave something for dinner, watch TV, and crash. But about six months ago, something changed. She never talked about it, but I think she was husband-hunting and decided to get serious—invest in it, you know? She must've been saving up and then decided what the hell, now or never. So she bought the armoire and started bringing tons of new clothes home and heading for The Flats a lot."

I hung up the pink dress and pulled out a snug silvery sheath. "So she was husband-hunting? Did she find any prospects?"

"This one guy used to call, leave messages—just 'Jenny, it's Jay—call back.' After a few weeks, he stopped calling, so maybe they broke up. And she went out once with a guy from this fitness center she belonged to. She never mentioned anybody else. But then, maybe she wouldn't have. Like I said, we weren't all that close. She never told me anything about this Jay, always went in her room and closed the door before calling him back. See anything you like?"

"Lots of things, but they're not practical. Not for the way I live."

"You and me both. I don't party much, either. She kept her more practical things in the closet."

The clothes in the closet were definitely more practical, also older and less expensive. These were probably the slacks and skirts and tops she'd worn to work—perfectly nice, not especially tempting. But there was one dress.

"Oh, my." I lifted it out reverently. A soft, rich material—I couldn't name it, but I could appreciate the way it felt between my fingertips. Maroon and black, a bold diagonal stripe. I never buy stripes or prints—solid colors are best for interpreting, so I stick to those. And the deep V-neck, the wide kimono sleeves, the way the skirt flared out subtly but assertively—this was a dream dress.

"That'd look fantastic on you." Had Lisa ever sold dresses for a living? "That maroon, with your hair, your skin—wow."

"It's too nice." I held it against myself, gazing at my reflection in the cheap mirror above the bureau. I want this, I thought. "I can't afford it."

"I haven't even decided what I'll charge for it. How do you know you can't afford it? Try it on."

I am not made of stone. I tried it on. Lisa had been right about my hair and skin. This brightened them in a way nothing else ever had. "How much do you want for it?"

Lisa hesitated. "Eighty dollars?"

We negotiated down to fifty—still more than I could afford, but for a dress like this, I'd damn well do without food for a while. To celebrate her first sale, Lisa threw in a pair of black heels, digging them out of a pile of shoes and purses and other stuff including, I noticed, a red-and-white "Try It Out!" tote bag identical to the one the receptionist gave me when I signed the contract for my trial membership.

I gazed at myself in the mirror, hating to take the dress off. "What I really need to go with this," I said, "is a perfect gold necklace."

"I know. Jenny had a great necklace she wore with

it—really thick, maybe ten strands twisted together. Not that it was real gold. I mean, it couldn't have been. If it was real, it would've been hundreds of dollars, and how could Jenny have afforded that?"

How had Jenny afforded any of it—all these amazing dresses, all these shoes? I didn't know how much dental hygienists made, but was it enough to pay for all this? "Maybe a boyfriend gave her the necklace. Maybe that man who used to call, Jay."

"Maybe. But like I said, they probably broke up after a few weeks. Who'd give a girl an expensive necklace after dating her such a short time?"

Someone rich, I thought, like the son of someone who owns a classy fitness center. And maybe they hadn't broken up. Maybe, when things got serious, he'd decided to be more discreet and call Jenny only on her cell phone. "Jay." Was that code for Jason? I thought of the gold ring on Jason's left hand. That hadn't stopped him from flirting with Rosa, or with me. And Jenny had been very pretty. Had Jason flirted with her? Had she been receptive? Could that be why she suddenly started buying expensive clothes, going out often but never telling her roommate about meeting anyone? Lisa thought Jenny was husband-hunting. Maybe she'd hunted up someone else's husband. Maybe, somehow, that led to her death.

"Could I see the necklace?" I asked. "If it's not real gold, maybe I can afford it."

Lisa shook her head. "Jenny wore it the night she died. So I guess the police kept it, or gave it to her parents."

I looked in the mirror one last time. The dress looked as beautiful as ever, but now it felt slightly creepy. This is a dead woman's dress, I thought. But I loved it. I pushed down my misgivings and reached into my purse. I'd save it for a really special occasion, I decided, when I had to make just the right impression.

Lisa seemed delighted with her first sale. "If you want a second look at anything, give me a call. Want a glass of wine to seal the deal?"

The deal was already sealed, but wine always sounds good. And Lisa might feel lonely in the apartment now Jenny was gone. It might be a kindness to spend time with her. And I might learn more about Jenny.

"So," Lisa said as we settled on the couch, "you're friends with Rosa. She did Jenny's nails. About the time she started buying all the clothes, Jenny started getting her nails done every week. She'd go Wednesdays during her lunch hour and meet friends from this fitness place she belonged to, Elise Reed."

"I belong to the Reed Center, too. Well, I don't exactly belong. I have a trial membership."

Lisa grinned wryly. "So you got a trial membership. Lucky you. Personally, I don't think the Reed Center's such a big deal. Why shell out all that money because some old lady won a few medals decades ago? We've got an exercise room at the clinic where I work—stationary bikes, treadmill, stairmaster. That's all you need."

"Absolutely. You can get a great workout with those. So, you work at a clinic? Are you a doctor? A nurse?"

"An R.N. Plus I'm in a physician's assistant program, part-time. When I told Jenny about it, she talked about putting some credits together and applying. But she lost interest." Refilling her glass, Lisa grinned again. "She lost interest in wine, too. At first, we took turns bringing bottles home, splitting them when we split a pizza. But then she stopped—never brought a bottle home, almost always said no when I offered her a glass."

"Maybe she started doing all her drinking at The Flats."

"Maybe." Lisa's large, pale eyes clouded. "The night she died, though—she brought a bottle home then. Not wine. Vodka. She had at least three glasses. Damn. I could see she was upset. She was jittery as hell. I should've told her not to go out."

Poor Lisa. "It wouldn't have done any good. If she was determined to party—"

"I don't think she was. She had all those great dresses, but that night she put on a gray pantsuit, and this white top with a high neckline, and that necklace, and flat shoes. Nice, but flat. She didn't look like she was going partying. She looked like she was going on a job interview. And she said—I'll never forget this—she walked to the door and turned around and said, 'I'll be back in an hour, Lisa. In one hour.' She never told me when she'd get back, because I was always asleep by then. That night, she told me."

I didn't know what to make of it. "It *does* sound like she was upset."

"Oh, yeah. And you're right—I probably couldn't have stopped her. But I feel bad I didn't try." Her eyes grew moist again.

"I'm sorry. It must be hard living here without—"

"I'm fine." She managed a smile. "My mom's called every night since it happened, like clockwork, and I've got great friends at work." Her phone rang. She looked at it and grinned. "Mom. Clockwork."

That gave me a way to leave. On Monday, I went to Walt Sadowski's office and told him everything. He didn't like it that I'd talked to some people on my own but spent only ten minutes lecturing me, stressing the obvious fact that I didn't know a damn thing about how to investigate anything and would mess up if I tried. Another stunt like that, he said, and I'd be out of a job. He was intrigued by my account of seeing Sam in a bar and pressed for details.

Did Sam's jacket look new? Did his watch look expensive? Mostly, though, Walt was upset to hear Jason had flirted with Rosa.

"Married, and over thirty," Walt said. "Damn! This is worse than her lowlife boyfriend. Why didn't you tell me sooner?"

"Because I wasn't sure it was important." And because you haven't been telling me things, I thought, and this is my petty, childish way of getting back at you. "It's hard to decide what's important, because I don't have any idea of why Rosa's father is worried. Is it drugs? Because it's possible Jason isn't flirting Rosa because he wants to get her in bed. Maybe he wants to sell her drugs."

"No way," Walt said. "A guy like that—rich family, drives an Audi, mother owns that ritzy center. Why would he sell drugs? And he flirted with you, too."

"Yes. Maybe because he wanted to get me in bed, maybe because he wanted to sell me drugs. Come on, Walt. It's hard for me to do this job if I don't know what I'm looking for. Is Rosa involved with drugs?"

Walt shifted his weight from left to right in his chair. "In some ways, that'd fit with things she's done. But it could be something else. Keep your eyes open."

"That's helpful." I forced my exasperation down. "What about Gary Nichols? Doesn't it look like he discovered something, or at least suspected something? Maybe he never reported much to you because he was waiting until he knew enough to write a big story about it. And he kept trying to talk to Jenny Linton, maybe because he thought she had information. Then someone kills Gary and takes his laptop and notebooks, and then someone kills Jenny. Doesn't it look like someone's covering something up?"

Walt sighed. "Gary sees a pretty girl at a fitness center, gets her number, and pesters her with calls, only she doesn't wanna bother with him because he's a kid. And of course burglars take laptops, and we got no reason to think Jenny was killed. So where do you get this stuff about covering up a drug ring?"

When he put it like that, it did sound silly. "Maybe it's not drugs. Maybe Jason's a chronic flirt. Maybe he flirted with Jenny, and maybe she said yes. Maybe that's what Rosa and Sam asked her about in Ginger's Pantry, and that's why she got upset."

Walt snorted. "You think that was Gary's big story? 'Married Man Screws Around.' That's a headline-grabber, all right."

"Jason's not just any married man. He's the son of a local celebrity, an executive in a fitness center that prides itself on its wholesome image. And Rosa's only nineteen. What if Jason also flirted with girls who were seventeen? What if it didn't always stop with flirting?"

"Still not front-page stuff. And you're getting off track with this Gary and Jenny thing. Put it aside. Focus on Rosa."

"Put it aside? Gary and Jenny died, Walt."

"Yeah, they did. Gary got killed by a panicky burglar, and Jenny drank too much vodka and fell in the river. And nobody's paying us to find out about Gary and Jenny. Rosa's the job, not them. When do you see her again?"

"Late this afternoon." I stood up. "I understand Rosa's the job. But in the last ten days, two people connected to her have died, and one or both of them might have been murdered, for reasons that might have something to do with her. If it's our job to keep Rosa safe, I think we have to worry about what happened to Gary and Jenny. I think we have to worry about whether Rosa's in danger, too."

Chapter 8

I arrived at the Reed Center half-sorry I'd agreed to meet Rosa. Much as I liked her, every contact with her felt off. She had secrets, and I had secrets. Whenever we were together, we signed busily, but the most important things never got said. I didn't feel like seeing her today.

As it turned out, she wasn't the first person I saw. Hector Connolly called out to me as I headed for the locker room. I didn't feel happy about running into him right now, not after six hours of battling filth at a seafood restaurant shut down by the board of health. But Hector didn't seem to notice how saturated my Cathy's Cleaning Crew tee-shirt was with sweat, and things worse than sweat.

"I hope you enjoyed volleyball," he said. "I meant to speak to you afterward, but I didn't get a chance."

No, you didn't, I thought. You were too busy nuzzling with Kirsten. I smiled. "I had fun. I couldn't believe how long and hard you kept playing—you, and your brother and sister, and Kirsten."

He chuckled. "One of these years, we'll do ourselves serious damage. But we've battled at these volleyball games since we were kids. I guess when we get out there, we still feel like kids, so we play like kids. And with our mother watching, we want to do our best. So, you're working out? For how long?"

"About an hour. I'm meeting a friend. That reminds me. When you interviewed me, I met a woman named Emily Davis. She applied for a trial membership, too. Can I get a message to her? I thought we might work out together some time."

"Oh. Emily Davis." He half-winced. "We weren't able to offer her a trial membership. I didn't see the right level of commitment to fitness."

I was surprised at how sad that made me feel. I'd liked her so much, and I'd thought we might become friends. Now, I'd probably never see her again. "That's too bad. She seemed excited about joining." I didn't have any right to question his decision, but I felt too disappointed to let it go.

"Sure she's excited. For now. She wants to slim down for her wedding. Fine. I can certainly see why. But it's a short-term goal. Somebody who lets herself get into that kind of shape probably won't make long-term changes. She hasn't developed the self-discipline. As soon as Emily reaches the end of the aisle, she'll lose interest in fitness and hit the nachos again. The center can't afford to invest its resources in someone unlikely to become a regular member for more than a few months."

I nodded, not willing to risk a comment. As a businessman, he probably had to make those calculations. But the way he'd talked about Emily sounded too condescending, too close to downright cruel.

"About this friend you're meeting," he said. "Not a male friend, I hope?"

That surprised me. "No. Rosa Patterson."

It took him a moment to place the name. "Rosa—the deaf girl? That's right. On your application, you said she told you about the center. You must know her professionally, right? That's great. Her trainer says Rosa has lots of potential, but it's hard for them to communicate. Could you interpret for them some time?"

"I'd be glad to." The tiny suspense created by his question about a male friend hung in the air, distracting me in a way that made no sense at all.

"Great." He smiled—a broad, warm smile, a smile that brought his eyes up to full intensity and made my throat go tight. "Do you and Rosa have plans for later? No? Then would you have dinner with me?"

He's not asking me on a date, I thought. He's got something going with Kirsten. Even if he didn't, no one wants to date a woman who smells of rotting catfish and stale mouse droppings. This must be part of the orientation process. He must want to give me more brochures. "That's nice of you, but it's been a long day, and—"

"Then dinner out is just what you need. And I've been craving shepherd's pie, and the Irish pub at Legacy Village serves a delicious one. Have you been there?"

"Not in a while, but—"

"Then it's time to go again. Do you think you'll be ready by seven?"

I'd have to shorten the workout, lengthen the shower. I'd have to lengthen the shower a lot. "Yes, but I'll need to go home and change."

"Don't bother. It's not a fancy place. Meet me at seven, by the fountain?"

"Or I could meet you at the restaurant. That might be simpler."

"Why take two cars? I'll drive us over, then drop you back here. It's on my way home. So, seven by the fountain?"

"Seven-fifteen." I managed a smile. "That sounds like fun."

I walked into the locker room. It's not a date, I told myself, but couldn't help thinking it might be. I didn't like the way he'd talked about Emily, but he'd grown up in a fitness-crazed family. Maybe he couldn't help being intolerant of the less fit. Maybe the right woman could set him straight. I've read enough Jane Austen to know romance is best when the man and the woman have something to learn from each other. He'd help me improve my sit-ups, and I'd broaden his mind.

As for Kirsten, maybe he'd found perfection exhausting and wanted to relax with a less intimidating specimen. One way or another, Hector had asked me to dinner. Hector—the most attractive, interesting man I'd met in a long, long time.

And I was disgusting, and I couldn't go home and change. Fortunately, I had fresh underwear and a clean shirt in my tote bag. Unfortunately, it was a Top Skorz tee-shirt—orange, with big gold letters. And my jeans were the shabbiest ones I owned, purposely selected this morning because I knew I'd spend hours kneeling in goo. Well, I'd brush them off with a wet washcloth, douse them with deodorant, hope for the best.

When Rosa showed up, crisp in a white blouse and soft gray skirt, I was spraying my jeans with deodorant for the second time. I explained about dinner with Hector. For a moment, a hesitant look came into her eyes. Then she smiled. "*Great. He seems really nice. Why don't you borrow my skirt? I'll wear my sweat pants home, and you can return the skirt tomorrow at class.*"

"*Thanks, but it's okay. If Hector can't take a little fish smell—*"

"*No, really.*" Rosa's signs were firmer now, more insistent. "*You can't go to a restaurant in smelly jeans. Please, Jane. You saved my purse. Let me do* you *a favor. And my skirt should fit you fine.*"

Yes, it should. We were about the same height, about the same build. If there were any discrepancies, the flare of the skirt should hide them. And gray goes with orange as well as anything else does. It might look strange to wear a skirt with a tee-shirt and sneakers, but compared to smelly jeans, it sounded like a solution.

"*Thanks*," I signed. "*You're sure you don't mind*?"

"*No problem*," Rosa signed, and we changed into our workout clothes. She had to send a text message, she signed, so I headed for the equipment room alone. Two minutes later, she joined me. We had the place almost to ourselves. Surprising—six o'clock on a weeknight should be a popular time for people to come by after work. But maybe most people preferred the pool or the handball courts.

After fifteen minutes on stairmasters, we moved on to a rack with dumbbells lined up neatly, colors ranging from pink to black, weights ranging from wimpy to ridiculous. Kirsten had inspired me—I'd become appalled by my undefined arms and was determined to build biceps. Ten-pound weights to start, I decided, and immediately wished I'd started with five. Rosa and I made it through a reasonable number of repetitions and moved on to fifteen pounds. Those were brutal. Since our hands were busy with the weights, we couldn't sign, but we communicated with grimaces and grunts.

I noticed two women walk into the equipment room, Diana Connolly and a short, solidly built woman with dark hair pulled back in a stubby pony tail. Diana pointed to us, said something, looked at us uneasily, and left. The other woman looked at us uneasily, too. Then she walked over quickly, positioning herself in front of Rosa.

"Rosa Patterson?" Her voice was unnaturally loud, and she moved her lips in an exaggerated way. Taking a leather holder from her purse, she held it out stiffly so

Rosa could see. A photo ID and a badge. "I'm Detective Bridget Diaz. I need to ask you some questions."

Chapter 9

I put down the weights. "*I'm Detective Bridget Diaz,*" I signed and said. Not that there was any need for that—Rosa could read the card for herself. But when I interpret, I interpret everything. "*I need to ask you some questions.*"

Detective Diaz let out a sigh. "Oh, fantastic. You know sign language? You can help us?"

"I'm happy to," I said, signing simultaneously so Rosa would understand. "Rosa, okay if I interpret?"

Rosa spread the fingers of her right hand and touched her chest. "*Fine.*" Her face didn't match the sign. She sat on a bench, eyes wide with apprehension.

"Fine," I said, and nodded to Detective Diaz.

"Fantastic," she said again. She looked about thirty, with deep beige skin, remarkably dark eyes, and a delicate, almost fragile nose and chin that contrasted with the severity of her black pantsuit. "Please tell Ms. Patterson I'm—"

"Excuse me," I said, still signing as I spoke. "Please don't speak to me. Please speak directly to Rosa—to Ms. Patterson."

Detective Diaz gave me a puzzled look. "But she can't hear me."

"I know. And I'll sign everything you say, voice everything she signs. But it really will work better if you speak to her directly. It may feel odd, but you'll get used to it. Just try to forget I'm here." I walked over to stand next to her, so she couldn't look at me without taking her eyes off Rosa.

She looked skeptical but locked her eyes on Rosa and spoke—still too loudly, still with exaggerated lip movements. "Ms. Patterson, I'm looking into the death of Jennifer Linton. You're aware she died in a drowning incident last week?"

"Incident," not "accident." Rosa's eyes filled with sadness, and with something more. Was it fear? She touched her open palm to her forehead. "*I know.*"

"Some questions have come up, so I'm trying to learn more about her. I came here because she evidently spent a lot of time here. And several people told me you and she were friends. Is that correct?"

Rosa shook her fist forward, just once. "*Yes.*" She took a deep breath. "*We worked out together sometimes. And I did her nails. I'm a manicurist at Nails by Ilana, in University Heights. That's how we met.*"

"I see." Detective Diaz took a notebook from her purse and started writing things down. "And how did you—I don't know how to put this, but I assume you communicated. How? Do you read lips? Do you speak?"

"*I don't read lips. I don't speak.*" Rosa made her signs more emphatic than necessary, especially since, according to her father, she probably could read lips and speak a little. This was a statement of principle, not simply a statement of fact. "*We wrote notes and used gestures. And I was teaching her some signs.*"

"I see." Already, she was focusing on Rosa, not me. Already, she'd started to forget I was there. And she'd stopped speaking loudly and exaggerating her lip movements. "Did she ever talk to you about anyone she wasn't getting along with? Anyone who threatened her?"

Rosa brought her index and middle fingers down to close against her thumb, shaking her head as she did so—a firm, definite "*No*."

"Did she ever talk about a man she was seeing socially? About someone she was dating?"

Rosa paused before answering. "*Not really. I once asked her if she had a boyfriend, and she said no. She said she liked to date, to meet new people*."

"Did she tell you about a particular person she was dating? Did she mention a name?"

Again, the index and middle fingers closed against Rosa's thumb, but not as decisively this time, and not with an accompanying head shake.

Detective Diaz seemed to notice the difference. "Did you ever see her talking to a man—here, at the fitness center?"

It took Rosa a moment to reply. When she did, her signs were precise, almost reluctant. "*She talked to men here sometimes*."

"Was there anybody special?"

Rosa hesitated again. "*Not really*."

Detective Diaz seemed to sense Rosa was holding back. She must be a good detective to pick up on subtleties in signing so quickly.

She sat on the bench, turning to face Rosa. "I understand why you don't want to single anyone out, to give the police a name. You don't want to get an innocent person in trouble. I don't want to get innocent people in trouble, either. I'll be careful with any information you give me. I won't jump to conclusions. Maybe it'd help you to know other people have already told me about someone who seemed very friendly with Ms. Linton. I'm simply looking for confirmation."

Rosa thought that over then started signing in a rush. "*Jason Connolly flirted with her sometimes. He'd come over while we were working out and talk to her. I don't know what they said, but the way he looked at her—it seemed like flirting. But Jason flirts with everyone. He flirts with me, too. Maybe it's his way of being friendly.*"

"That's helpful. You said he flirts with you, too. Did he flirt with you in front of Ms. Linton?"

Another hesitation. "*He didn't start flirting with me until last week. Until after Jenny died.*"

Detective Diaz made a note. "Did Ms. Linton ever say—scratch that. Did she ever communicate with you about Jason Connolly in any way?"

Rosa half-smiled, sadly. "*She said he has a nice butt.*"

I wondered how Jenny had communicated that particular sentiment—not, I bet, in a note.

Detective Diaz half-smiled, too. "Do you think she had a relationship with him?"

"*I don't know.*" But this time, when she signed "know," Rosa tapped her forehead sharply, just once, and she didn't raise her shoulders or shake her head, as people often do when they sign "don't know." She doesn't know, I thought, but she suspects. I kept my voicing neutral. If Rosa wanted to convey more than "don't know," she'd have to sign it more explicitly.

"That takes care of my questions." Detective Diaz looked over her notes. "Let me ask, in a general way, if there's anything else I should know. Have you had any thoughts about Ms. Linton's death? Is there anything that would help my investigation?"

Rosa looked stricken. "*I've told you everything I know,*" she signed, with an emphasis on "know" again.

"Are you sure?" Detective Diaz watched her closely. "Because I hope you won't mind my saying this, but if Ms. Linton had a secret, she might've thought telling a deaf person would be safer than—"

"*She never told me secrets.*" Rosa made each sign distinct. "*Is that all? I have to get home for dinner.*"

"Yes, that's all. Thanks for your help." Detective Diaz turned to me. "I'd like to thank you, too. Is it okay if I speak to you directly now? I'm sorry—I don't know your name."

"Jane Ciardi. I was happy to help."

Rosa looked impatient. "*I have to go, Jane. I'll leave the skirt by your locker.*"

"*Fine,*" I signed. "*I'll see you in class. And thanks again.*"

Detective Diaz watched as Rosa practically ran to the locker room. "That's the first conversation I've ever had with a deaf person. You were right. Speaking to her directly worked better. I *did* almost forget you were here, and I feel like I picked up on more. Did it seem to you she was holding back about something?"

"I'm sorry," I said, "but I can't comment. I'm a professional interpreter, and we never comment on anything we interpret. It wouldn't be ethical." Never before had I felt so grateful for the restrictions of the code of ethics.

"I understand," she said, not looking as if she really did. "So you're Rosa's interpreter? Were you around when Jason Connolly flirted with Jennifer Linton? Why didn't you interpret for Ms. Patterson when she and—"

"I'm not Rosa's interpreter." I realized how awkward this could get. Why hadn't I run off when Rosa did? "We're just friends. We didn't meet until recently."

The skepticism was clear on her face—maybe because she was good at knowing when people weren't telling the full truth, maybe because she didn't believe what I'd said about professional ethics. But that, at least, was perfectly true. "So, you didn't meet Ms. Patterson until recently? Not until after Ms. Linton's death?"

Damn. Why had I volunteered that information? "We met at about the same time she died. I should go, too—I have a dinner date."

"Sounds like fun," she said, but didn't smile. "Let me get your phone number. If I need to talk to Ms. Patterson again, I may ask you to interpret. Your last name's Ciardi? Would you spell that, please?"

I gave her the information, headed for the locker room at a speed that rivaled Rosa's, grabbed my shampoo and two towels, closed myself into a private shower, and turned the water on maximum volume, almost maximum heat. If only it could wash away all the complications that had come up today, along with the fish smells. I agreed with Detective Diaz. Rosa had been holding back. Now I had to worry about what she'd held back, and why.

I'd been holding back, too. It was the first time I'd been questioned by a police officer, and I hadn't lied, but I hadn't been completely open, and Detective Diaz seemed to know it. If Rosa were my client, as her interpreter I could legitimately refuse to say anything that might violate her privacy. But she wasn't my client. And I thought private detectives could refuse to talk to police about their clients—at least, I remembered that from television shows—but I wasn't really a private detective. Where did that leave me? The police must have a list of sign-language interpreters officers could call. Probably, Detective Diaz asked for my phone number not because she might want me to interpret again but because she might want to question me. If she demanded details about how I met Rosa, what should I do?

Maybe I should tell her everything. Even if that violated one set of professional ethics or another, it might be the right thing to do. If Jenny Linton had been murdered—if Gary Nichols's murder wasn't a burglary gone bad—the truth should come out. What excuse could I have for not revealing everything I knew?

Except that some things I knew might focus suspicion on Rosa and Sam in an unfair, ridiculous way. If Detective Diaz found out Rosa's father had hired a private detective to watch her, wouldn't she think that Rosa must be capable of doing terrible things, that even her own family saw her that way? If she questioned Rosa more harshly, if she took her to the police station, that would be a frightening experience. And focusing on Rosa might distract Detective Diaz from going after the person really responsible for Jenny's death.

Assuming, of course, Rosa wasn't the person responsible.

Of course she isn't, I told myself.

Then the next problem hit me. I'd interpreted for Rosa, so I had an ethical obligation to keep her communications confidential. But Walt was paying me to watch Rosa, so I had an ethical obligation to tell him everything I observed. How could I honor my obligations to Walt without violating my obligations to Rosa?

I turned off the water, wrapped one towel around my hair and the other around my body, and vowed to stop thinking about all this. For the first time in months, I was going to dinner with a man I found attractive and charming. I should focus on trying to be attractive and charming myself. Enough drama, I decided. From this moment on, I refuse to think about anything except having fun.

I walked to my locker. There was Rosa's skirt, neatly laid out on a bench. And there, next to it, hands on hips, stood Dr. Kirsten Carlson, buck naked.

Chapter 10

Hey, Jane!" Tossing her head, Kirsten flipped her long, wet hair onto her back. "I hear you and Hector have a date tonight. Awesome!"

Was she being sarcastic? Was she in fact furious about Hector's betrayal, ready to pound me to a pulp with those powerful arms? If so, I hoped she'd let me get dressed first. Getting beat up is never dignified, but wrestling in the raw—no. I'd be too embarrassed to defend myself.

"It's not really a date," I said. "He probably just wants to show me brochures."

"Of course it's a date. Hector told me." She looked at me closely and then laughed. "You're afraid I'm jealous, aren't you? Honey, I'm never jealous about Hector. Hector and I have a bond. He dates lots of people, I date lots of people, but the bond goes so much deeper than any of that. It's who we are. It's okay if you don't understand that. Most people don't. The point is, I'm glad you're going out with him. I'm sure glad you're not going out with Jason. I heard he tried to hit on you yesterday, and it made me want to spit. Jason's *such* a loser."

How should I respond? Agreeing wasn't safe, disagreeing wasn't safe, and I had no idea of what was going on. "Well, Jason's married, isn't he?"

She seemed surprised, as if that detail hadn't struck her as important. "Yeah, there's that, too. Not that I blame him for stepping out—his wife's a sarcastic bitch—but I hate the way he runs after every new girl who joins the center. I mean, we're not monks. I've screwed lots of guys who come here. But there should be some discretion about time and place. You know?"

Now what? Should I agree that one should show discretion about when and where one screws center members? "Jason does seem to be a flirt."

"A flirt?" She laughed. "Sweetie, Jason doesn't waste time flirting. He sees someone he wants, and pow! Sometimes it's in his office, sometimes in the sauna, sometimes in a handball court. I once caught him in the rock-climbing room, doing it standing up with this girl barely out of her teens, plastering her against the rock wall. I made him stop, but her back was already such a mess I had to give her first aid. You wouldn't believe how deep the indentations went."

How much more uncomfortable could a conversation get? "That's right," I said, hoping to steer talk in a more normal direction—though with Kirsten naked, real normalcy was not an option. "You're a doctor. Do you have a specialty?"

"Gynecology." Why did that not surprise me? "I used to do obstetrics, too, but the hours messed up my social life. And popping babies out is boring. I mean, if things go wrong, it can get interesting, but usually it's just don't push, push, grunt, groan, gush."

And how much variety, I wondered, did gynecology offer? I didn't ask. I didn't want to hear her answer. "I see what you mean," I said, though I didn't.

"You bet." She snapped her fingers. "Hey, I'll give you my card. All the volleyball girls come to me. It builds team spirit. And not to brag, but I'm the best. Fast, painless, good. Damn good. I'll be right back."

She strode off, and I snatched my clothes and sprinted to a dressing room. Kirsten wasn't the only woman who didn't mind going naked in the locker room. After the game yesterday, several of my teammates stood around chatting in the raw.

But I'm not that liberated. I toweled off and pulled on my clothes. Kirsten and Hector looked intimate yesterday, but she didn't seem upset about my date with him. She seemed delighted. If they really were intimate, that wouldn't be possible. Would it? And she didn't talk like any doctor I'd ever met, didn't act like any doctor I'd ever met. What the hell was the deal with her?

I headed back to my locker. No Kirsten. Gratefully, I went to the station at the end of the row of lockers, blew my hair dry, and peered into the mirror to do my makeup. Just as I finished, Kirsten came back. Her hair was dry now, too, full and glorious, and her makeup was perfect. Still no clothes.

"You look great," she said. "Cute shirt. Top Skorz—what's that? A band?"

Exactly the same question Ulysses Patterson had asked. But imagining two human beings more different than Ulysses Patterson and Kirsten Carlson would take some effort. "It's a place where I work," I said, fighting off waves of *déjà vu*. "We help students prepare for the SAT."

She looked shocked. "Oh, man. How boring can you get? And I bet it pays shit. Hector said you were patching jobs together, but I didn't know it was *that* bad. You've gotta find something better, girl—something fun, something that pays. So, here's my card. Center members get a discount on paps. I'm glad we got a chance to talk about Jason. He's caused lots of girls here lots of grief. You'll stay away from him, right?"

I fussed with my hair. It gave me a way of not looking at Kirsten directly—I could still see her in the mirror, but not as much of her. "I always stay away from married men."

She shrugged. "Whatever. As long as you stay away from Jason. I don't know how Hector turned out so great. Both Jason and Diana are rank."

I turned around, surprised. "Diana? She seems very nice, very smart."

"Smart, but bossy as hell. She tries to run her brothers' lives."

Jason could probably use help running his life. "She's quite a bit older than they are, isn't she? Maybe she feels maternal toward them."

"Yeah, she's older. I guess after she was born, her parents had to work up the nerve to try again, scared they'd get stuck with another ugly baby. But Jason was gorgeous, so they went ahead and had Hector." Kirsten pursed her lips. "And yeah, Diana was like a mom to them. Hector's said that. Elise and Ray were focused on the center, so Diana picked up the slack. Fine. But they're all grown up. She should back off."

Neutral response, I decided. "It's probably hard to let go."

"Especially if you're a bitch." Kirsten sniffed. "Perfume. I don't smell perfume."

Oh, God. I smelled bad. "Do I smell like fish?"

"Fish? No. Why would you smell like fish? You smell like shampoo. But you're going out with Hector. Shampoo's not good enough." She grabbed my wrist and started running. "I've got Shalini. It's his favorite. Come on!"

Once we got to her lockers—she had three, all stocked solid with stuff—she found her Shalini and doused my pulse points. I didn't protest.

She *is* a goddess, I thought—an all-powerful, demented goddess. Resistance is futile.

"Earrings!" she cried, and ordered me to take out my silver posts and put on dangly gold-and-amber things that, I had to admit, set my Top Skorz shirt off perfectly. She decided my hair lacked luster, made me bend over while she back-brushed it, worked some sweet-smelling substance through it with her vigorous hands, re-parted it, and stood back. "There!" she said.

I looked into the mirror lining the door of one of her lockers and gasped. My hair had never looked this good before in my life. What had she done, and could I ever duplicate it?

"Wanna see what I'm wearing tonight?" Kirsten reached into a locker, pulled out a black satin sheath with silver spaghetti straps, and gazed at it affectionately. "My getting-laid dress. It's magic. Whenever I get horny—and I'm horny as hell, it's been three days—I head out wearing this, and pow! It's hard to get them to buy me dinner first. Not because they're cheap. They always spring for nice hotels, and they always get me Dom Perignon and whatever I want from room service afterward. They're just so *eager*. Isn't that sweet?"

I am so out of my depth here, I thought. Three days, and she's horny? If she had to live my life, she'd have slit her throat years ago. But it felt wrong not to caution her. "Isn't that dangerous? To go to a hotel with someone you don't know well, I mean. Don't you worry about—"

"It's dangerous if you're stupid," Kirsten cut in. "I'm not stupid, so I don't worry. I can spot freaks and losers a mile off. But most guys are fine." A dreamy look came into her eyes. "I *love* men. Don't you? I love meeting new ones. So many are great—really smart, really fun. And even ones who aren't outstanding can be interesting. I love figuring out how to make them happy, showing them how to make me happy. It's intellectually stimulating. Well, here goes."

In seconds, she'd pulled the dress over her head, smoothed it into place, and slipped into silver stiletto heels. No bra, no underpants, no slip, no hose—just large green earrings that looked like real emeralds, a generous dose of Shalini, a final flip of that magnificent hair. She lifted both arms in the air, leaned her head back, and yowled. Dr. Kirsten Carlson was ready for a night on the town.

"You look gorgeous," I said, and meant it. No way would she get to eat dinner in a restaurant tonight. I hoped that the hotel would have a good room-service menu, that the Dom Perignon would be properly chilled, and that she'd be safe, and that she wouldn't catch cold with no underwear on. "Have a nice time."

"You, too." She reached out, cupping my face in both hands, and kissed my forehead. When she backed away, she had tears in her eyes. "Tell Hector I said hi. You'll have a very good time tonight, Jane. Remember what I said about great men? Hector's one of the best. And he's fantastic in bed. So strong, so confident, so really, really sweet. Trust me—I know."

Good grief. "It's just dinner. I hardly know him. It won't—"

She pressed a finger against my lips. One tear made its way, slowly, down her cheek. "I told you Jason doesn't waste time flirting. Neither does Hector. You'll have a very good time tonight. But don't forget—tell him I said, hi."

She picked up her purse and coat, slammed her three locker doors shut, and walked off without glancing back. Dear God, I thought. What kind of people are these? What have I gotten myself into?

Chapter 11

Twenty minutes later I sat at a small wooden table, savoring the warm smells of cabbage, onion, and beef, smiling at Hector Connolly. We had the best table in the place, the one framed by two leaded glass windows set deep in sharply peaked stone arches, the one directly in front of the rustic fireplace only slightly disfigured by a big-screen television perched above the mantel. Had we landed at this table by chance, or had Hector called ahead, promising to slip the hostess a twenty or two? He'd definitely slipped her something. Normally, I'd consider that sweet. Tonight, after talking to Kirsten, it put me on my guard. What payoff did he expect for all this studied romance?

The hostess asked about drinks. Alcohol only in moderation, I remembered from my interview with Hector. So no Jameson's, good as a cold, hard shot of Irish whiskey would feel after my encounters with Detective Bridget Diaz and Dr. Kirsten Carlson. And Hector's a jock, and jocks like beer.

"Michelob Light, please," I said. There, I thought. How's *that* for moderation?

"Orange juice," Hector said. "Thanks."

Damn. "I'm sorry," I said after the hostess walked

away. "I don't need anything alcoholic. We can call the hostess back."

"Jane, it's fine." He reached across the table to close his hand over mine. "I don't disapprove of alcohol. I simply don't choose to use it."

Well, hell. I don't think of myself as "using" it, either—I don't feed an addiction with it, I don't rub it into my armpits or lubricate my knees with it, and I don't drink it to excess. "I've heard," I said, "that alcohol in moderation promotes good health."

Hector nodded. "I've heard that, too. It may be true. But I can't forget what my father said: 'If you never take that first drink, you can never become an alcoholic.'"

"You mean you've never had a drink? Not one?"

"Never." He smiled. "Not one."

I couldn't believe it. "Did you go to college?"

He laughed. "University of Akron, physical education major, *magna cum laude*. And I went to lots of parties and always enjoyed myself. Whenever I felt tempted, I simply reminded myself of my father's saying."

Abby told me something once, something her grandfather once told her: "When you arrive at the World to Come, you'll have to answer for every innocent glass of wine you denied yourself, every time you refused the pleasures of the world God created for us to enjoy." On the whole, I thought that saying beat Hector's father's saying, hands down. "Your father must've had a big influence on you," I said idiotically. Now I really wanted that Jameson's.

He nodded. "He was my hero. Lots of sons say that. For me, it's literally true. I've never met anyone else I admired half as much. Not one tenth as much."

Even after all these years, his face tightened with pain. Poor thing. I wanted to hug him. True, I'd wanted to hug him before he'd talked about his father, but now the desire intensified, and not for purely selfish reasons. "He died in a car accident?"

"Yes." The waitress brought our drinks; Hector waited for her to leave. "I was fifteen, at camp in Maine—the last summer I went to camp. The director woke me up at 3:00 in the morning, to tell me my father was dead. My mother had called and insisted I be told right away. So I packed—that took ten minutes—and I sat on my bunk, watching the other boys in the cabin sleep, listening to them snore, thinking about my father, vowing I'd always be true to everything he'd taught me. That's when I decided I'd never take a drink."

If I'd been your mother, I thought, I'd have let you sleep. I'd have asked the camp director to tell you in the morning, when you had friends and counselors around you. I wouldn't have let you face that night alone. But Elise Reed must've been wild with grief. She couldn't be expected to think coherently. "That sounds incredibly hard."

"I got through it. The next day, I took a bus and a plane. Jason was sick, so sick he couldn't come to the funeral, and Mom was hysterical, but Diana had things under control, and I helped with final arrangements. It was a beautiful funeral." He sipped his orange juice and smiled. "How'd we get started on this? We shouldn't talk about funerals on a first date. Jane, you look great. I love what you've done with your hair. And your shirt's very striking. Top Skorz—the SAT place, right?"

Thank goodness he didn't ask if it was a band. He must've remembered that from my application, I thought, giving him points for a good memory, and for being interested enough in me to remember. I picked up the menu. "That's right. So, you said the shepherd's pie is good. But it's got to be loaded with calories."

"You don't have to worry about calories," he said, "as

long as you work them off. Order shepherd's pie—that's what I'm having. And let's have soup and salad and dessert. We'll find a way to work the calories off later."

Somehow, I didn't think he meant going back the center and hitting the treadmills. Let it pass, I decided. Pretend you don't think he meant anything by it. "I'll try shepherd's pie, maybe a salad. But no soup, no dessert."

He grinned. "I'm not giving up on dessert. The bread pudding's incredible. Did you enjoy your workout?"

"Very much." Not that I worked out much, I thought. I was too busy interpreting for a police detective who probably suspects your brother of murder. At least my code of ethics kept me from having to agonize about whether to tell Hector that. I couldn't—end of story. "It's a wonderful facility."

"It is. I'm glad you're taking advantage of it so often."

"I want to make the most of my one-month membership." I caught myself. "And then I hope to get a regular membership. I've already grown used to coming to the center. If I had to stop, I'd miss it."

"I'm sure you would. Well, who knows? Maybe things will work out. Say, I ran into Kirsten. She said you two had a nice chat tonight."

A nice chat. That's one way to describe it. "She's quite something."

"She sure is." His voice was warm with affection. "And she looked great, all decked out in her getting-laid dress. I hope she meets someone nice."

So he knew about the getting-laid dress. "I hope she'll be safe. It sounds risky."

"Kirsten's a risk-taker, that's for sure. Bungee jumping, hang gliding—she'll try anything. But when she goes out, she doesn't take risks. She's smart. That eliminates risks. And she enjoys sex, and she's good at it. Why should she deny herself?" He smiled at some memory.

"She's the second woman I ever had sex with. She taught me a lot. She *still* teaches me a lot, every time."

Was he really saying these things? Part of me wished we'd stuck with talking about the center's facilities. Part of me felt fascinated. "So you still get together? And you don't mind that she gets together with other men?"

"Why should I mind?" He lifted his glass, lifted an eyebrow. "I 'get together,' as you put it, with other women. Kirsten's my best friend. I've known her forever, and we can talk about anything. Basically, it's a platonic relationship."

"Except that you have sex."

He shrugged. "So it's a neo-platonic relationship. The important thing is, we always have a nice time, whether we play a great game of tennis, or cook a great dinner, or have great sex. We also have nice times with other people. What's wrong with that?"

I thought I knew the answer to that question. "I guess if neither of you has any interest in having an exclusive relationship or settling down—"

"I want to settle down. One day, when I find the right woman. Kirsten loves her freedom too much to want that. But I want to fall in love, and stay in love for the rest of my life. I want to get married and have children. I want what my father had. And once I find the right woman, that's it. No other women, ever."

"Not even Kirsten?"

"Especially not Kirsten. I've told her that. She doesn't believe me. She says I'll never cut her off. But when I find the right woman, I will. Kirsten will always be a friend, but the right woman wouldn't want her to be more. I wouldn't want it, either." He looked at me and then laughed. "What? You don't think I can do it?"

I lifted my beer in a half-salute. "Remember what you said about Emily? You said she doesn't have the right level of commitment. Once she makes it down the aisle, she'll hit the nachos again. You said she hasn't developed the self-discipline to resist. Well."

"This is different. I've always wanted marriage and a family, but I've always known I wasn't ready yet. When I'm ready to make the commitment, I'll keep it. The night my father died, I made a commitment to not drinking. I've kept it. When I make a commitment to the right woman, it'll be the same. Until then, why shouldn't I enjoy myself? Who am I hurting?"

Again, I thought I knew the answer. Luckily, the waitress came over, so I didn't have to articulate it. We placed our orders, Hector said we'd decide about dessert later, and I smiled. But no way was I having dessert. I was sure Hector could come up with clever arguments about working off calories without hurting anyone, and I didn't trust myself to find clever ways to refute him. Skipping dessert felt safer.

He handed the waitress our menus. "How's the job search? I know you had problems with one interpreters' agency. Are there others?"

"Yes, and I submitted resumes to all of them, long ago. But once you have trouble with one agency—I'm not holding my breath."

"Is it that ethics problem? Have all the agencies blacklisted you?"

"It's nothing that formal. But word gets around." I folded my hands on the table. "I don't want you to get the wrong idea about what happened. I really didn't—"

"As I said, it's none of my business. And it's so subjective. What seems unethical to one person seems fine to another, and who's to say who's right?"

"You're trying to make me feel better. That's sweet, but—"

"I'm not trying to make you feel better. These words

we throw around—ethical, unethical, moral, immoral, legal, illegal. They're *all* subjective. Laws, for example. Most just reflect the preferences of the people with power. So you don't have to explain."

"I *want* to explain. But it's a long story." I took a deep breath. Could I cram it into a few sentences? "About a year ago, I was a last-minute replacement at a murder trial—my first and last time in criminal court. A deaf man was accused of killing his boss."

"At the School for the Deaf, right? I read about that."

"Everybody read about it. It got national attention. I worked with a co-interpreter, a highly experienced woman with lots of connections in the interpreting community. We agreed I'd sign for hearing witnesses, and she'd voice for deaf witnesses."

"Voice for them? You mean she watched what they signed and translated it into speech?"

"She interpreted for them, yes." It'd take too long to explain the difference between "translation" and "interpretation," to explain there's no such thing as exact translation between American Sign Language and spoken English. "As I watched what one crucial witness signed and listened to what the co-interpreter voiced, I became convinced the co-interpreter was prejudiced against the defendant and was deliberately distorting the witness's testimony. I think she was trying to keep suspicion focused on the defendant, obscuring details that pointed toward other people. During a recess, I told her about my concerns. Naturally, she denied doing anything improper."

"Did she keep doing it?"

"No. Maybe, after I confronted her, she was more careful. The defendant was acquitted—the case against him was weak—and no one else has been charged. The media started saying it'd probably been a burglary gone bad, and the police and the prosecutor seem content to let it go."

Hector lifted his hands, spreading his fingers. "So how come you got in trouble?"

I sighed. "Because I filed an ethics complaint with the agency. The director didn't want to take action, but I insisted he watch the videotape of that witness's testimony. I thought the co-interpreter shouldn't be allowed to interpret in court again. He finally watched the tape, and he issued a mild reprimand to the co-interpreter, saying perhaps her voicing could've been more precise. She's still interpreting in court. And the agency hasn't given me a job since. No agency has."

"Now I get it." He sat back in his chair. "You got branded as a troublemaker. And nobody wants to hire a troublemaker."

"Not even if she's right," I agreed. "He *must* know I was right. But if word got out, it'd embarrass the agency. So he's protecting the agency by discrediting me. I'm sure when another agency calls for a reference, he says he stopped giving me assignments because I was involved in an ethics dispute. I'm sure he makes it sound as if I'm the unethical one, not the one who reported someone else."

"I'm sorry. That's very unfair."

"That's not the worst of it. I think the real murderer was in the courtroom that day. I think that witness's testimony pointed in that person's direction. The testimony aroused *my* suspicions. If it'd been interpreted properly, I think other people would've suspected that person, too."

"Really? Who do you think the murderer was?"

I shook my head. "I don't have proof, so I shouldn't gossip about my suspicions. The truth should've come out at the trial. If the co-interpreter hadn't covered things up, it might have. But it didn't, so I have to let it go.

Someone got away with murder, and now there's nothing I can do about it."

"And now you also can't get an interpreting job. All that training, and you can't use it." He sighed. "I guess that experience taught you something. Getting all upset about some ethics thing doesn't pay. If you could go back in time, I bet you'd do things differently."

"Yes, I would," I said. "I'd stop the trial. I'd go to the judge and insist he call experts in to watch the videotape immediately."

He stared at me. "But that would've created a public scandal. You would've gotten in even more trouble."

"Absolutely. That's why I didn't do it. I thought about doing it, but I chickened out. It was my first time in criminal court, and I felt overwhelmed. I let myself believe that I didn't have to take a stand, that I could let things go and hope they'd work out. That was wrong. Someone got away with murder, and maybe I could've prevented it. Maybe not. But I should've tried. And every day, for the rest of my life, I'll have to live with the knowledge that I didn't do the right thing because I was afraid."

Even as I spoke, I could hear my voice growing harsher, more bitter. I hadn't meant to say all that. But this had been the central moral test of my life, a test I'd failed. I couldn't let Hector shrug it off as proof it doesn't pay to make a fuss. I don't know why, but I could not stand to let him do that.

The waitress brought our salads and retreated. We both stayed silent for a long moment. Finally, he reached across the table to put his hand on mine again, to put his hand on my clenched fist.

"Jane," he said. "I was too flip. I didn't realize how much this meant to you. I'm sorry."

"It's all right." I picked up my fork and attacked my salad. "It's funny. When I was working toward national certification, I took an ethics course. I got impatient. Why spend a whole semester discussing every ethical dilemma that could ever come up? Now I wish it had been a two-semester course. I've encountered so many ethical dilemmas the course didn't cover." Just in the last week, I'd encountered several. But if I told him that, he'd ask me to explain, and I couldn't. It wouldn't be ethical. "So, you were a physical education major. Would you like to teach?"

"Definitely. It's what I've always wanted to do. Get a job at a high school, teach, coach. I volunteer now as the soccer coach at a private school, and I love it. The practices are always the best part of my day."

I could picture him as a coach, with his enthusiasm, his good humor, his overall niceness. His players must adore him. And his father had been a coach. Hector hadn't said that was one reason he wanted to coach, too. Some things are too obvious to say. I hesitated, not wanting to be tactless. "But you decided to work at the center."

"Oh, I love working at the center. But it's temporary." He laughed. "Long-term temporary. Over ten years now. When I graduated, the center was in rough shape. The national chains attract so many people. It's hard for a local business to compete. And my mother's health kept her from promoting it as much as she'd like, and Diana knew we needed renovations but had a hard time paying for them. Paul Kent helped—he's been with us since before my father died. But Diana said she needed me to turn things around. And we seem to be pulling it off."

Interesting—when Hector spoke of people helping to keep the center going, he didn't mention Jason. Probably, he thought of Jason as useless, or worse than useless. Probably, he was right. "That must've been a tough decision," I said. "To put your own dreams on hold for years so you could help your family. That's so unselfish."

Hector lifted a hand. "No big deal. It just felt like the thing to do. Don't make it sound like something noble."

"It *was* noble." This time, I was the one to reach across the table, to take his hand and squeeze it. "You worked hard in college—*magna cum laude*—so you could pursue the career you'd chosen. But when your family needed you, you made a sacrifice. You did something generous and good. I admire you for that."

He blushed. He looked at his plate, pretending to be absorbed in cutting lettuce. "You wouldn't admire me so much if I told you about the dumb mistakes I made during my first years on the job. I had this big inspiration for promoting the center. We'd give Elise Reed Spirit of Cleveland Awards to community volunteers, get local news to cover the ceremony. To advertise our ice rink, we'd hold the ceremony there, have people skate across it to get their certificates. Oh, man! Was *that* a disaster."

He described award recipients flailing and falling, glass shattering as framed certificates fell from numb hands halfway across the ice. I reciprocated with an account of my misadventures at the seafood restaurant we'd tried to rescue today. By the time our shepherd's pie arrived, we were both laughing, trading stories about childhood embarrassments, about pets, about teenaged dates gone horribly wrong. I couldn't remember the last time I'd felt so relaxed and comfortable with a man. When the waitress asked about dessert and Hector again recommended bread pudding, I said sure—remembering, too late, the possible consequences of consuming calories that'd need to be worked off. Damn.

He left a tip and smiled at me. "Jane, I've had a fantastic time. Thanks. Shall I drive you back to the center?"

"I've had a nice time, too. Thank you. And yes, I'm ready to go."

But he won't really want to go back to the center, I thought as he helped me with my jacket. Halfway there, he'll suggest we go to his apartment for a quick drink—or, actually, a quick shot of orange juice. And I'll have to find a gentle way to say no. Too bad. Such a lovely evening, and it had to end with awkwardness.

He drove straight to the center, pulled into the parking garage, and asked me to point out my car. He parked next to it, got out, and opened my door. When I got out, he shook my hand.

"Thanks again, Jane," he said. "This has been special." And he kissed me, quickly, on the cheek.

Kirsten had said I'd have a very good time tonight. She'd meant, obviously, that I'd have sex with Hector, that he always had sex with women he took to dinner. If he'd tried, I would've refused. I'd rehearsed ways of wording my refusal. But I felt almost hurt he hadn't tried. What—was I that much less attractive than every other woman he'd ever taken to dinner?

Not knowing what else to do, I kissed his cheek, making my kiss even quicker than his. I unlocked my car door, and he held it open as I got in.

Just before he closed the door, he smiled, a little sadly. "I'll call you," he said.

No, you won't, I thought. I did something wrong, or I'm just wrong. You'll never call.

Chapter 12

He called the next afternoon. I was at the seafood restaurant, in the men's room, scrubbing mold off wall tiles. He left a message on my cell phone.

He'd had a wonderful time last night, he said. And he hoped he wasn't rushing things, but tomorrow, Wednesday, was his mother's birthday, and it was a family tradition to gather at her house for a potluck dinner. If I was free, he'd love it if I'd come with him. Please call back.

I replayed the message twice, then sat on the steps behind the restaurant, staring at my phone. He'd invited me to dinner with his family. And we'd known each other less than a week, we'd gone out only once, and he hadn't even tried to have sex with me.

Maybe this explained why. I'd thought last night was unusually wonderful. Maybe he'd thought so, too. He'd come close to saying so. Maybe he'd actually meant it. Maybe his dinner dates were usually one-night stands, but maybe, at some point, he'd decided he wanted our date to be the beginning of something more.

You're reading too much into this, I told myself, but didn't believe it. After one date, he'd invited me to have dinner with his family. That isn't what people usually do.

It had to mean something.

I called back to accept, and we negotiated. I wanted to get his mother a gift and make something for the potluck, he said no to both, and we eventually agreed I'd skip the gift but bring a salad. I hung up feeling very happy. In some ways, it'd be awkward. I suspected Jason Connolly of murder. That'd make it tough to chat comfortably as he passed the salt. But I'd manage.

And I had the perfect dress. I thought of the maroon and black dress I'd bought from Jenny Linton's roommate, thought of how often I'd gazed at it since then, longing to wear it. Now I had my chance. It was modest enough for a family celebration, flattering enough to hold Hector's interest. I didn't have the right necklace to wear with it, but I had a decent gold bracelet.

Thinking of the bracelet, I looked down at my hands and felt appalled. Two days of heavy-duty restaurant cleaning had left my nails ragged. Luckily, I knew a manicurist.

Lisa had said on Wednesdays, Jenny used to meet friends from the Reed Center at the salon where Rosa worked. During her lunch break, Lisa said—probably, that meant around noon. I could make it to Nails by Ilana around noon tomorrow. It'd been years since I'd gotten my nails done professionally, but this was an emergency. I could splurge. And maybe, if Jenny's friends showed up, I could learn more about her.

That night, before class started, I spotted Rosa. "*Your skirt's in my car*," I signed. "*I'll get it dry-cleaned and return it Thursday*."

"*Not necessary*." She made it emphatic. "*I'm sure it's fine, and I'm planning to wear it tomorrow. How was your date*?"

"*Fantastic. We had an amazing conversation.*"

"*Great.*" She looked toward the mats. "*Want to warm up*?"

I nodded but felt disappointed. I'd expected more enthusiasm, I'd expected lots of questions, and I'd looked forward to being coy, to making her work at getting me to bashfully admit he'd already asked me out again. Maybe she felt awkward. The session with Detective Diaz had upset her, and this was the first time she'd seen me since then. She'll get over it, I thought, and joined her in twists and toe-touches.

Class went predictably. I did well on kicks and punches, did well on joint locks, did well on sparring, couldn't fall. This time, Sam stopped me after five minutes.

"That's enough," he said. "You don't have to keep trying. You obviously don't want to do this. Until you do, it won't happen. Your turn, Robert."

Grim-faced, Robert took my place on the mat, threw himself forward, and aced it. I joined several others in applauding, and he flashed me a grin.

I walked over to a group practicing kicks. Sam's given up on me, I thought. Good. Now I won't have to endure those humiliating minutes on the mats. But I felt like a failure.

Later, in the parking lot, I returned Rosa's skirt. "*Are you working tomorrow*?" I asked. "*I'd like to get a manicure. My nails are in rough shape.*"

She winced. "*I noticed. Is it that cleaning job, the one that spoiled your jeans? You shouldn't have to do jobs like that. You should be interpreting. It's not fair.*"

I lifted a shoulder. "*The job's not so bad—best hourly rate of any of my jobs. Can you save my nails*?"

"*I'll try. I work from noon until six tomorrow. Does that fit your schedule*?"

I formed the "P" shape with both hands and brought the middle fingers together. "*Perfect.*" She hadn't asked, but I couldn't resist telling her. "*It's for a special occasion. It's Elise Reed's birthday tomorrow, the whole family's having dinner at her house, and Hector asked me to come. Can you believe it? He hardly knows me, and he's invited me to a family celebration.*"

She smiled, but those large, dark eyes looked sad. "*Family celebrations are hard when you've lost someone you love. You keep thinking about the person who should be there but isn't. I'm sure Hector will be missing his father tomorrow. If he thinks having you there will help him, he must really like you.*" She gave me a card with the salon's address. "*No charge for the manicure.*"

"*No, you'll get in trouble with your boss if you don't charge me.*"

"*Come at 1:00. My boss is at lunch then—everyone else is. It's just me. Please, Jane. I really don't want you to pay.*"

She made it emphatic. I was surprised to see tears standing in her eyes. "*We'll figure it out tomorrow,*" I signed.

She nodded, and we both got in our cars.

She seemed emotional these days. She'd been emphatic about lending me the skirt, too. Tonight, I understood the emotion. When she'd talked about Hector missing his father, she must've been thinking about her mother, about how poignant her own family celebrations had become. I couldn't offer her sympathy, though. She'd never talked about her family, so officially, I didn't know her mother was dead.

I got home minutes before Abby returned from having dinner with Nate. She joined me in the kitchen, where I was poaching chicken. Leaving it to simmer, I poured us two cold, stiff Diet Cokes, and we sat down for a serious chat.

I said what a good first impression Nate had made,

and she demanded details about Hector. The issue of jewelry for tomorrow night came up, and Abby ran to her room to fetch a string of black beads with gold specks—costume jewelry, but classy. We were going through my jewelry box, arguing about earrings, when the phone rang. I glanced at the clock. Ten minutes past ten.

Hector, I thought—he can't get through the night without talking to me. No, that was silly. It was probably my mother. She sometimes called this late, to make sure I was stuck at home as usual and not out enjoying myself.

It was Frederick Patterson. "I'm sorry to call this late. But Rosa came to my apartment to ask some questions, and I'm worried. Could I see you?"

"Of course. I'm working tomorrow, but by noon I should—"

"Could I see you tonight? This might be serious."

I felt stunned, and scared. Frederick had seemed so cool, so calm. What had Rosa said to get him this upset? "Fine. I live in Richmond Heights, on Loganberry Drive."

"I'll be there in fifteen minutes. What's the address?"

I gave it to him. Good grief, I thought, and explained the situation to Abby. She started clearing away clutter in the living room, and I focused on the kitchen. At least the chicken was done. I had it safe in the refrigerator and had just sponged off the counter when the security door buzzer sounded.

Chapter 13

Abby stayed in the living room long enough to be introduced, then retreated tactfully to her bedroom. Tonight, Frederick wore jeans, a casual shirt, and a brown leather jacket. Worried as I was about Rosa, I couldn't help noticing how snugly the jeans fit, how well a more casual look suited him. I should have been ashamed of myself, and I more or less was.

"Would you like something to drink?" I asked. "We have Diet Coke and—"

"I'm fine." He sat on the couch, not resting back, arms propped on his legs. "And I'm sorry. It's ridiculously late. But with the way Rosa's been acting, I didn't know what to think."

"It's not that late. What happened?"

He ran his hand back over his scant hair. "She showed up at my place maybe an hour ago, with notes already written out." He reached into his jacket pocket, pulled out several sheets of jagged-edged paper, and read the first note out loud. "'I need help. I need to ask you questions. But you have to promise not to tell Dad. Otherwise, I'll leave, and you can't help me.'"

"Good grief," I said. "That put you in an awkward position."

"Damn straight. She wouldn't make me promise unless it was serious. I hated to promise to keep something like that from my father. But if she walked away without anyone to help her—I couldn't let that happen. So I promised. And she handed me the second note."

He held it out to me silently.

"'If the police question you and you don't tell the whole truth, is that a crime? If you don't lie, but you don't say everything you know, can you go to jail?'" I set the note down. "I see why that upset you. And I think I know what the note's about."

"I thought you might. When I read that note, I almost lost it. I tried asking her what had happened—I wrote her notes, used every sign I know. She wouldn't tell me anything. Finally, I wrote that she had to tell me if she'd been arrested, if she'd been taken to the police station. And she wrote this." He moved on to the third note. "'No. It happened at the Reed Center. A friend interpreted for me. Now answer my questions.' I'm hoping the friend was you."

"It was." Desperately, I tried to sort out the ethical issues I'd put on hold. I'd known I'd have to report to Walt tomorrow, but I hadn't expected Frederick to show up tonight. "I'd like to tell you everything, but I can't. I think it's all right for me to confirm that a police detective came to the Reed Center yesterday and questioned Rosa. I think it's all right to say I interpreted for her. I can't tell you what the detective asked her or what Rosa said. Deaf people rely on interpreters to communicate with the hearing world. If they had to worry that what they said might be repeated, they wouldn't feel free to communicate. So confidentiality is essential."

He nodded slowly. "It's like attorney-client privilege. And I'd never ask you to violate your professional ethics. But if you could give me any idea of what happened, I'd be grateful. I'm afraid Rosa's suspected of a crime and isn't doing what she should to protect her rights. I'm worried sick I should be taking action on her behalf, but I don't know what to do. Can you help me?"

I looked at his face—so earnest, so open, so miserable. There had to be a way. "I'll get us some wine," I said, and headed for the kitchen. By the time I came back, I had a plan. I handed Frederick a glass of Chianti. "I'd like to set your mind at ease. And I could, at least to some extent, if I could speak freely."

Some of the tension went out of his shoulders. "That's good to hear. Thank you."

"I haven't really said anything. I'm simply commenting on the situation. I can't reveal the content of Rosa's conversation with the detective. Maybe I shouldn't have said the conversation took place, but she'd already essentially told you, so I went ahead."

"That seems right." He sat forward. "Now, if you weren't paid for your services yesterday, was it really an interpreting job? Would the rules about confidentiality apply?"

I shook my head regretfully. "I think so. When you do *pro bono* work, you still respect your client's confidences, don't you?"

He nodded, half-smiling. Probably, he'd known that dodge wasn't valid but hoped I wouldn't realize it. "True."

"On the other hand," I said, "I think I can tell you about my own experience. I don't see why I can't tell you what the detective said to me."

"That works. Go ahead."

"All right. While Rosa and I were working out, a police officer identified herself as Detective Bridget Diaz and said she wanted to ask Rosa some questions. I asked Rosa if she'd like me to interpret. About ten minutes later, Rosa left the room. I think I can legitimately tell you about the brief conversation Detective Diaz and I had after Rosa left. Then you can draw any inferences that seem appropriate."

He took a sip of wine but didn't speak.

"Essentially, Detective Diaz asked if I'd ever interpreted for Rosa and a woman named Jenny Linton. She asked if I'd seen a man named Jason Connolly flirt with Jenny Linton."

Frederick's brow furrowed. "Jenny Linton—the woman who drowned at The Flats. Walt Sadowski told us she and Rosa were friends. And Jason Connolly is Elise Reed's son, right? Sadowski said you saw him put his arm around Rosa." He took a moment to sort the information out. "So Diaz is evidently looking into Linton's death and suspects she had a relationship with Connolly. Maybe she considers Connolly a suspect in Linton's death. Is that right? That's why she questioned Rosa? She doesn't suspect Rosa herself of any crime?"

"I'm sorry. I can't reveal anything about Detective Diaz's conversation with Rosa. As I said, you have to draw your own inferences."

"Right, right. Sorry." He grinned. "And you can't comment on the quality of my inferences?"

I shrugged. "I can comment, in a general way, that I'd expect anyone who made law review at Princeton to draw good inferences."

"Don't believe everything you hear about Princeton," he said, grinning again, "but thanks. Well, if Rosa isn't a suspect, if she was questioned only about Linton's relationships, that's a relief. But she couldn't have told this detective everything she knew, or she wouldn't be worried. I wonder what she held back, and why?"

"I can't help you there, and not because of ethical restrictions. I honestly don't know."

"No. None of us knows. Sadowski's watched her for over a month, and he doesn't know, either. Rosa's mixed up in something. I wish I knew what the hell it is."

I hesitated. Rosa had already put Frederick on the spot tonight. I didn't want to do it to him again. But I could help more if I knew more. "May I ask why you're sure she's mixed up in something? After the questions she asked you tonight, yes—I see why you think so. But why did your father hire Walt in the first place? Is it only because he doesn't like Rosa's boyfriend?"

"Not just that." He took a longer drink and set down his glass. "My father would be furious if he knew I'd told you. But he'd also be furious if he knew I hadn't told him about Rosa's questions. If I can keep one secret from him, I guess I can keep two. Since Rosa started dating Sam Ryan, she's changed. Some of it's standard-issue rebellious teenager stuff—staying out late, getting even less communicative than usual. But there are other things. I told you she was very close with our mother?"

I nodded, remembering the image of Rosa and her mother curled up on the couch, reading and signing and laughing.

"Well," Frederick said, "my mother never cared about jewelry, or clothes, or other things lots of rich people care about. But she loved books. She collected books. She had a special passion for early editions of the girl-detective books she'd loved when she was younger. Nancy Drew was her favorite, but she also collected Trixie Belden, the Dana girls, Cherry Ames—"

"Cherry Ames isn't a girl detective," I objected. "She's a nurse."

"So you know the books." He smiled. "I can't form an independent opinion—I never read them—but according to my mother, Cherry Ames qualifies as a girl detective because she's always solving the mystery of the secret patient, the mystery of the silent doctor, the mystery of the stolen bedpan—"

"There was never," I said firmly, "a mystery about a stolen bedpan."

"Maybe not. Anyway, my mother built her collection for years. Those books were special to her, and to Rosa. When they were both learning sign language, they used those books to practice—signing passages to each other, sometimes pretty much acting scenes out. Rosa would sign Nancy Drew's lines, and my mother would sign the lines for George and Beth and—"

"Bess," I corrected.

"Whatever. When my mother died, she left the books to Rosa. Rosa treasured them. My father had a special bookcase built in her room, and she reread them constantly." He took a long, deep breath. "Then, last month, she started selling them."

"Selling them? The books your mother left her?"

"Yes. My father noticed about a dozen of the most valuable ones were missing—first-edition Nancy Drews, Trixie Beldens signed by the author. My father says he happened to notice the books were missing when he was putting away a sweater Rosa left downstairs. Maybe. Or maybe he was searching her room for drugs. Either way, he noticed, and he hired Walt Sadowski. Sadowski located the books at two rare book stores downtown. The owners said they'd bought the books from a man named Samuel Ryan."

Oh, Sam, I thought. Oh, Rosa. Those precious books—how could you? "Did your father ask Rosa about it?"

"No. He says she wouldn't have given him a straight answer, and she might've gotten mad and moved in with this Ryan character. I don't know if he's right, but he's her father. It's his decision."

I supposed so. "It's sad—Rosa will regret it someday—but they *were* her books. If she needed money—"

"Why would she?" He stood up and started pacing. "She lives at home, and my father doesn't charge her for rent, board, anything. When she graduated from high school, he gave her a new car. When she decided to join that fitness center, he paid for a year's membership. And she works thirty hours a week and doesn't spend much on clothes or anything like that. She doesn't care about those things, any more than my mother did. So why would she need money? Why did Ryan sell four more books last week?"

I couldn't come up with a comforting answer. "You think it's drugs."

"Drugs, gambling, something worse." Frederick's voice got sharper, louder. "He's got a habit, and my sister's feeding it. Or he's setting up some shady scheme, and she's financing it. And you saw him at a bar, wearing expensive clothes and a gold watch. Where did he get the money for those? From selling my mother's books, that's where."

"It looks like that. But I've gotten to know Sam. It's hard to believe he'd use Rosa that way. His affection for her seems genuine, and he seems like a good person."

"Is that so?" His upper lip curled with derision. "Then tell me this. You've gotten to know Rosa, too. Do you think she could kill someone?"

"No. Of course not."

"Of course not. But when that policewoman questioned her about Jenny Linton's death, Rosa held something back. She held back even though she was afraid she'd go to jail." He took a step forward. "If she wasn't hiding her own guilt, she must've been protecting someone else. Whom would she be likely to protect?"

I felt like hiding behind the couch. "There could be another explanation."

"That's a theoretical possibility," he said, his tone heavy with sarcasm. Then he turned his face aside, as if he'd been struck. "Damn. Jane, I'm sorry. I barge into your home late at night, I pressure you into compromising your professional ethics, you help me, and this is how I pay you back. I shout you down and stomp all over you."

"I don't feel all that stomped on. And you're a lawyer. You like to make arguments, and you like to win. I understand that."

He grinned—a nice grin. "So I'm no worse than other lawyers. Is that a compliment, or a way of saying it'd be foolish to expect decent behavior from me? No, don't answer. Anyway, sorry I got so loud. I hope I didn't disturb your roommate."

"Don't worry about it. She's deaf."

"Damn." He sat down again. "So now I sound like an idiot. A lawyer, and an idiot. Bad combination."

"You sound like a big brother, and you're worried. That's natural. And you're sad about your mother's books. That's natural, too."

He looked up. "I'm very sad about my mother's books. After Sadowski found them, I went to those stores, thinking I'd buy the books back, give them to Rosa when all this is behind us. But the books were gone. Every last one had already been sold."

"I'm sorry. And I'm also sorry to say another problem just occurred to me. Walt's paying me to keep an eye on Rosa and report to him. I can't tell him about what she and Detective Diaz said to each other. But there's also the question of whether I should tell him about the questions Rosa asked you."

"You can't," he said, alarmed. "He'd tell my father.

I'd essentially be breaking my promise to Rosa. And my father would be angry at me for not telling him myself."

"I know. I don't *want* to tell Walt, but maybe I'm obliged to. He's my employer."

"Damn." He thought it over. "He's paying you to watch Rosa and report what you learn. You didn't learn about Rosa's questions while you were watching her. You learned about them while talking to me. Sadowski isn't paying you to report on conversations with me."

I winced. "That sounds like a technicality."

"Technicalities have their uses. Sometimes, they promote justice. This technicality would let me keep my promise to Rosa."

"And also keep your father from getting mad at you. But that's a legitimate goal, too. All right. I won't tell Walt about our conversation."

"Thanks." He stood up. "I've taken enough of your time."

I walked him to the door. "About those books. Keep an eye on e-Bay. Some people buy books like those as an investment. They wait for prices to go up, offer them for sale when they can make a profit. Those books may turn up again."

"They might—probably at ten times what Rosa got for them. Well, Rosa's young. She's got lots of birthdays coming, and those books would make good presents. Thanks, Jane—for the suggestion, and for everything else. Maybe we could have lunch some time. I'd like to show you I can actually be pleasant company."

"I've never doubted that," I said, "and lunch sounds nice." Forty-eight hours ago, it would've sounded fantastic. Now, I was so fixated on Hector that I felt barely a flutter.

I locked the door behind him. He was right. Rosa was young—young enough, I hoped, to recover from any mistakes she'd made in the last few months. Was Sam Ryan one of those mistakes? I didn't want to think so, but it was getting harder to deny.

Chapter 14

From the street, Nails by Ilana didn't look like much—a narrow white-washed brick storefront wedged between a kosher bakery and an optician's shop, part of a long, squat strip mall at the corner of Cedar and Green. A weathered purple-and-blue sign hung above the door, and stenciled blue letters on the windows confirmed the salon's name. Everything seemed faded, old, borderline shabby.

Inside, it looked better. Someone had studied design magazines and painted the walls a rich, deep gold, with dark brown hanging shelves for accents. Large, luxuriantly padded dark brown chairs lined one wall. In two of the chairs sat women I recognized from volleyball—Bethany, the one who suggested a moment of silence for Jenny Linton, and a lively brunette whose name I couldn't remember. Rosa sat in a chair with a tray attached to it, working on the brunette's nails, wearing navy slacks and a pink blouse.

Bethany waved when she spotted me. "Jane! I didn't know you come here."

"It's my first time," I said, signing a greeting to Rosa. Smiling, she asked me to take the third chair. Both women watched with interest.

"That's right," the brunette said. "You're a sign-language interpreter. Is that how you know Rosa?"

"We're in the same martial arts class," I said and signed. "Then Rosa suggested I join the center."

Rosa shook her head. "*You don't have to sign. I can't watch anyway—I have to focus on work.*" So I stopped.

"You joined because of Rosa? Well, she joined because of us." Bethany pointed to her "Try It Out!" tote bag. "She noticed my bag and wrote a note asking about the center. So now we're all members!" Bethany seemed to find that an amazing fact.

"Well, I'm a trial member. And you've got the tote bag, so I guess you are, too."

"That's how I started," Bethany said. "Ashley, too. But we've both been regular members for over two years."

"Almost three for me." Ashley looked very different than she had on Sunday—hair and makeup just so, black pencil skirt and red cashmere sweater. "And we've been coming here for months, because Rosa's the best. The best!" She raised her voice for the last two words, lifting one arm in a gesture presumably supposed to express "the best!" Rosa recognized it as a compliment and smiled.

"Yeah, we used to go to this place in Beachwood. It was classy." Bethany pursed her lips, as if acknowledging the other place's merits grudgingly. "But it's so crowded and noisy. Ilana's isn't as fancy, but it's a better place to relax."

"Especially if you come when Rosa's the only one around." Ashley lowered her voice. "It's a good chance to catch up on gossip, since Rosa can't hear what you're saying. She can't read lips, either."

It was insensitive, I thought, to talk about Rosa as if she weren't here, to take advantage of her deafness by gossiping in front of her. But they didn't seem to mean anything by it.

Bethany looked wistful. "We had another friend who used to meet us here. Jenny Linton. She drowned last week. You probably heard about it on the news."

"Yes, I did," I said. "Rosa mentioned it, too. I got the impression she and Jenny were friends."

"Oh, yeah," Bethany said. "After Rosa joined the center, they got real close. Jenny showed Rosa how to use the equipment, introduced her to people. I think she felt Rosa might need extra help, since she's deaf and all. They used to work out together, have lunch together. They were always scribbling notes back and forth—it was cute." Sighing, she looked at Rosa. "I bet Rosa misses her. I do, too."

"Yes, we all miss Jenny." Ashley sounded impatient. Maybe she was afraid Bethany would get gloomy. "And it *was* cute seeing her with Rosa. You know what else was cute? One day, Rosa's boyfriend came here. He moved stuff in the storeroom for her. It was *so* cute to see them signing to each other."

"It sure was." Bethany smiled. "*He's* pretty cute, too. A big guy—athletic looking. He and Rosa look adorable together, since she's so tiny. It's ironic—a big, strong guy like that, and he's deaf."

Rosa's boyfriend isn't deaf, I started to say, but caught myself in time. Maybe Sam had played deaf that day, just as we'd played deaf in the restaurant last week. But one thing didn't make sense. "Was Jenny with you that day?"

"No," Bethany said. "I remember thinking it was too bad she didn't get to see him. Why do you ask?"

"Just curious," I said and felt relieved when she let it go at that. On that first day in Ginger's Pantry, Rosa had introduced Sam and Jenny. They couldn't have met before, and Jenny hadn't seemed surprised Sam could hear.

If Bethany and Ashley had told Jenny that Rosa had a deaf boyfriend named Sam—but maybe they hadn't mentioned his name. And Rosa hadn't introduced Sam as her boyfriend. It had just been "my friend Sam." Was any of that significant?

"So, Jane," Ashley was saying, "where do you usually get your nails done?"

"Actually, I haven't had them done in years, but they're in unusually rough shape." I held out my hands to prove it. "And I'm going out tonight."

"With Hector?" Ashley asked.

I looked at her, surprised. "Yes. How did you know?"

Ashley shrugged. "I didn't. But I saw you two talking on Sunday, and he seemed interested. Anyhow, fantastic. He's really nice."

"Yeah, he's a sweetheart," Bethany agreed. "You'll have a great time."

This was getting to be a pattern: Other women telling me what a great time I'd have when I went out with Hector. How many of the recommendations were based on personal experience? Had he gone out with Bethany, too, or Ashley, or both?

As Rosa finished Ashley's nails and moved on to Bethany, talk shifted to other subjects. We took turns whining about our jobs. Ashley's a bank teller, Bethany an administrative assistant. Both had valid complaints, but neither could top my stories about the seafood restaurant. We talked about movies, shopping, television. Bethany described her vacation in Cape Cod last summer, and Ashley said she planned to spend a week in Mexico this winter. The hour passed pleasantly.

Before Rosa finished my nails, both Bethany and Ashley left, saying they hoped I'd come again next week. I smiled but knew I couldn't afford to. Once they'd gone, Rosa and I argued about whether I'd pay. Finally, I gave in, on condition that I buy her lunch soon.

Time to face Walt Sadowski. Of course, he was annoyed. I told him about Detective Diaz and tried to explain about confidentiality. He didn't buy it. Ulysses Patterson, he said, would not be pleased. If he decided to question me himself—good luck.

At least Walt hadn't fired me. As for being questioned by Ulysses Patterson, I'd have to try not to worry about it. I'd have to try not to have nightmares about it.

I put in a quick shift at Top Skorz and raced home to get ready. The dress looked even more perfect than I remembered. When I walked into the living room, Abby clenched both fists, brought them to face level, spread her fingers, and lifted her hands still higher, up and out. *Amazing*. An understatement, I thought, but it would do.

Just as I finished tossing the salad, the security buzzer sounded, and I opened the door for Hector.

I swear he did a double-take. "My God," he said. "You look gorgeous."

I couldn't deny it. I smiled. "Come meet my roommate," I said.

It was good to see how comfortable he was with Abby. I never blame friends who aren't used to being around deaf people for acting self-conscious or speaking too loudly. It's understandable. But when they respond to a deaf person as they would to any other person, I'm impressed. When Hector stepped into the kitchen to get the salad, Abby slipped me a quick sign, circling her face with her pointer finger, putting her palms together and sliding her right hand down the length of her left—*handsome*. So Abby approved.

As we drove to his mother's house, Hector filled me in on the other guests at the dinner. I'd already met most of them, he said—Diana and Jason, of course, and also Paul Kent and Kirsten. They were old friends of the family.

And naturally Jason's wife, Mara, would be there, and their six-year-old son, Kevin. I hadn't known Jason had a son. And he evidently cheated on his wife constantly, and if he was involved in Jenny's death—God. That poor little boy.

As I'd expected, Elise Reed's house was huge. But I'd pictured something white and sprawling, with chimneys and columns. This was a massive two-story concrete block rectangle, with tall borders of turquoise tiles at top and bottom. Probably, in the sixties, this had been somebody's idea of the future of American architecture—contemporary, functional, bold. Fortunately, American architecture had turned in less drastic directions, leaving Elise Reed's supermarket-style house behind as a memorial to bad taste.

Hector looked at it affectionately as we got out of the car. "This is where we all grew up. It's really too big for Mom now that it's just her and Diana. But she loves it. And we've got lots of memories here."

The front door opened directly into the living room—no foyer, just an immense white-walled, white-carpeted room that stretched clear from the front of the house to picture windows at the back. Near the door, a pink-and-yellow area rug defined a conversation area outfitted with acrylic benches facing each other across a glass coffee table, with a white grand piano to the left. The room was dominated, though, by a much larger area near the windows—five steps leading down to a conversation pit larger than my living room, framed on three sides by a built-in white sofa, lined with oversized pink and yellow throw pillows. You could fit twenty people on that sofa without nudging elbows.

Just four people sat there now, directly below the windows: Elise Reed in a long, silky pink dress with flowing sleeves; Kirsten to her left, her black dress short, close-fitting, and sleeveless; Paul Kent to her right, in another impeccable suit; Diana next to him, wearing a beige pant-suit, looking anxious.

She came to greet us. "I'm glad you could come, Jane. And you brought a salad—how nice. Hector, would you put it in the kitchen? Jane, come meet Mother."

It felt like approaching a throne. She didn't stand. I wouldn't have expected her to. "Thank you for having me, Mrs. Reed," I said, shaking her hand. "Happy birthday."

"Call me Elise." She looked me over, tilting her head to the side. "Diana says you were at the volleyball game, but I don't remember—well. I'm glad you came." The corners of her mouth twitched. "You look—healthy."

Oh, God. I looked fat. I shouldn't have worn maroon. It was too close to red, and red always makes me look huge. I slunk off to a seat on the northern wall of the sofa.

Hector bounded down the steps, put a brightly-wrapped package next to the others on the coffee table, and kissed his mother on the forehead before sitting next to me. "You look beautiful, Mom. How are you today?"

She lifted an arm, the long, loose pink sleeve floating gracefully. "Oh, well. I never feel very good anymore. Today was hard. When I tried to get up this morning, the vertigo was too much. The room was positively swimming. I had to lie back down. Diana came over at noon and made soup. I tried to eat it—really, I did—but I felt so weak. And I've had those pains in my legs all day, and my shoulders, and the small of my back. Then Paul came over and insisted I take my temperature."

"Ninety-nine point two," he said, shaking his head. "Ninety-nine point *two*."

She smiled at him. "He thought I should cancel dinner, but I knew you were all looking forward to it, so I thought, 'Well, I'll just go through with it.' But enough about that. Don't worry about me, Hector. How are *you*?"

"Fine." He looked at the floor, as if he felt guilty for feeling fine. "I'm sorry you had a rough day."

She sighed. "*Every* day is rough. But *you* feel fine, and that's what matters." She turned to me with a sweet, fragile smile. "Hector tells me you're a sign-language interpreter."

"She used to be," Kirsten said. The harshness of her tone surprised me. "She can't get interpreting work anymore. She's a waitress and a cleaning woman."

"Really?" Elise's eyes grew wide. "Aren't interpreting jobs available? There are still deaf people around, aren't there?"

Damn. "Yes. But it's a long story, and—"

"And there's no need to get into it now," Hector cut in. "Did Jason say when he'd get here?"

"He said he'd get here on time." Diana stood up. "So much for that. I'll start putting things in the oven."

"I'll help." I leapt up. Maybe there'd be a back door in the kitchen. Maybe I could sneak out and walk home.

The kitchen must've been remodeled recently. Hardwood floors, stainless steel appliances, granite countertops—those hadn't become required proofs of affluence and good taste until long after the sixties. I bustled about helping Diana, afraid she, too, would try to get me to reveal more than I should about Rosa and Detective Diaz.

Instead, she asked which exercise machines I'd tried and recommended several others. It wasn't an especially warm conversation—I don't think warmth was Diana's strength—but after what happened in the living room, it was a relief. When we heard new voices coming from the other room, she looked up.

"Sounds like Jason's here," she said. "Mara's bringing ice cream—I should get it. Can you finish the relish tray? Thanks." She dried her hands on a dishtowel, started toward the door, and turned around. “Hector hasn’t brought a woman home since he was in college. He’s thirty-three. It’d be good for him to settle down. I think that’s what he really wants. And he’s basically an affectionate person.”

She walked out briskly, not giving me time to reply. Good grief —another woman recommending Hector to me. But this recommendation I liked. So I evidently had the big sister’s approval. Since the mother’s approval seemed doubtful, that felt comforting.

As I fussed with carrot sticks and cucumber slices, I heard someone walk into the kitchen. I looked over to see Jason with grocery bags in both arms.

“Hello, Jane,” he said flatly, barely glancing at me.

“It’s nice to see you. Can I help with those things?”

“No thanks.” He threw two containers of ice cream into the freezer and started shoving champagne bottles in the refrigerator.

Fine. Be that way. I turned back to the relish tray, focusing on achieving rough symmetry between radish roses and black olives.

Behind me, the refrigerator door slammed. And then Jason grabbed my arm and yanked me around to face him. Before I realized what was happening, he had me by both arms, pushing me back against the counter, staring, his face rigid.

“That dress!” he said. “What the hell do you mean, showing up here in that dress? What are you up to?”

“What?” I said, stunned. “I don’t understand—”

“Don’t give me that. You’re trying to get to me.” His face was red now, his voice fierce. He pulled me closer. “Tell me. How the hell did you get that dress?”

My God. Jenny’s dress. Jenny’s very distinctive, unusual dress. He obviously recognized it—maybe he gave it to her. What kind of idiot must I be, coming to a dinner with Jason Connolly and wearing Jenny’s dress?

Chapter 15

His grip on my arms tightened. Enough, I thought. I brought my hands up, turned the palms out, and struck his arms aside with a jerking motion. To give myself more room, I shoved him in the chest, not hard, and stepped to the side.

"Don't touch me," I said. "I don't know what you're talking about."

"Like hell you don't." He moved toward me. "That dress—"

I shoved him again, not so gently this time. "Get control of yourself. You're not making sense. What's wrong with my dress?"

He was still red in the face, still breathing heavily, but he kept his distance. "Tell me how you got it. And don't say you bought it at Macy's or Nordstrom, or anywhere in Cleveland, because I know that's not true."

"I bought it in Cleveland," I said evenly, "this morning, at a consignment shop in Shaker Heights."

That slowed him down. "A consignment shop?"

"Yes." I scraped indignation up frantically. "Not that it's any of your business, but I wanted to wear something nice tonight and couldn't afford something new. I've been having employment problems—ask Hector. So I went to a consignment shop. It's probably closed now, but you can call in the morning."

I could practically see him trying to think it through, trying to figure out how Jenny's dress could end up in a consignment shop so quickly, trying to decide if I might be telling the truth. "A consignment shop?"

"Yes," I said impatiently. "So what? You think I'm not good enough for your brother because I'm wearing a used dress? Fine. Tell him that. We'll see if he listens."

I hated to turn my back on him, but I made myself go back to arranging radishes and olives. If Jason has a brain in his head, I told myself, he'll let it go. He doesn't want to make a scene about this, not in front of his family. Not in front of his wife.

He let it go. He snarled some particularly foul words and flung open a cabinet door. I heard him pour something and stalk out. After waiting fifteen seconds, I looked at the bottle on the counter. Scotch. Good choice, I thought, and wished I could join him.

My nerves were shot. Why had he gotten so worked up about the dress? If he'd had an affair with Jenny, if he'd given her the dress, I could understand why seeing another woman wearing his dead mistress's dress would upset him. But he'd gotten almost violent, and he'd accused me of trying to get to him. What did that mean? And had my consignment shop story been quick thinking or a stupid mistake? I hadn't considered trying to explain about Rosa, Jenny's jacket, Jenny's roommate. I hadn't thought he'd believe the truth. Did he believe the lie? What if he called the consignment shop in Shaker Heights? *Was* there a consignment shop in Shaker Heights? I didn't know. I'd made everything up on the spot. If Jason checked, if he realized it was all a lie, what would he do?

No time to think about that now. Diana returned and

started taking things out of the oven. Breathing in deeply, I picked up the relish tray and carried it to the dining room.

People were gathering around the long, unnaturally glossy black table. Not wood—some space-age plastic, maybe. I got my first glimpse of Jason's wife, a marginally heavy woman with too-blonde hair. I could trace remnants of prettiness in her face, but it hadn't held up well. She sat next to their son, a chubby, beautiful little boy with curly red hair.

Hector and I helped Diana carry out casseroles, platters of chicken, baskets of breads, bowls of vegetables. It was an extensive spread, and Diana had cooked most of it. Kirsten's contribution, I learned later, was a package of heat-and-serve rolls. The heating and serving had been left to Diana.

Kirsten sat across from me at dinner but never looked at me, never spoke to me. She hardly spoke to anyone, just ate methodically, brooding with every bite. Why such a drastic change? She'd seemed delighted when I went out with Hector, took it for granted I'd have sex with him, almost literally gave me her blessing. But it obviously bothered her that he'd invited me to a family dinner. Their relationship couldn't be as open and uncomplicated as Hector thought. Things seldom stay open and uncomplicated once sex gets involved.

Dishes got passed around the table, and I found myself, like everyone else, watching anxiously to see what Elise would eat, if she would eat. She put bits of things on her plate and dipped her fork into them, occasionally brought her fork to her lips. When my salad reached her, she leaned forward, then drew back.

"Oh, my," she said. "Who brought this? Jane? Isn't that lovely. What are those white things? Are they noodles? Are they fried?"

"It's maifun," I said. "Rice sticks. And yes, I put them in hot oil, for just a moment. That's what makes them puff up. But I drained them on paper towels."

"Try it, Mom." Hector put a delicate portion on her plate. "It's fantastic."

Elise poked it with her fork. "Oh, look. Peanuts. I've never seen peanuts in a salad before." She pushed the peanuts aside, along with the maifun and chicken, and risked a scrap of lettuce. "My—that's sweet. Is there sugar in the dressing?"

"A little," I said. "It's mostly oil and vinegar."

"Oh, oil," she said. "That's why it's so heavy. But thank you. " She put down her fork. "Could someone pass the relish tray, please?"

Damn. Why had I tried to show off? Why couldn't I have brought a regular salad, just lettuce and celery and other irreproachable vegetables, dressed with vinegar but no oil and definitely no sugar? I noticed Jason's wife, Mara, watching me, lips curled in a wryly sympathetic smile.

"Champagne," she said. "Jason, we brought champagne. Why haven't you served it?"

"Forgot." He went to the kitchen, coming back with bottles of champagne and ginger ale. "Here we go. Ginger ale for Hector and Kevin, champagne for everyone else. Let's have a birthday toast for my beautiful mother."

He made an elaborate, dramatic business of uncorking the champagne, with plenty of pop and fizz. Amateur, I thought. If you know what you're doing, there's very little pop, practically no fizz. As he poured, Elise made an elaborate, dramatic business of turning her champagne flute over and setting it down on the table.

"I hope nobody minds," she said. "But I almost never drink."

"We don't mind." Mara downed her champagne without waiting for the toast. "With all the pills you take, you probably *shouldn't* drink. Hell. You probably don't *need* to drink."

Jason stopped pouring. "What's that supposed to mean?"

"Nothing." She paved a heat-and-serve roll with butter. "But prescription painkillers kill all kinds of pain. If you can sweet-talk your doctor into writing you another permission slip, who needs booze? You must have a nice little permanent buzz going, Elise. Jason, I'm ready for a refill."

He thrust the bottle into her hand. "You're always ready for a refill."

Judging from what I could see, she'd had a few refills already. I understood why. If I'd known what was coming, I might've had a shot or two at the apartment. Damn. This was one of those nightmare dates. I'd be lucky to get out of here alive.

I kept my own champagne sips small as one person after another rose to toast Elise. We finished with eating dinner, with watching Elise pretend to eat dinner, and Diana brought out a meticulously frosted strawberry layer cake with one candle in the middle. She watched closely as Elise blew out the candle, eased her fork through the corner of her slice, and raised up a crumb.

She tasted it. "Oh, my. That's so sweet."

"It's a cake, Mom," Hector said. "It's supposed to be sweet. Diana, it's delicious."

"Of course it's delicious, dear," Elise said. "I never said it wasn't. Diana, thank you. It's a very nice cake." She set down her fork.

Mara shoveled down four bites without intermission. "I love this cake. Best damn cake I've had in years. May I have another slice, Diana?"

"Oh, goodness," Elise said. "Mara, dear, please don't

feel you have to. I know you want to make Diana feel better about her cake, but if you think you shouldn't—"

"Why would I think that?" Mara asked. "Diana, make it a big slice, please. How about you, Kevin? Isn't Aunt Diana's cake the best ever? You want more?"

"Please, Mara." Elise looked pained. "Don't encourage him."

"I don't need to encourage him." Mara absorbed another forkful and smacked her lips. Kevin, grinning, imitated her. "Look—he's eaten it all. He wants more. Diana?"

We made it through the cake—it *was* good, but I felt too self-conscious to eat much—and adjourned to the conversation pit, Paul holding Elise's arm to help her down step after painful step. Jason and Kevin built a tower of throw pillows, taking turns collapsing on top of it and knocking it over, laughing wildly, rebuilding it and attacking it again. He's forgotten about the dress, I thought. He's just happy now. And look at how much he loves his son.

We came to the unwrapping of presents. A stunning cut-glass vase from Paul, Cary Grant DVDs from Kirsten—Elise exclaimed over them and set them aside. Diana brought her offering forth shyly.

"Oh, look." Elise unwrapped the delicate ceramic sculpture. "Why, it's a little like the statue from the fountain, isn't it?"

"It *is* the statue from the fountain." Diana reached out, closing a hand over her mother's. "I found a local artist who does miniatures, I gave him the original drawings for the statue of you, and he copied it exactly."

"Isn't that nice." Elise held it up, squinting. "Yes—I can see it's supposed to look like the statue. Where's the switch to turn on the water? Oh—there's no water? It's not a fountain? Well, it's still a nice present, dear. It's sweet. It's very, very sweet."

My God, I thought. She's the best I've ever seen. My own mother's pretty damn good, but Elise makes her look like an amateur. Every word she speaks is sweet and gentle—if you accused her of cruelty, you couldn't find a single quotation to back it up—but every word cuts straight through the soul.

I didn't for one second doubt she knew exactly what she was doing. Diana's shoulders drooped with shame as she stuffed that beautiful little statue back into its box. And now Hector handed his gift to his mother. My body went stiff with dread.

"*This* looks interesting," Elise said, unwrapping it. She looked at it and paused. "Oh. It's one of my wedding pictures. Did you take this from my photograph album, dear? That was clever."

"No, that's the picture that was in the *Plain Dealer*." Hector sounded pathetically eager. "Dad always said it was his favorite picture of the two of you, but we never had the photograph itself—just copies on newsprint. So I talked some people from the *Plain Dealer* into looking through some files. That's the original photograph—I got them to give it to me. The frame's special, too."

"It is," Elise agreed. "All those tiny pink bumps—they're so shiny!"

"They're Montana sapphires," Hector said. "If Dad were still alive, next month would've been your forty-fifth anniversary, and sapphires are the traditional forty-fifth anniversary gift. So I got a frame made with Montana sapphires because we always went to Montana to ski, and I asked for pink ones because that's your favorite color."

Elise stared at the frame, her brow furrowed. "I must be confused. I thought sapphires are blue."

"Some are, sure," Hector said. "But sapphires come in almost all colors. Blue sapphires are for sixty-fifth anniversaries, so I thought those might not be right. And you've always preferred pink."

"I certainly have," Elise said, "and I'm certainly glad you didn't waste your money on *real* sapphires."

Hector looked crestfallen. "They *are* real, Mom. They're high-quality pink Montana sapphires."

"I'm sure they are," she said. "And I couldn't like them more even if they *were* blue. Really, Hector. I *prefer* these, and I'm *very* glad you didn't splurge. Goodness! Did anyone ever get so many nice, pretty little presents!"

"You haven't opened mine, Mom." Jason took a small, flat box from his coat pocket. "It's an original composition."

She opened the package. "A CD?"

"Yes. I composed a medley of songs you skated to at the Olympics, and I performed it on the piano and recorded it."

Elise gasped. "What a thoughtful gift! Oh, Jason! I can't think of anything I could ever want more! Should we put it on right now? Or would you—would you perform it for me?"

He smiled. "If you want, sure. I brought the sheet music, just in case."

"Oh, *thank* you!" I couldn't tell if she actually had tears in her eyes, but her voice sounded weepy. "That would make me *so* happy!"

I wanted to hate Jason's performance, but I couldn't. It wasn't the music itself—songs from *Carmen*, some other big, melodramatic operatic pieces I vaguely recognized. It seemed like standard fare. I'd seen other women skate to the same music at other Olympics. The way Jason played, though!

It wasn't showy, but it was passionate. He seemed to have thought about how each note should be played, and he'd found seamless ways to weave each piece into the next.

His face was transformed. Whenever I'd seen Jason before, he'd been angry, or leering. Only when he'd been romping with his son had he seemed natural and happy. Now, he seemed to have forgotten about himself, to be drawn in by the beauty he was creating. God. He was a real musician.

Throughout the evening, Elise had been controlling emotions—manufacturing her own, manipulating everyone else's. Now she sat forward, fists clenched, eyes deep with rapture as she watched her son play. Mara watched him, too, tears flowing down her cheeks. At one point, she reached for her son's hand, squeezed it, and smiled at him, sharing the joy of his father's triumph.

But Kirsten looked bored, and Paul looked deeply unhappy. Halfway through the performance, Diana walked to the kitchen and started washing dishes. Hector took out his BlackBerry to check messages.

I couldn't blame them. I especially couldn't blame Diana and Hector. Jason had trumped them all, and for Diana and Hector, the hurt must go especially deep.

Jason played the last notes and sat with his hands in his lap, his body limp with spent emotion. Forgetting her pain, Elise leapt up, holding her arms out, calling his name. He ran down the steps, embraced her, and kissed her forehead. Then he looked away from her and shot a triumphant glance at Hector. Okay, I thought. That was a nice break. Back to nastiness.

Diana served coffee, and Elise accepted a cup and actually drank it. That was a surprise. Well, maybe that's how she kept herself minimally functional—practically no food, but generous doses of pills and caffeine. She used sweetener, I noticed, not sugar. Why would someone so skeletal deny herself sugar?

It made no sense. But I thought I understood.

Just as we finished our coffee, just as I dared to hope we might be released soon, the doorbell sounded. Elise set her cup down with a bump.

"Goodness! It's after ten. Who'd come at this hour? Oh, my—I should answer the door." Wincing, she tried to stand.

"Of course not, Mother." Diana jumped up. "I'll get it."

We heard a murmur of voices. Then Diana walked back toward us, her face blank. Detective Bridget Diaz and two uniformed policemen followed a step behind her.

"Jason," Diana said, "some people would like to talk to you. Hector, Kevin needs to wash his hands. Maybe you could take him upstairs."

"Oh, my God!" Elise cried. "Police, so late at night? What's wrong? Jason, what's happening? Please, please, somebody, tell me what's happening!"

Hector scooped his nephew into his arms. "Come on, buddy," he said, heading for the stairs. "Those hands look sticky. And I want to show you my old room."

The rest of us sat frozen. I saw Bridget Diaz glance around the room, saw her eyebrows arch when she noticed me. She waited until Hector got Kevin upstairs.

She walked over to Jason. "Mr. Connolly, I need to ask you some questions regarding the death of Jennifer Linton. I'd like you to come with us, please."

Mara reached out to touch her husband's arm. He shook her off and gave Bridget Diaz a cold, measuring look. "What the hell is this? You got a warrant?"

"I do. I don't necessarily need to use it at this time. I'd like you to agree to come with us. And I'll read you your rights."

Jason sat through it, staring at the floor, then stood. "You want me to come, I'll come. Paul, find me a lawyer. I'm not saying one word until he gets to the station. Mara, careful what you say to Kevin."

Elise cried out, tried to stand, winced, half-collapsed. Paul ran to support her.

"Jason!" she cried. "I'm so frightened, Jason! So very, very frightened!"

Diana tried to take Elise's other arm. "It's all right, Mother. We'll take care of it. Please, try to stay calm. We have to think about Kevin."

Pushing her aside, Elise let out a loud wail, falling to the sofa, convulsed with sobs. "Jason! My baby!"

"We should go, sir," Bridget Diaz said.

"Fine," Jason said. "I don't care." He led the way out. Bridget Diaz cast one more glance at me before leaving the house.

At least there had been no handcuffs. I hated to think about how hysterical Elise might've gotten if there had been handcuffs.

She lay on the sofa, sobbing noisily, both Paul and Diana trying to comfort her. Mara sat off to the side, pulling at a loose thread in a throw pillow. I noticed Kirsten staring at me. All through the evening, she'd barely glanced at me, but now she stared.

Finally, Hector came back. "Kevin's okay. I read him a story, and he passed out. How's Mom?"

Forcing herself to a sitting position, Elise pressed the back of one fragile hand to her forehead. "They took him away. They took away my son. Why? Why?"

Diana looked at Hector. "The detective said she wanted to talk to Jason about Jenny Linton."

"Jenny Linton?" Elise echoed. "She's a volleyball girl, isn't she? The one who drowned? Why would they want to talk to Jason about her?"

Mara snorted, not softly, and looked away.

Paul stood. "Jason wants me to find a lawyer. I'll call Mike Hemson, ask him to recommend someone."

"Why can't Mike go himself?" Elise asked. "He's our lawyer. Why can't he go?"

Paul squeezed her hand. "Mike doesn't handle this sort of thing. But he'll recommend someone good. I'll go to the kitchen to call him."

"Don't stay away long," Elise said, clinging to his hand. "I feel so weak, Paul, so afraid. I need you. I don't know what I'd do without you."

"Don't worry, Mom." Hector sat down next to her. "It's some stupid misunderstanding. Jason will be back soon."

"But she said she wanted to talk to him about Jenny's death," Elise said. "Why? She can't—my God. She can't think he had anything to do with it, can she? Jenny just fell in the river."

"It's a misunderstanding, Mother," Diana said, "just as Hector says. We'll get it cleared up. Hector, do you remember when Jenny died?"

"Last week," Hector said. "Monday, I think."

"Monday, October twenty-fourth." Mara's voice was cool, matter-of-fact. "Between 8:30 in the evening, when she left her apartment, and 1:00 the next morning, when her body was found."

Poor woman. Obviously, she'd been following the news about Jenny. Obviously, she'd wondered about Jason.

"A week ago Monday," Diana said. "There was a singles' night last Monday. Those go until midnight—Jason probably stayed later, to help clean up. You see, Mother? Jason just has to tell the police that, and this will all be over."

Hector shook his head. "Jason left around eight. He

was on edge and said he needed a drink. He put Amber in charge, and he took off."

Diana looked taken aback. "But it's Jason's program. He's supposed to stay until it's over."

"Probably he does, sometimes. But he was on edge, like I said. And Amber pretty much runs singles' nights anyway. Maybe he came back later. I don't know—I left about an hour after he did, and he wasn't back then. We'll check with Amber."

"You shouldn't have let him go." Elise's voice turned shrill. "You should've talked to him and made him stay. Or you should've gone with him. He's your brother. You should look after him."

"He's my older brother, Mom." Hector rubbed his forehead. "I can't tell him what to do. And Jason doesn't want my company when he hits the bars."

"Hits the bars!" Elise said. "What a way to talk about your brother! Maybe he went home to have a drink. Mara, what time did Jason get home last Monday?"

Mara kept pulling at the loose thread. "I went to bed after around midnight. Jason was still out. When I got up, he was in the shower. I don't know if his bed had been slept in. I've stopped checking."

Paul came back from the kitchen. "Mike knows some good people. He's making calls."

"I don't understand," Elise said. "Why did they take Jason away? How did they know he'd be here tonight?"

"They're the police, Elise," Kirsten said. It was the first time she'd spoken since she gave Elise her present. "The police find out about things."

"We'll see." Mara stood up. "I'm getting Kevin. We're going home."

Hector stood, too. "There's nothing we can do now, Mom. A lawyer's practically on the way. He'll straighten things out. You should lie down and get some rest. And I should drive Jane home."

Elise grabbed his hand. "No! Don't leave me!"

He drew his hand away gently. "You've got Diana and Paul, and I'll be back in half an hour."

"Oh, God!" She fell back on the sofa. "Your brother's in jail, and you're leaving me!"

I walked over to Hector and kept my voice low. "I'll text my roommate. She'll pick me up. Or I'll call a cab."

Kirsten stood up. "I'll drive her home."

Damn. "I'll text my roommate. She can be here in—"

"Don't be stupid," Kirsten said. "I'll drive you."

"Thanks, Kirsten," Hector said. "Jane lives in Richmond Heights. It's practically on your way." He turned to me. "Jane, I'm sorry. But my mother's so worried about Jason. I don't want to give her one more thing to be upset about."

"I understand." I really, really did not want to get into a car with Kirsten, not after the way she'd been acting. "But we shouldn't inconvenience Kirsten. If I text my roommate—"

"It's not an inconvenience." Kirsten picked up her purse, walked to the door, and held it open. "Get in the car."

Chapter 16

For the first fifteen minutes, we said almost nothing. I thanked Kirsten for the ride, and she nodded but didn't reply. I gave her directions, and she nodded again. I made some idiotic remark about being concerned about Jason, and she let it drop into silence, not even nodding this time.

I couldn't think of another topic. Chatting about volleyball would be insensitive with Jason possibly in jail by now. Fine. I'd been afraid she'd want to confront me about whatever I'd done to upset her. But maybe she'd just wanted to show Hector how nice she is by solving a problem for him. And maybe she, too, couldn't think of appropriate things to talk about. We wouldn't talk, then. It felt awkward, but what the hell.

A few minutes from my apartment, she broke the silence. "Hector says you're taking *sogu ryu bujutsu*."

Good—she'd found a safe topic. "Yes, I'm really enjoying it. Have you ever taken martial arts?"

"I have a fourth-degree black belt in tae kwon do." She didn't take her eyes off the road. "I also have black belts in judo and karate. Hector says you're having trouble learning to fall."

"That's true. But I'll figure it out."

"It's not something you figure out. It's something you just do. I could show you."

Not on your life, I thought. "That's nice of you. Maybe, some time when we're both at the center—"

"No time like the present." She pulled into the parking lot at my apartment building and got out of the car. "Come on."

I got out of the car, too—what else could I do?—but kept my distance. She couldn't be serious. I looked down the long, narrow strip of parking lot and didn't see a soul. It had gotten dark, very dark and cold. I forced a laugh. "Right. Thanks for the ride. I'll see you at the center."

She took a few quick steps and stood in front of me, blocking my path to the door. "I'll show you right now. Throw a punch at me."

I tried to laugh again. "Be serious. This is my best dress. I'm in heels."

"I'm in a dress and heels, too. I don't want to mess them up—I won't get rough. I just want to teach you a few things. Throw a punch at me."

She lifted her fists in a fighting stance. And she smiled—a broad, grim smile. My God. What was wrong with her?

"Very funny," I said, and started toward the door.

She stepped forward and grabbed my right wrist. Before I could even think about breaking free, she turned around, pulled me onto her hip, and slammed me down on the concrete. I fell on my back, hitting my head. Still holding onto my wrist, she pulled me up and punched me in the face, twice, before releasing me and letting me fall again.

I'd never felt pain like this before—in my head, my back, everywhere. I lay gasping, hardly able to think, hardly able to breathe. I put my hand to my face and felt blood flowing from my nose.

Kirsten stepped back, breathing heavily, and looked down at me. "See what happens? If you'd fallen right, you could've absorbed most of the impact on your side. And you forgot to slap the pavement. That spreads the impact out. It makes a big difference, especially on a hard surface. And if you'd tucked your chin, you wouldn't have hit your head. Then you could've thought more clearly, and maybe you could've gotten up or twisted your wrist free before I could punch you. Hector said you've studied other arts, so you must have some skills. But you can't use them, because you're hurting too much and feeling too disoriented. Want to try again?"

Get up, I told myself. Get away from her. Panting, I struggled to my hands and knees and tried to stand. Kirsten brought her knee up sharply and hit me in the ribs. Desperate to break the fall, I stuck out my elbow, cracking it against the concrete. Pain and dizziness suffocated me as I fell onto my back again, hit my head again.

"I'm disappointed in you, Jane," she said. "You keep making the same mistakes. You didn't tuck your chin, did you, and you didn't slap the pavement. How many times do I have to tell you these things? And never stick your elbow out. It's a natural reaction, but you'll only hurt yourself more."

I could barely hear her—something was terribly wrong with my ears. I wanted to call for help but couldn't find my voice. The pain overwhelmed me completely this time. It throbbed all through my body, blocking out everything else. I couldn't even think about getting up. I didn't feel sure I was still alive. I rolled onto my side and moaned.

Kirsten stepped closer, leaning over me. "Hector can't end up with you. Maybe he has to end up with someone someday, but it can't be now, and it can't be you. You'd destroy everything that's strong and free and beautiful about him. You'd make him into nothing. I said you could fuck him. I never said you could fuck with his mind. So now you're not allowed to be with him at all. Stay away from him, or I'll kill you."

I heard her walking away, closing her car door, driving off. Still I lay there, afraid to move, afraid of making things worse. Someone will come, I thought. Someone will help me.

No one came. I heard a car drive by, and a new fear hit me—she's coming back. I had to get up, had to get inside. Gasping for breath, I made it to my hands and knees and found my purse. Stand up, I told myself, and did it. Not sure I could walk, afraid I'd pass out at any second, I dug for my keys and stumbled to the door.

I don't know how long it took me to make it to the second floor. Clinging to the banister and leaning against the wall, I had to plan each step, wincing every time my foot touched down on a stair. Finally, I reached the top. I could see our door. Sobbing with relief, I hardly felt the last steps.

Abby sat on the couch, reading, waiting for me. She looked up with a smile and then froze, horror spreading over her face. She jumped up and ran to me. I collapsed into her arms and wept.

She started to guide me to the couch, but I shook my head and pointed to the bathroom. When we got there, she took a step back.

"*Bastard*!" she signed. "*Jane, call the police. You have to*."

Lifting my arms to sign was incredibly hard. "*He didn't touch me. No police. Give me ten minutes, and I'll explain*."

She looked at me doubtfully, then left me alone, closing the door behind her. I could hear her moving in the kitchen, opening cupboards, running water. She was probably making me tea. Part of me wanted a very large drink instead, but that wouldn't be smart.

Still shaky, I washed the blood off my face, rubbed cold water across the back of my neck. That would do for now. Soon, as soon as I could stand it, I'd take a long, hot shower. I took off my dress and looked at it. Blood, all down the front. Maybe, if I soaked it in cold water right away, I could salvage it.

I looked at the dress for another minute. Then I stuffed it into the wastebasket and stumbled to my room.

By morning, the pain had dulled, but everything ached deeply, and shifting my weight the wrong way made me gasp. Abby wanted me to call the police, but I refused. Even if Kirsten went to jail, she wouldn't stay there long, and when she got out, she'd hurt me again.

Abby also wanted me to call in sick. I couldn't. I'd traded shifts with another waitress to go to the dinner last night. If I didn't show up for the lunch shift, I could lose my job. After all, nothing was broken. Just a swollen nose, a blackened eye, a throbbing elbow, bruises, pain. In a few days, every trace would be gone, and I'd be fine. Probably, Kirsten had been careful not to do any permanent damage, not to do anything that would force me to go to the hospital and file a police report. She was a doctor and a black belt. She'd know how to be careful about those things.

Midway through the morning, Hector called. I saw his name on caller ID and let it go to messages. He'd done nothing wrong, but I couldn't stand to talk to him. I hadn't decided what I'd tell him. And I was considering never going to the Reed Center again, never talking to him at all.

With my arms and back so sore, it wasn't an ideal day for carrying trays of food, but I got through it. I got some unusually large tips, too. Chances were, people noticed what my face looked like and thought if I had extra money, I might be able to leave my abusive boyfriend. On the drive to Top Skorz, I found the courage to listen to Hector's message.

He was sorry about the way the evening turned out, he said. After Kirsten and I left, his mother got worse. He'd spent the night at her house—he was still there now. Jason's lawyer had called, saying the evidence against him seemed circumstantial. Hector hoped that meant it wasn't much. He didn't know when he could call again. In a few minutes, he'd take his mother to her doctor, for adjustments in her medications. Maybe we could get together tomorrow. Anyway, he was glad Kirsten could drive me home. He hoped we'd had a nice talk. He wanted us to become better friends, because we were both such great people.

Top Skorz was easier than waitressing, just the usual irritation with teenagers unwilling to make an effort to match the money their parents spent on tutoring. At least I could sit. At least I didn't have to lift anything heavier than sample tests. And at least I had something to distract me from the monotony of vocabulary drills.

Kirsten, Hector had said, was his best friend. He must've confided in her about our date, and she must've sensed feelings powerful enough to make her decide to beat me up and threaten me. Hector must really like me. And I liked him, very much. Now I had to decide just how crazy Kirsten was. I had to decide whether I liked Hector enough to risk having her kill me.

I continued to think it over as I drove to the community center and ate my tuna sandwich. I arrived fifteen minutes before class started, while Sam was laying out the mats. He looked up.

"God," he said. "What happened to your face?"

"Teach me how to fall," I said.

Chapter 17

At 9:00 on Friday morning, I went to the Reed Center for a swim. If Kirsten wants to start something, I thought fiercely, she won't find me such an easy target this time.

She wasn't there. I'd sort of figured she wouldn't be. I'd figured that at 9:00 on a weekday, Dr. Kirsten Carlson would be at her office.

And I'd decided a swim was exactly what I needed. I'd worked on falling for the full hour last night. I'd gotten damn good at it, but now I felt stiff. Swimming would loosen me up. Half an hour of slow, easy laps, alternating between crawl stroke and breast stroke, and I'd be in shape for carrying trays.

And I'd have the pool almost to myself—just one other woman, also doing laps, but hard, fast ones. For a moment, I thought it was Kirsten, and my stomach clenched. But no, it couldn't be, not unless she'd cut her hair. And this woman's arms looked strong, but not toned to an obnoxious level. I looked again and realized it was Diana.

She reached the deep end just as I approached it, noticed me, and swam over to the side, resting her arms on the edge so we could talk. "Good morning. God—is that a black eye?"

I forced an embarrassed laugh. “A little bit of one. I tripped on the stairs at my apartment building.”

It was the same explanation I’d given Sam and Rosa, and they obviously hadn’t believed me. Diana might not either, but she let it go.

“A swim should help,” she said. “And I’ve got good news. Jason was released yesterday afternoon.”

“That’s wonderful,” I said, not sure how I felt. If Jason were innocent, of course it was good he’d been released. But I’d been assuming he was guilty. “Hector left me a message yesterday. He said the evidence was circumstantial.”

“That’s what the lawyer said. He didn’t say much more. He probably can’t. But I don’t think that’s why Jason was released. He has an alibi.”

“He *did* go back to the singles’ night, then?”

“Nope.” She looked both amused and exasperated. “That would’ve been a nice, respectable alibi. That’s not Jason’s style. Anyway, Hector felt bad about not calling you again. Things got too crazy. You should call him.”

After what she’d just said, I’d definitely call. I wanted to hear more about Jason’s alibi, the one that wasn’t nice and respectable.

Hector didn’t need much prompting. We compared schedules, deciding we could squeeze in dinner before I interpreted at Abby’s synagogue. Hector suggested Jack’s, but I pushed for a decent but less distinguished deli. Jack’s is world-class, constantly packed. Tonight, I preferred half empty. Tonight, I’d compromise on the quality of corned beef so we could eat in a quiet place where Hector would feel free to tell family secrets.

Like almost everyone else I’d talked to lately, he began by exclaiming about my eye. He didn’t buy the tripping-on-the-stairs story.

“If some guy did that to you,” he said. “I’ll—”

"No guy did it to me." I took a deep breath. "I swear, Hector—no man has ever given me a black eye. Now, I've had the turkey club here. It's not bad."

By the time our sandwiches arrived, he'd relaxed enough to talk about Jason. "I'm glad he's got an alibi, of course. I just hope it doesn't finish off his marriage."

"Oh," I said. "That sort of alibi."

"In spades. He got drunk last night and bragged about it. He said he'd stonewalled the police for hours, refusing to say where he went after leaving singles' night."

"So he tried to protect the woman's reputation."

Hector shook his head. "He couldn't remember her name. That embarrassed him, though I bet it's happened before. Finally, he broke down and said he'd gone to a bar and picked up a woman named Susie or Sally or maybe Mildred. No clue about the last name. He did remember her apartment building, a classy one in Beachwood. How'd you like to be the cop assigned to checking *that* alibi—knocking on door after door, saying, 'Excuse me, Miss, but did you screw Jason Connolly on Monday, October twenty-fourth?'"

"Good grief. Did it really come to that?"

"No. Luckily for Jason, the building has a security camera in the lobby and keeps tapes for two weeks before re-using them. A security guard recognized the woman entering the building with Jason, and she confirmed his story."

"That's good. Does Mara know about the alibi?"

"She must. And she must realize the police think Jason was involved with Jenny, and she must figure they've got good reasons for thinking so. That's what I figure, too." He shook his head again. "Damn. I would've thought Jenny had more sense. Well, that marriage has been hanging by a thread for years. There've been lots of other women, and Mara's no fool. I've wondered why she's stuck it out this long. Probably, she's still in love with him. She despises him, but she loves him, and she can't let him go."

I remembered the tears running down Mara's face while Jason played the piano. Yes, some love still lingered. "And Jason still loves her, too?"

"Or he's staying because of Kevin. He adores that kid. That kid and my mother—the two great loves of Jason's life. Frankly, I never understood why he married Mara. Oh, she was cute back then, lively, lots of fun. And she's turned out to be a successful tax accountant. She works hard as hell, makes at least twice what he does. But I'd never thought she was special to him. I didn't even meet her until after my father died. Then they got married four months later, before she'd even graduated from high school. Two crazy kids carried away by passion, I guess. Or Jason just had to find one more way to mess up his life."

Poor Hector. He tried to joke about it, but I could see it pained him. "Jason has a history of messing up?"

"You bet. When he was in high school—God, the battles he and my father had! You name it, Jason did it. Drinking, drugs, plagiarizing, shoplifting. Then he got kicked off the soccer team for sneaking a bottle into the locker room. Dad nearly lost it that time. He talked about sending Jason to military school. But of course my mother said no. Too bad. That might've straightened Jason out."

"Maybe this scare will straighten him out," I said, not believing it. "Now it's behind him, maybe he'll take a hard look at his life and make changes."

"I don't know if anything could make Jason take a hard look at his life. And I don't know if it's really behind him. Detective Diaz told him not to leave town. The police actually say that. I thought it was a movie cliché, but she said it."

"I don't understand. It sounds as if he has a good alibi."

"He does. It proves he couldn't have murdered Jenny himself. I guess Diaz thinks he might've hired someone." Hector lifted a shoulder. "Or gotten someone in his family to do it."

It took me a moment to absorb that. "You think she suspects someone in your family?"

"I know she does. After she let Jason go, she questioned each of us. She did it at my mother's house, not the police station, but she was damn thorough. She spent almost an hour grilling me."

He'd turned pale. "I'm sorry. Why would she suspect you?"

"She probably assumes I love my brother. So if big brother's mistress threatened to go to his wife, or got too demanding, or just got boring, maybe I solved his problem for him. And I've got no alibi. None. After I left the singles' night, I went home, watched television, went to bed. No visitors. No phone calls."

He couldn't really be in trouble, could he? "Did she question Diana, too?"

"Oh, yes. Diana wouldn't talk about their session. She laughed it off, but I don't think she found it all that funny. Diana *has* cleaned up lots of Jason's messes. So it might not seem like a stretch to think she'd murder an inconvenient mistress for him."

"Does she have an alibi?"

"Better than mine. She was at this big fundraiser at the Rock and Roll Hall of Fame, to benefit community youth organizations—exhibits, musical performances, food, time to mingle. The Reed Center was a sponsor, but Mom didn't feel up to going, so Diana filled in. She went around eight, left around midnight. I'm sure lots of people saw her. But Jenny's body wasn't found until 1:00. Diana could've killed her after she left, ridiculous as that sounds."

It *did* sound ridiculous. "Did Detective Diaz question anyone else?"

He nodded. "Mara, of course—the jealous wife who might've decided to eliminate the competition. She was at home with Kevin, could've sneaked out after he went to bed. And Diaz questioned Paul Kent, even my mother. She can't think Mom killed Jenny—Mom can barely walk—but Paul and Mom spent the evening together. Diaz could think Mom's lying about that to give Paul an alibi. And Paul's so devoted to Mom that Diaz might think he'd commit murder to protect her son. Not that he's capable of murder. Not that any of us are. But Diaz probably thinks we all have motives. If she finds evidence that seems to point to one of us, it could get bad."

"It'll blow over," I said. "The person she really suspected has an alibi, so she questioned everyone connected to him. She'll probably look in other directions now."

"I hope so. I can't even see why she thinks Jenny was murdered. Why would she think it was anything but an accident?"

"I don't know." She must have reasons. I had reasons, too. Were hers the same as mine? I glanced at my watch. "I should go. I can't be late for services."

"Damn," he said. "Time went too quickly. Jane, I'd like to take you out for a real dinner, maybe a movie or play. Would tomorrow be too soon?"

I winced in apology. "I'm waitressing. Saturday's my best night—lots of customers, big tips. And I can't cancel at such short notice. I'm sorry."

"Don't apologize for having to make a living. But I'll see you Sunday at volleyball, right?"

I winced again. "I might not make it."

He grinned. "Your mother talked you into going to church?"

"It's not that." I couldn't tell him the truth, not all of it—he'd confront Kirsten, and she'd hurt me. "There's some tension between Kirsten and me right now. If I go, it might get uncomfortable."

"Yeah, I noticed she was acting weird the other night. Well, she's always been moody—big highs, deep lows. How about playing on my team? Then you wouldn't have to deal with her so much."

Then she might *really* get mad. But I'd vowed not to let her intimidate me. I should at least consider keeping that vow.

He walked me to my car and kissed me, on the lips this time. Then he stood looking at me, running his hands up and down my arms, as if reluctant to turn away. "Good night, Jane," he said. "Take care of yourself."

After services, several members of the congregation came over to shake my hand. They'd been moved by my interpreting, they said. They couldn't understand the signs, but it had seemed so passionate, so deeply spiritual—they'd never seen me sign like that before. That's because Hector Connolly never kissed me in a parking lot before, I thought, and felt faintly embarrassed.

Abby came up, too, and drew me aside. She'd brought Nate with her tonight. He usually went to a Conservative synagogue, but she'd persuaded him to try Reform. Next Friday, he wanted her to try Conservative. She'd like to have him over for Shabbat dinner first. Would that be okay, even though it meant there wouldn't be an interpreting job for me that night? Could she dominate the apartment for the evening? And would I help her cook?

I answered the questions with one firm fist shake, a nod, a broad smile. *Yes.* Abby's an artist at almost everything, except cooking. This would be fun. I'd research some Jewish recipes and give them my own spin. I felt deeply happy. For months, neither Abby nor I had dated much, or met anyone we much wanted to date. Now, within days of each other, we'd both found men we cared about. What a sweet addition this was to our friendship, what a treat for us to share this hope.

I got up the next morning feeling wonderful. My eye looked better, the bruises had dwindled, and the pain was an unconvincing memory. The day ahead didn't look like fun—a cleaning job that'd soak up the afternoon, a waitressing shift that'd stretch past midnight. But I had the morning to myself.

I researched recipes on the Internet for a few minutes before deciding to look for inspiration at Shaker Square Market. It was a beautiful day, brisk but not oppressively cold, bright and utterly clear. I felt like being outside. It was a little soon to buy produce for Friday's dinner, but Shaker Square is the best farmers' market in town, and it's open only on Saturdays. I'd find some interesting things, experiment with them during the week, do the final shopping at the Cleveland State Market on Thursday.

Abby decided against coming along, so I set out alone. The market stretched down both sides of Shaker Boulevard—two long, inviting lines of tables and booths crowned with awnings, offering not only fruits and vegetables but also baked goods, fish, meats, home-made cheeses, other good things. I lingered over my choices, chatting with vendors, watching a cooking demonstration by a local chef, enjoying the smells of the place, the music provided by a mariachi band, the crisp sunlight, the bustle of friendliness and good spirits. As I stood by a table spread with Amish fare, trying to decide between strawberry and blueberry jam, someone tapped my shoulder.

I turned around to see Detective Bridget Diaz. “Good morning, Ms. Ciardi,” she said. “Your roommate informed me that I could find you here, and I—God. How did you get that black eye?”

Chapter 18

That wasn't fair. The black eye had faded so much I hadn't thought anyone would notice it. I forced the usual laugh. "Oh, that. I tripped on some stairs."

She didn't even try to look as though she believed me. "Really. Well, we need to talk. Why don't you make your purchase, and we'll find a place to sit."

She didn't present it as a matter of choice. Flustered, I turned back to the genial white-capped woman selling jam and chose blueberry at random. Detective Diaz pointed to a bakery stand. We got some lemonade and sat at a small table covered with a blue-and-white checked plastic tablecloth.

"Thank you for agreeing to talk to me," she said, though I couldn't remember agreeing. "I checked into what you said about not being able to comment on conversations you interpret. You were telling the truth."

Already, I felt offended. "I generally tell the truth," I said.

"Good. Let's start with your eye. Did you really trip on the stairs?"

If I lied again about that, she'd suspect me of lying about everything. "No. But it's not a police matter. It's personal, and I don't want to discuss it."

Her voice got gentler. "Women in your situation usually don't want to discuss it. But it *is* a police matter, and it'll get worse unless you take action. We have an officer who specializes—"

I held up a hand. "You're assuming I'm in an abusive relationship. That's a natural assumption, but this time it's wrong. No man hit me. That's the truth."

It'd worked with Hector. Not with her. "So it was a woman. Your roommate?"

"Abby? Don't be ridiculous." I could take Abby.

She leaned forward. "Ms. Ciardi, tell me the truth. Was it Diana Connolly?"

This time, I didn't have to fake a laugh. "No. And in case you're wondering, it wasn't Mara Connolly or Elise Reed. You could say it happened during a martial arts lesson."

She sat back, looking skeptical. "Which art?"

She had me there. "It'd be hard to say. Look, you must've come here with other things to discuss. Can we move on?"

She paused and then nodded. "Okay. Frankly, Ms. Ciardi, when I spoke to you last Monday, I got the impression you weren't being completely open. It wasn't just that you couldn't comment on my conversation with Ms. Patterson. Something else felt off. And I was surprised to see you at the Connolly house Wednesday. I have to wonder what your involvement in this whole situation really is."

Keep it casual, I decided. "There's nothing mysterious about it. Last week, I applied for a trial membership at the Reed Center. Hector Connolly interviewed me. We were attracted to each other, we've gone out a few times, and he invited me to his mother's birthday dinner. That's all."

She didn't look convinced. "And Rosa Patterson—you

happened to meet her at a martial arts class, and you both happen to belong to the Reed Center. Is there anything more to it?"

Why hadn't I asked Frederick about the legal consequences of withholding information from the police? "I'd rather not answer. I have ethical concerns—not relating to interpreting this time, but ethical concerns of another sort. Am I legally obliged to answer your question?"

She shrugged. "You're not under arrest. You're free to walk away at any time."

"Thank you." I stood up.

"Except," she said, "a woman died under questionable circumstances. I'm investigating her death, and you may have information that could help me. I'd think any conscientious citizen, any decent human being, would want to help."

I sat back down. "I *do* want to help. But I'm honestly not sure if it's ethical for me to talk to you."

"Think it over. I'll buy you a cookie."

She bought me a ginger snap—not a dry, brittle ginger snap like the ones that come in boxes but a soft, chewy ginger snap, rich and fragrant, its crinkled surface flecked with sugar. "This is a good bribe," I said.

"It's not a bribe. Citizens sometimes attempt to bribe cops. Cops don't bribe citizens. The cookie's an inducement. Ms. Ciardi, I understand you want to be careful about ethics. I know you've had problems in that area in the past."

Damn. "You called the interpreting agency."

"I called several agencies, to assess your reliability as a witness. All the agencies said they're no longer giving you assignments because you were involved in an ethics dispute. Now, you—"

"Look," I said, "I didn't do anything unethical. I filed an ethics complaint against another interpreter. It embarrassed the agency, and now the agency won't place me and is destroying my reputation. You can believe that or not. I really don't care."

She looked at me. "I do believe that. I think you've told me the truth—about the ethics dispute. You didn't tell me the whole truth about your eye, and you haven't told me the whole truth about Rosa Patterson. What's your relationship with her, Ms. Ciardi?"

I gave up. "A private detective hired me to keep an eye on her. He hired me because I know sign language. That's why I'm taking the martial arts class and why I joined the center."

She looked pleased with herself. "I wondered if it might be something like that. I checked Rosa Patterson out—I know who her father is. So Ulysses Patterson got scared when his daughter's friend drowned. He worried it might be connected to the Reed Center, and his daughter might be in danger. But he couldn't talk to her about it, because teenagers never listen to their parents. So he hired a private detective. Who?"

She'd made too many assumptions, and she'd made some mistakes. But it might be prudent not to point them out. "Walt Sadowski."

"I've heard of him. So Sadowski hired you to babysit Rosa, try to find out if there's anything funny going on at the center. Is dating Hector Connolly part of the job?"

"No. That just happened."

"A fringe benefit, huh?" She smiled, a moderately friendly smile. "Have you come across information that might help me?"

"Possibly. But I *do* have ethical concerns. I'm not a private detective, but I work for one, and I have the impression private detectives are supposed to keep things confidential, even from the police." It'd feel embarrassing to admit I'd gotten that impression from television. "I don't know what's appropriate. I'd like to ask Mr. Sadowski for advice."

She grimaced. "I respect you for wanting to honor your professional responsibilities. I'll tell you what. I'll call Mr. Sadowski and find a time for the three of us to meet on Monday. Then we can get everything out in the open."

"Fine," I said, relieved she hadn't pushed more. "I'm available any time before noon on Monday, and any time after six."

"Good." She started to stand and then sat down again. "Your eye—was it Rosa Patterson?"

Again, I didn't have to fake the laugh. "Good grief. No."

Walt called two hours later, and I took a break from power-washing rides from a traveling children's carnival to talk to him. He was in a surprisingly good mood. "So we're set to meet with Diaz at 10:00 Monday morning. She thinks Patterson didn't hire me until after Jenny Linton died. That's good. That means she thinks he hired me just because he's afraid Rosa's in danger, not because he thinks she might be up to something herself. We gotta be real careful, make sure she keeps thinking that."

"I understand," I said. "You want to protect Rosa. So do I. But shouldn't we tell Detective Diaz about Gary Nichols? If there's a connection—"

"Not one word about Gary. That's an order. Then Diaz would want to know why he was watching Rosa before Jenny died. She'd want to talk to Rosa—she might start suspecting Rosa killed Gary, or Jenny, or both. And the last thing we wanna do is make Ulysses Patterson's daughter a murder suspect."

"I agree. But—"

"But nothing. Right now, Diaz isn't interested in Rosa. She's interested in Jason Connolly's family, and she thinks you might've stumbled across information about them. That's all she wants to know about. So that's all we're gonna tell her."

"But she's investigating a possible murder. Maybe she should be investigating two possible murders. If we told her about Gary, if we cooperate with the police—"

"I'm all for cooperating with the police. If we do, next time we need their help, maybe they'll cooperate with us. But we don't have to answer questions they don't ask. That's how we're playing it with Diaz. Understand?"

Two people might have been murdered. It didn't feel right to hold anything back. But Walt knew more about these things than I did. "Understood," I said.

On Sunday, I found the courage, or stupidity, to go to volleyball. Bethany and Ashley looked confused when I walked to Hector's side of the net, but they smiled and waved. Kirsten saw me and said nothing. That match was a grim, nearly silent echo of the one the week before. Again, Elise Reed gave her welcoming speech and made the first serve. Then she almost collapsed, and Paul Kent took her home.

Kirsten played even more fiercely this time, but she didn't cheer her teammates on or whoop when they scored. She swore when things went wrong, but aside from that said nothing. Diana seemed tired. Twice, she sat down, holding her head in her hands, letting others take her place. Hector pursued the ball with the same energy he'd shown last week, but he seemed distracted and faulted. Jason, back on his family's side of the net, was the only one whose mood had improved. He played vigorously and well—he was the reason our team won. Cursing, Kirsten stalked to the locker room. No shower for me, I decided, grabbed my red-and-white tote bag, and got the hell out of the gym.

Hector caught up with me in the hall. "It feels like forever since we've talked. And Diana thinks we should go stay with Mom now, and tomorrow we've got a stupid singles' night—Diana wants me to go keep an eye on Jason. Could we sneak in a quick, early dinner? I'd have to be back here by seven."

Inspiration hit. "How about making it a quick, early picnic? We could meet at Squire's Castle. It's near my apartment. That way, we don't have to worry about getting served in time. I'll pack a picnic basket. Of course, the evenings are getting cold."

"Not a problem for me, if it isn't for you." He looked delighted. "Fantastic idea. Maybe we can fit in a walk. I love the hiking trails around there. But don't spend much time cooking. Keep it simple, okay?"

"Absolutely," I said, and immediately began planning the menu.

I headed to the equipment room to meet Rosa. There she was, with Jason, in the middle of a sign-language lesson. He'd mime an action, she'd show him the sign, he'd imitate it, she'd smile and nod. She seemed to find him charming, and she didn't seem to mind when, after getting a sign correct, he embraced her, lifting her off the floor and planting a kiss on her lips.

No more, I decided, and joined them. "Hi, Rosa," I said, signing as I spoke. "Jason, nice to see you. How's Mara?"

Anger instantly came to his eyes. "Fine."

"Great." I turned to Rosa. "I met Jason's wife. She's very nice. And they have an adorable son, Kevin. How old is he, Jason? Five?"

"Six." The anger had escalated to hatred.

"That's right," I said and signed. "I hope you get to meet Kevin, Rosa. I could see how much he loves both his daddy and his mommy."

"Cut it out." Jason stepped between me and Rosa. I

started to sign what he was saying, but he knocked my arms aside with a rough sweeping motion. "Mind your own business. And I haven't forgotten that dress." He strode off.

I looked at Rosa and shook my head. "*He's married. And he's not a nice man.*"

She shrugged. "*I don't take him seriously. You know I'm with Sam. Let's get started.*"

After an hour, Rosa had to go. I still owed her lunch. We both had Wednesday morning free, so we agreed to meet for a serious workout, followed by early lunch in the café. And during lunch, I decided, we'd have a real conversation. Walt was paying me to find out what was going on, and in almost two weeks I'd learned almost nothing.

I decided to shower at home—only, I assured myself, because that was more private, not because I half-feared Kirsten might be lurking in the locker room. It'd been almost two hours since the game. I'd have to be paranoid to imagine she'd waited in the locker room that long.

She'd waited in the parking garage. She stood behind a concrete pillar near my car, still wearing the shorts and sports bra she'd worn during the game. Probably, she hadn't showered, had stood there the whole time. I didn't see her until I was barely four feet away. No one else was around.

She stepped out from behind the pillar. "I told you to stay away from him. Wasn't I emphatic enough?"

Should I drop my bag and take a fighting stance? No, that'd be an invitation. Better to stay cool, to keep things from escalating, to hope someone, anyone, would enter the garage before she killed me. "I don't want trouble, Kirsten. I could've reported you to the police. I didn't."

"If you don't want trouble, stay away from Hector. That's simple enough. But no. You just had to come this morning, you had to play on his team, you had to help him beat me. You wanted to humiliate me."

"No one wanted to humiliate you. It's just a game."

"It's *never* just a game." She stepped toward me. "You can't understand that. You'll never understand Hector, either. You know how old he was, the first time I screwed him? Fifteen. I was on my way to med school—there weren't many teenagers I'd bother with. But Hector was special. Even at fifteen, he was special. I've screwed him hundreds of times since then, and he's always been special. He's screwed lots of other women, too. Hundreds. He's wild and strong and free. You really think you can handle a man like that? You really think you're up to it?"

When she put it like that, no, I didn't think so, not really. But she might be lying about hundreds of women. I looked at her coldly. "Maybe we should let Hector make that decision."

She took another step toward me. "*I* make Hector's decisions."

Then, miraculously, I heard voices coming from the stairway, and there they were—a father and two sulky teenagers, talking and arguing and heading for their car.

I jumped up and down, waving my arms and shouting. "Hey! It's Jane Ciardi. And this is Kirsten Carlson. Hope you had a great workout!"

"Thanks," the man said, looking confused. "Hope you did, too."

I sped past Kirsten and got into my car. But she grabbed the door before I could pull it shut.

"I won't warn you again," she said. "The next time I see you anywhere near him, I'll do it."

Chapter 19

Now," Detective Bridget Diaz said, "tell me everything you know about Jason Connolly."

We sat in Walt Sadowski's shabby, oddly cheerful little office. Even with Walt behind the desk, Detective Diaz was clearly running the meeting.

I took a deep breath. I told her what I'd learned from Jenny's roommate, and she nodded but didn't take notes. Obviously, she'd heard it before. When I described Jason's reaction to Jenny's dress, she took extensive notes, pressing me to remember exactly what he'd said. God, I thought. If Jason gets charged with murder, I may have to testify. I told her about the times I'd seen him flirt with Rosa, about dinner last Wednesday, about tensions between Jason and his wife, about his love for his son.

"What about Paul Kent?" she asked. "Do you think he's Elise Reed's lover?"

"Or her lackey. I'd guess lackey. He adores her, but I'd bet she's kept him at a distance, an intimate distance, ever since her husband died. That's not based on much. It's only an impression."

"All right," she said. "Tell me about every other impression you've gotten."

When we finished with Paul, we moved on to Mara,

then Diana, then Hector. Talking about Hector felt uncomfortable, but no code of ethics gave me an excuse for holding back. When I mentioned Hector's deep love for his father, I also mentioned what he'd said about conflicts between his father and Jason, and she started taking notes again. Good, I thought. Jason's the one she's really interested in.

"So his father tried to whip him into shape," Walt commented, "and his mother pampered him. Bad combination. Bad for the kid, bad for the marriage."

Detective Diaz half-nodded. "There was another woman at the dinner. Elise Reed identified her as Kirsten Carlson, a family friend. I haven't questioned her. Should I?"

"Well, she's odd," I said. "Very, very odd. Extremely odd. Maybe the oddest person I've ever met."

"Any connection with Jenny Linton?"

"The only connection I know of is that they played on the same volleyball team at the center. But Kirsten *is* odd. She's obsessed with Hector Connolly."

"With Hector. Not with Jason?"

"Right. She once called Jason a loser."

She pursed her lips, lifted a shoulder, and didn't write anything down. "Okay. Let's go back over something you said about Mara Connolly."

I could see what she was thinking. An obsession with Jason would give Kirsten a motive for killing his mistress. An obsession with Hector didn't. And I had no reason to think Kirsten killed Jenny—except I thought she might be capable of killing people, since she'd seemed damn convincing when she'd threatened to kill me. It didn't seem fair she got crossed off Detective Diaz's list so easily.

We went on for another half hour. She didn't ask about Rosa. As Walt predicted, her interests focused sharply on the Connollys, especially Jason. So no ethical conflicts, no chance I'd get Rosa in trouble. I thought Detective Diaz should know about what happened in Ginger's Pantry, and about Gary Nichols. But Walt had ordered me not to bring up either subject.

She checked her notes. "That takes care of my questions. Thanks for your help."

Walt sat forward. "If you really wanna thank us, give *us* some help. I got a client worried sick about his daughter. Ever since Jenny Linton died, he's been afraid there's something wrong about this fitness center, afraid Rosa's in danger. I've been telling him to stop worrying, that Linton's death was an accident. Should I stop telling him that? What I mean is, have you got solid reasons for thinking she was murdered?"

As far as I knew, Walt was making all that up. When Ulysses Patterson talked to me, he hadn't said one word about Jenny. Probably, Walt was trying to reinforce the illusion Ulysses Patterson had hired a detective only because he feared his sweet, innocent daughter might be in danger. If that's what he was doing, it worked.

"I understand your client's concerns," Detective Diaz said. "I can honestly say I have no reason to think there's a serial killer associated with the Reed Center, or anything like that. I do consider Jason Connolly's interest in Ms. Patterson disturbing, and I'm glad Ms. Ciardi's advising her to stay away from him. As to your question—yes, I have solid reasons for thinking Ms. Linton might've been murdered."

I couldn't stop myself. "We probably know some of those reasons. Jenny wasn't dressed for partying at The Flats—she was wearing a pantsuit. And a gold necklace. Her roommate thought it wasn't real gold. Was it? Was it a gift from Jason Connolly?"

She smiled. "I can't share that information. If we *had*

determined the necklace was worth nearly a thousand dollars, if we *had* traced the purchase to Jason Connolly—yes, that might've made us suspicious. I can't comment further."

"I understand," I said. "I respect you for wanting to honor your professional responsibilities."

She grinned, recognizing her own words. "Here's something I *can* tell you. Technically it's public knowledge, though almost nobody knows about it. You know Ms. Linton's car was found in the parking lot of a bar at The Flats. Two nights later, the owner of that bar called a local late-night radio talk show. He was upset because his bar's getting a bad reputation—people are staying away. So he told the talk-show host some things he'd already told us. We'd asked him to keep those things quiet, but we couldn't order him to do so."

"I missed that," I said. "I don't listen to late-night talk radio."

"Apparently, not many people do. The owner said he didn't think Ms. Linton had actually been in his bar that night. He'd spoken to all his employees and several regular customers, and nobody remembered seeing her. An attractive woman in a pant suit—he thinks somebody would've noticed her, in a bar where most women wear low-slung jeans and low-cut tops."

"Interesting," I said.

"Yes. The owner also repeated something one of his employees told us. He was standing outside the back entrance sometime between nine and ten that night, smoking, and saw a red car pull into the lot and park near the back. A tall person wearing jeans and a hooded jacket got out but didn't enter the bar. Instead, he or she ran out of the lot—sprinted, the employee said—heading east."

"'He or she,'" I said. "The employee couldn't tell if it was a man or a woman?"

She shrugged. "It was dark. The person wore a hooded jacket, with the hood up."

"And was Jenny Linton's car parked at the back of the lot? Is it red?"

Standing up, Detective Diaz slung her purse over her shoulder. "The color's called Chianti. Sort of a maroon. Yes, it was parked at the back. That's not confidential information. And as it happens, after our technical team finished with the car, I drove it to the lockup." She shot me a smile. "You and I are about the same height—about the same height as Jenny Linton. And if someone told me the last person to drive that car was considerably taller than you, or I, or Ms. Linton, I couldn't disagree. Again, thank you for your cooperation."

We waited until we heard the outer office door close. "So when Detective Diaz got in the car," I said, "the seat was too far back, and the mirrors were wrong."

"Yeah." Walt grinned slightly. "Amazing. Even if you plan everything out real careful, you can forget something like that. Besides, most killers are amateurs. They've never killed anyone before, they don't know what cops look for at crime scenes, and they're nervous as hell. That's why they mess up."

"So Jenny never went to that bar," I said. "Maybe the killer arranged to meet her a mile or so downstream, knocked her out, put her in the river, and held her under until she drowned. Then the killer drove Jenny's car to the bar, left it in the lot, and sprinted back to his or her own car. `Sprinted'—the killer sounds athletic."

"That fits almost everybody in the Connolly family. Plus Paul Kent."

Plus Kirsten Carlson, I thought. "Do you think the police also have other evidence of murder?"

"They might. Marks on the body that don't fit with drowning, maybe. And they'd check her phone records.

An amateur might call her from a pay phone, thinking that's clever. But it's a red flag. It doesn't sound like the cops have much pointing to somebody in particular, though. Jason had an affair with her, but he's got an alibi. So they gotta look at his family."

And Hector's his brother, I thought, and he doesn't have any alibi at all. "But anybody who committed murder would set up an alibi. So if someone doesn't have any alibi, doesn't that almost prove he or she wasn't the murderer?"

Walt grinned again. "Sorry, honey. It only proves it probably wasn't premeditated. Say Jenny was blackmailing Jason. He's too upset to deal with her, so he asks somebody to take care of it. This person sets up a meeting, but Jenny keeps demanding more. And this person gets mad, drowns her, tries to cover up. No time to set up an alibi. Make sense?"

Damn. It did.

I hurried through the rest of the day, cleaning an empty apartment that was already in good shape before racing home to put our picnic dinner together. Not fried chicken, I'd decided yesterday. That's a picnic cliché. Instead, I'd roasted a turkey breast and made fresh cranberry relish. Using produce from Shaker Square Market, I'd made potato salad with sun-dried tomatoes and tarragon, marinated green beans, and concocted an apple-and-pear variation on Waldorf salad. I'd baked hand-sized oatmeal cookies spiked with raisins, pecans, and chocolate chips. Now, all I had to do was slice turkey thin and fold it into wraps with cranberry relish, sprouts, and provolone. As I crammed containers into the basket, I felt proud. As I'd promised Hector, I'd kept it simple.

Grabbing a jug of cider and a blanket, I got in my car and headed for Squire's Castle. The park where it's located has plenty of picnic tables, but I wanted to have dinner in the castle itself. I'd eaten there before and found it pleasantly creepy. With Hector there, it should be romantically creepy.

Carrying the picnic basket and my other supplies, I walked across the grassy clearing leading to the castle—a large, gray stone shell of a building, stark against the darkening sky, bordered on three sides by trees thick with orange and gold leaves. As I'd expected, the cold had driven people away. We'd have the castle to ourselves.

It's not really a castle, of course, despite the turrets and arches and tall stone chimneys. A wealthy businessman with the conveniently chivalric last name of Squire built it in the 1890s, seeing it as the gatehouse for an estate he never completed. After using the gatehouse as a summer cottage for a while, he sold the property, and it eventually became part of the city park system.

Local legends say Squire's wife hated staying here and was afraid to live in what was then an isolated spot. One night, while passing through the trophy room her husband had decorated with heads of big-game animals, she took fright at something, panicked, screamed, ran, fell, broke her neck, and died.

It's not true. She may never have lived in the gatehouse at all. She definitely didn't die there. She died of a stroke, in her house in Wickcliffe, years after her husband sold the property. That doesn't stop people from insisting that her ghost haunts the gatehouse, that on dark nights they can see her red lantern burning in an upstairs window, that they can still hear her terrified screams.

As I stood in the center of the castle, I thought of the legends, enjoying the small thrill of foreboding ghost stories can create even when we know they're based on nothing. The place definitely has a spooky feel. Over the years, after repeated incidents of vandalism, the city had stripped the gatehouse almost to its bones, tearing down interior walls, knocking out windows, filling in the basement and putting down a hard gray floor that looks like cement. Two massive fireplaces remain, though, one framed with red bricks, the other with gray stones. I set my things down and walked over to the stone fireplace to read the plaques mounted above it. As I stood reading, I heard footsteps behind me. Hector's here, I thought, and turned around.

Kirsten stood in the middle of the floor, wearing black sweat pants and a black tank top, her long blonde hair pulled back hard and gathered into a pony tail. Despite the cold, despite her bare arms, she didn't shiver. She put her hands on her hips.

"I warned you," she said. "Twice."

Chapter 20

Calm down, I told myself. I thought of the legends about Squire's wife, dying when she ran from imaginary danger. I looked at Kirsten directly.

"You don't want to try anything here," I said. "It's a park, for God's sake. It's a public place."

She moved her eyes to the left and the right, smiling a small, tight smile. "It's a public place," she said. "But no one's here. Just you and me."

"Hector's arriving any minute. You don't want him to see you acting crazy."

"Hector's been delayed. He's got car trouble." Again she glanced left and right, not moving her head, not taking her focus off me. "This must've been beautiful once. What a shame vandals kept defacing it. Those damn teenagers. And now a mugging. A fatal mugging. Those damn teenagers."

She's a doctor, I reminded myself. She's an intelligent, educated woman. I can reason with her. "Kirsten, stop and think. You've got a successful career, a reputation to protect. Why risk all—"

She screamed and sprang forward, hands in fighting position, bringing her right knee up and snapping her foot out sharply, aiming for my chest. Surprised, I had barely enough time to bring my left arm up. It took the full force of the kick and hurt like hell, but at least she hadn't knocked the air out of me—not a textbook block, but good enough.

Then she tried the same move she'd used last time—grabbing my right arm, putting an arm around my waist, pulling me up on her hip and throwing me down.

This time, I remembered to tuck my chin and slap the cement floor. Pain shot through my already-injured arm, nearly taking my breath away, but it spread the impact out. And I hadn't hit my head. I lay flat on the floor, and she had me by the arm, but I could still think, still act.

She started to pull me up, forming her right hand into a fist. Before she could punch me, I yanked my arm down, pulling her head forward. Forcing all my desperation into a yell, I brought my left foot up and kicked her in the face.

She let go of me, putting her hand to her face, stumbling backward. Jumping up, I ran toward her and caught her in the stomach with a right side kick, knocking her breathless. Again she stumbled back, still holding her face, surprised by the pain.

Gathering my breath, I stood a few feet from her and put my hands up to block. "Walk away. We'll pretend this never happened. I won't tell Hector. But Kirsten, you've got problems. You should see a counselor."

She took her hand away from her face and stared. Then, screaming, she took a half step forward. I saw the spin beginning. Shit, I thought, and stuck my right arm up to protect my head.

She spun around, bringing her right leg up, aiming for my forehead. I got my arm up in time, but the force of the kick knocked me sideways, sending me stumbling against the wall.

For a moment, I'd had the advantage. But I'd blown it. And she's stronger than I am, I thought, and a better fighter. It's over. I stood frozen, trying to gather my wits for the next attack, knowing I couldn't last long.

Then I heard Hector's voice, saw him running toward us. "Kirsten!" he cried. "Stop it! What's wrong with you?"

She backed away but stayed in a fighting stance, eyes wide and blank. He ran to me and held me by both shoulders. "Are you all right?"

"Fine," I said, but didn't protest when he eased me against the wall and stepped in front of me, putting his body between me and Kirsten.

"What the hell, Kirsten," he said. "Why are you here? What did you do?"

"You can't end up with her," Kirsten said. Her voice sounded utterly calm. She could've been discussing treatment options with a patient. "She'll ruin you, Hector. She'll make you weak. We have to get rid of her."

"God," he said. "Listen to yourself. You sound absolutely out of your mind. And I saw you kick her." He turned to me. "That black eye—was it Kirsten?"

I tried to shrug. "It doesn't matter."

"It *does* matter." He turned back to her. "I don't know what's gotten into you. I'm—I'm pulling your membership. You're suspended from the center for a month."

If I hadn't been so scared, I might have laughed. It's junior high, I thought. He's the assistant principal. She tried to kill me, so he suspends her from the Reed Center for a month. I put my hand to my mouth to stifle the hysteria welling up.

Kirsten didn't see it as a joke. "You can't suspend me! I'm on the board! And you need me, Hector."

"Not if you keep acting like this. We'll talk tomorrow. But now, you have to leave. Stay away from Jane, and stay away from the center for a month. Otherwise, you're out for good."

She stood motionless, staring. I half-expected her to attack us both. Then she ran off—not a word, not a sound, not a flicker of emotion on her face. She simply turned her back on us and ran. Hector took me in his arms, holding me close. I pressed against him, finding comfort in the hard strength of his chest and arms.

"I'm sorry," he said. "What happened? Did she hurt you? Did she scare you?"

"Hurt me? Not too bad." But both arms ached, and I knew I'd have huge bruises. "Scare me? You bet. But it's all right. You're here." I pulled back and smiled. "My cavalry—arriving in the nick of time. Kirsten said you'd be delayed. She said you had car trouble."

He shook his head, as if still not able to believe it. "I did. When I got to the garage, all four tires were flat. At first I thought it was some kid getting back at me because I'd made him stop horsing around in the pool or something. Then I remembered the look in Kirsten's eyes when I told her we were having a picnic at Squire's Castle. I ran back upstairs, got Diana's keys, and drove her car straight here. Thank God."

"Amen." I smiled again. "Letting the air out of your tires—damn. This *is* like junior high."

He looked puzzled but let the reference go. "What now? You're probably too upset to eat, and you must want to get out of here. Should we go to your apartment, so we can talk?"

"Actually, I'm starving. And if you don't mind the cold, we can talk right here. I brought candles."

He didn't mind the cold. We spread out the blanket, lit the candles, unpacked the basket. The gray stone walls surrounding us felt oddly comforting, and the gathering darkness soothed me. I couldn't picture Kirsten jumping out of these shadows. I felt safe here, alone with Hector.

As we ate, I told him about what happened when Kirsten drove me home, what happened today. He had trouble taking it in.

"I never expected anything like this," he said. "Kirsten and I have never had an exclusive relationship. She's never wanted one. She goes out with other men, and I go out with other women. She encourages me to. She's never been possessive before."

"I guess she just doesn't like me."

"I don't think that's it." He took my hand. "Do you?"

I looked into those intense blue-gray eyes. "I hope that's not it."

"It's not." He brought my hand to his lips and kissed it. "Kirsten must've sensed it's different this time. It *is* different. *You're* different. When I asked you to dinner last week, I thought it'd be just another date. But when you told me about reporting that other interpreter—I don't know many people who would do that."

I shrugged, embarrassed. "It wasn't a big deal."

"It was. You put your career on the line because you thought it was the right thing to do. You surprised me, Jane, and nothing's been the same since."

He leaned toward me and kissed me, and I put my arms around his neck and kissed him back. It was awkward—sitting on a concrete floor, the blanket bunching up between us, both of us half-conscious that if we got much closer, the candles might topple over and set the blanket on fire. We didn't dare keep it up long. But it was sweet.

With a glance at the candles, he pulled away and smoothed out the blanket. We laughed, both embarrassed, I think, by the things he'd said, and by the promise the kiss held. He switched topics. "Kirsten must be unbalanced. I'd never seen that before. I knew she's more passionate than most people, sure—big highs, deep lows, like I said—but I thought that just made her more fun, more interesting. This afternoon, though. We were playing handball, I told her about our picnic, and she started saying vicious things." He grinned. "She said you're after me for my money."

"I'd hate to think of myself as being 'after' anybody, for any reason. But if I *were* after you, it wouldn't be for your money."

"That's good," he said, "because I don't have any. People think we're rich. We probably were, once, and Mom's still got that house. And the center looks upscale, but we have to keep it that way, or people wouldn't come. Every cent we make goes into keeping the center looking good. Some months, when things get tight, I don't take a salary. And Diana has an MBA from John Carroll, and she pays herself a thousand dollars a month. She lives with my mother, so that covers most expenses. But I don't think she has five cents to her name."

I thought of Jenny's clothes, of the gold necklace she wore the night she died. "And Jason?"

He laughed again. "Jason makes a nice salary. Mother wouldn't have it any other way. And Mara makes plenty, and he—well. Jason does all right."

I remembered how Jason strode into Hector's office that first day, how upset he'd been about "accounting changes" Hector and Diana wanted to make. Had Jason been skimming funds from the center? Had Hector and Diana proposed "accounting changes" designed to stop him? That worm, I thought. That's how Jason paid for Jenny's clothes, for her necklace, for all the things he'd probably given other women. His brother and sister are sacrificing so much for the center, and Jason sees it as a cookie jar he can raid. "I'm sorry it's been so hard," I said.

"It's the damn chains. We have to offer everything they do, even if we go broke doing it. When my parents started the center, most of the chains didn't exist. We had the best facility in town, and people joined so they could catch a glimpse of Elise Reed. Mom did half-hour performances at our rink twice a week—the place was always packed. But it's been years since she could skate, and she won those medals long ago. Most people in Cleveland don't know who Elise Reed is. They've all heard of the chains, though."

"It's a beautiful facility," I said. "You could still turn things around."

"That's what I keep telling myself. I keep thinking we'll find the perfect gimmick to draw people in. Or the United States will grab a bunch of skating medals at the next Olympics, and the rink will become a real attraction again." He sighed. "Or we'll just keep making it month to month, never quite going under. I'm sure as hell not giving up. This center was my father's dream, his last dream. He'd wanted to coach a professional team. That didn't happen, so he poured all his hopes into the center. Now it's up to us to keep it going."

I put my hand on his. "I'm sure you will. I just hope you don't neglect your own dreams too long."

"I'll get to those. Once the center's on a solid footing, I'll definitely get to those." He looked at his watch. "Damn. Why does time go so quickly when I'm with you? I should go. And you should get inside. Your hand feels like ice."

"I *am* getting cold. I'm sorry we didn't get to the hiking trails. Maybe we'll try those another time."

"I'd like that, if you wouldn't mind coming back. After the stunt Kirsten pulled, I wouldn't blame you for wanting to avoid this place forever."

"From now on," I said, "whenever I think of Squire's

Castle, I'll think of our picnic. Kirsten's a dim memory by comparison."

He stood up. "So we exorcised the place. Well, not completely. Poor Mrs. Squire's still here. But if the ghost of Kirsten is gone, that's good enough."

He helped me up and then pulled me closer. I put my arms around him, and we kissed several times. His cheek felt cold against mine. A tightness grew inside me. If he hadn't had to leave, if it hadn't been so cold, I don't know what might have happened.

He pulled back, reaching out to touch a strand of my hair, tucking it back in place behind my ear. "I want to have a real date with you, Jane. Not a quick dinner before one of us has to rush somewhere else, but a chance to spend real time together. Can we make that happen?"

I thought quickly. "Friday night? I'm helping Abby make dinner for a friend, but I'll be done by seven. Will that work?"

"Yes." Pulling me to him again, he kissed me hard. Friday night, I thought, and felt that tightness again. I had big decisions to make before Friday night, and not just about what I'd wear.

Chapter 21

The next morning, I still hadn't calmed down all the way. I was in an office building downtown, in a public relations firm's reception area, washing walls. I had my back to the glass door leading to the hallway, I had my I-Pod turned up, and I was singing along to "Walking on Sunshine." Maybe my arms felt sore. I don't remember. All I could think about then, all I remember now, is the sweet coolness of Hector's cheek, the strength of his embrace, the things he'd said.

Kirsten had never been possessive before, he'd said. She hadn't cared when he had sex with other women. That had to be because she knew that, to Hector, sex was just another pleasant physical activity, like tennis or swimming. She hadn't minded because she knew no matter how much he slept around, she was the most important woman in his life. Now, she minded. That had to mean she thought Hector saw me as more than just another woman. And Kirsten wasn't stupid.

He must really care about me, I thought for the thirtieth or fortieth time, and felt excitement surge through me again. Then I felt a firm, hard hand on my shoulder. Letting out a yell, I spun around, hands in fighting position.

Frederick Patterson took a step back, holding up both

palms. "Take it easy. I was walking by, and I thought it was you and wanted to say hello."

I took off my earphones and tried to get my heartbeat down to normal. "Sorry. I'm slightly on edge. It's nice to see you. What are you doing here?"

He gestured upwards with his thumb. "Meeting with a client, ninth floor. What are *you* doing here?"

"I'm working. The firm's redecorating, and the owner wants everything washed down before the painters arrive."

I could see him trying to figure it out. "The owner's a friend of yours?"

"No, it's just a job." I pointed to the "Cathy's Cleaning Crew" insignia above my shirt pocket. "I help students prepare for the SAT, I waitress, and I clean. We do residential jobs, too, but lately it's been mostly commercial."

"But you're a sign-language interpreter. That's got to pay better than those jobs."

Not again. I made myself smile. "I haven't gotten much interpreting work lately. It's a long story."

He glanced at his watch. "I have ten minutes. Can you take a break?"

Might as well get this over with. "I can take a break," I said, and we cleared the tarps off two chairs.

As concisely as I could, I told him the story. The corners of his mouth twitched downward.

"You should've gone to the judge during the recess," he said. "He could've called experts in to review the tapes right then. He might've declared a mistrial."

"I know. But it happened so quickly, and it was my first time in criminal court. I couldn't decide what to do. If the jury had found the defendant guilty, I definitely would've gone to the judge, right away."

He winced. "You couldn't know what it's like. But

I've stood next to clients when the jury's brought in a guilty verdict. Even when the charge isn't murder or anything close, it's a devastating experience. Even for people who are probably guilty, it's devastating. For an innocent man to have a jury declare him guilty of murder—I wouldn't wish that on anyone. But you got lucky. The jury found him not guilty anyway. And I'm sure you wouldn't make that mistake again."

"I wouldn't." I tried not to show how stunned I felt.

"Good. Well, I hear the police took Jason Connolly in but released him. Do you know if he's completely off the hook? Or did they let him go for lack of evidence?"

I didn't see any problem with answering. "They released him because he has an alibi, but I think they're still investigating him."

"Good. He sounds like bad news, and I don't like it that he's flirting with my sister. You should tell Rosa to stay away from him."

"I *have* told her. Just the other day, I reminded her he has a wife and son, and I said he isn't a nice person."

He winced again. "Not a nice person—that's putting it mildly. Next time, don't mince words. Rosa shouldn't get mixed up with him. This Sam Ryan jerk is bad enough."

I tried to keep irritation out of my voice. "I don't know Sam well, but I haven't seen or heard anything to make me think he's a jerk."

He raised an eyebrow. "He's pressuring a teenaged girl into selling her mother's books so he can buy expensive clothes and hang out in bars. To me, that makes him a jerk. And God knows what else he's using that money for. I wish you could find out what he's up to. My father and I thought you'd have learned more by now."

Keeping irritation out of my voice was no longer an option. "It's difficult. I'm supposed to act like I'm Rosa's casual acquaintance. If I start interrogating her, she'll avoid me. And I'm not a professional private detective."

"Yeah, I know." Was that sarcasm? "But try to move things along. My father and I are worried, and you're not making any progress. I should get to my meeting. But I haven't forgotten I owe you lunch."

"You don't owe me anything," I said. "And, as you see, I'm very busy. Now that I can no longer get interpreting jobs, I have to work long hours to support myself. I seldom have time for a lunch break. And since most of the work I do is menial, I'm seldom dressed suitably for going to restaurants. If you'll excuse me, I have to get back to washing walls."

He looked puzzled. "Jane, what is it? Did I say something wrong?"

"You? Say something wrong? Impossible." I turned away, put my earphones back on, and picked up my sponge.

Even with my back to him, even with my I-Pod blaring, I knew he stood staring at me for a long minute before walking away. You smug, self-righteous prig, I thought. Hector thinks I'm a saint because I sacrificed my career to take an ethical stand, and you look down at me for not acting sooner. And yes, in many ways I agreed with Frederick. Every day since the trial, I'd blamed myself for not going to the judge right away. But that didn't give *him* the right to blame me. It took me a while to gather my courage, but I'd insisted on an inquiry, even though I knew it'd anger the agency. In a similar situation, would Frederick do as much? Would he endanger his career as an attorney? If he didn't know for a fact that he would, what right did he have to judge me? Hector had said he didn't know many people who'd do what I did. And, damn it, he was right.

And Frederick's cracks about my lack of progress, his assumptions about Sam—those weren't justified, either.

Smug, self-righteous prig, I thought again, congratulating myself for finding exactly the right words, scrubbing walls so viciously the painters probably wouldn't need to strip them. So he was Ulysses Patterson's son after all—smoother on the surface, but basically an arrogant, judgmental boor. No wonder Rosa lost interest in learning to speak to them. Well, Frederick can damn well starve to death waiting for me to have lunch with him. I have Hector, and Hector thinks everything I do is wonderful. Who needs Frederick Patterson?

I put in five more hours of cleaning, changed into my Top Skorz tee-shirt, and drove to my next job. Three hours later, ignoring the apple and the slice of pumpkin bread in my glove compartment, I pulled into a McDonald's drive-through and treated myself to a cheeseburger. I was still steaming about Frederick, I was headed to martial arts class, and I was spoiling for a fight. I needed serious protein.

We started with falls. I hurled myself down full force every time—forward, backward, to the left, to the right, slapping the mats so hard my hands turned red, yelling so loudly even some deaf students took notice. Robert watched gape-mouthed, Rosa looked almost scared, and Sam told me to take it easy.

"It's only practice," he said. "You don't have to prove anything to anybody."

But I did. With every fall, I was proving things to Kirsten, to Frederick, to myself. I am fearless, I thought as I threw myself down again. I am proud. Nobody messes with me.

Tonight, after the first fifteen minutes, Sam and Charlie gathered the whole class for a lesson. Sam spoke and signed simultaneously, finger-spelling the foreign phrases.

"Tonight, we'll discuss a fundamental principle of

sogu ryu bujutsu: ichi-go, ichi-e. That's Japanese for 'one encounter, one chance.'" He brought his right index finger forward. "One." He brought his fists together, index fingers raised. "Encounter." His right index finger came forward again. "One." He brought both hands up and bounced them down. "Chance."

Charlie took over, with Sam signing for him. "It's not only about martial arts. It's a way of life. It means you make the most of every opportunity. The phrase comes from the tea ceremony, and the idea is you make even an everyday activity, like making tea, into something special."

I nodded. *Carpe diem*. Seize the day. I understood that.

"So when it comes to self-defense," Sam said and signed, "it means when someone threatens you, you gotta realize this could be it. That doesn't mean you respond with lethal force if a drunk takes a swing at you in a bar. Of course not. But if your life's in danger, don't mess around, because you might not get a second chance. Let's try a demonstration. Any volunteers?"

My hand shot up. With Kirsten out there, I wanted to learn as much as I could, as fast as possible.

"Okay, Jane," Sam said and signed. "Come up front. Let's say you're walking down a dark alley, and a bad guy comes up to you with a knife and tells you to give him your purse. What would you do? Charlie, you be the bad guy."

"Typecast again," Charlie said, and got a rubber knife from his gym bag. To amuse the younger students, he growled as he advanced toward me, holding the ten-inch black knife in his right hand, twisting his face into a menacing grimace. "Hey," he snarled. "Gimme your purse."

Some people giggled, but I kept my focus serious. He's going to attack. I realized. I have to be ready. But the first step, always, is trying to avoid conflict. "First, I'd toss him my purse," I said, miming the gesture. "I wouldn't risk my life to save my purse. If he picks it up and walks away—"

"Your watch, too," Charlie said, stepping forward, bringing the knife up.

Time to protect myself. With a sweeping motion of my left hand, I blocked Charlie's move, knocking the knife away from me. That left his ribs exposed, so I landed a punch, stopping just short of contact. I jumped back, took a fighting stance, and waited.

He lunged forward, grabbing me around the neck with his left arm, pulling me forward, and lightly stabbing me in the stomach five or six times. He let me go, stepped back, and grinned.

"Jane's dead now," Sam commented. "She demonstrated a good technique to use if your neighbor attacks you with a rolled-up newspaper. With a bad guy in a dark alley, it could get you killed. Charlie has a knife. That makes it a life-or-death situation. She gave him her purse, and he didn't back off. He came toward her. She stopped him, but only for a moment. She hurt him, but only enough to make him mad. Then she stood around waiting for his next attack. That's how you end up dead."

It's the same mistake I made with Kirsten last night, I realized. For a moment, I'd had the advantage: I'd hurt her and knocked the breath out of her. Then I'd backed off and advised her to see a counselor. Good grief. What had I been thinking? "What should I have done?" I asked.

"You should've treated that moment like it was your one chance to save your life," Sam said, "because maybe it was. You don't wait to see if one punch will make him walk away. You don't try to reason with him, you don't try to cooperate—"

"That's important," Charlie cut in. "Lots of people get

in trouble because they think they'll be okay if they co-operate. Somebody says `get in the car,' and they get in the car. Don't do that. Don't let anybody tie you up. Don't go along with the guy, hoping you'll get a better chance to fight back later. For all you know, this is the one chance you'll get."

"So if someone tells you to get in the car," Sam said, "*that's* when you fight back. Fight back as hard as you can, for as long as you have to. Don't stop for a second until the attacker is incapacitated and you can get away."

A younger student raised his hand. "You mean we should kill the guy?"

Sam shook his head. "I said incapacitate, not kill. I mean, yeah, if killing the guy is the only way to save your life, you gotta do it. But it probably won't be the only way. You'll probably have to hurt him, so bad that he can't come after you. That's a hard idea to get used to. You're nice people—you don't wanna hurt anyone. You'd never do it to show off, or because someone insults you. But if your life's on the line, if this is your one chance to save yourself, do what you gotta do."

"Okay," I said. "May I try again?"

"If you want," Sam said. "Don't be so nice this time."

I got ready. Charlie went into his act, brandishing the knife, growling, demanding my purse. I pretended to toss it to him, and he stepped forward, asking for my watch, raising the knife.

Moving quickly, I turned sideways and kicked his kneecap—a tap, but if it'd been full force, his kneecap would be broken. He'd be in real pain. I grabbed his right wrist with both hands, lifting his arm in the air. Then I spun around, facing away from him, and pulled his arm down over my shoulder. Full force, that'd break his arm. Charlie howled with pretended agony, dropping the knife. I aimed a front kick at his stomach, stopping an inch short, and he collapsed. Snatching the knife, I ran like hell to the door of the gym.

Sam led the applause. "Good job. The sidekick to the kneecap was smart. The kneecap's vulnerable—even if your kick's not perfect, you can shatter it, and the guy's gonna have a hard time coming after you. To be safe, you broke his arm, and you knocked him down. Maybe the last kick wasn't necessary, but maybe it was. Maybe he's got a gun in his back pocket, and he can fire it with his left hand. And you got the knife and ran. Now you can call the police, and chances are he'll still be lying there moaning when they arrive. Congratulations, Jane. You saved your life."

I felt as if I really had. With all my heart, I hoped Kirsten would never try anything again. With all my heart, I hoped she'd see a counselor, become a better and happier person, and channel all her aggression into volleyball. If she did, I'd forgive her. If Hector wanted to invite her to the wedding, I wouldn't fuss. But if she did try to kill me again, this time I'd really be ready.

Chapter 22

At 7:30 the next morning, Rosa and I met at the Reed Center. She beat me easily at handball, we worked out hard on stretching machines and treadmills, and we spent an hour in the pool, alternating between races and long, relaxing laps. At 10:30, I stuffed my bathing suit into my red-and-white Try It Out! tote bag, and we headed for the café—ridiculously early for lunch, but Rosa had to be at work by noon. And after three hours of exercise, I felt plenty hungry.

We both ordered sandwiches with faint hints of chicken and plenty of sprouts and cucumbers to make us feel less guilty about the bread and mayonnaise. Time for serious conversation, I decided.

"*You did a great job on my nails*," I signed. "*It's been a week, and they still look nice. Do you like working at Nails by Ilana?*"

"*It's okay. Everybody's friendly, and doing nails is fun.*"

"*Would you like to have your own nail salon some day?*"

"*No.*" She made it emphatic—bringing her index and middle fingers down to close against her thumb twice, shaking her head. "*It's just for now, to have money of my own so I don't have to get everything from my father.*"

I understood. Asking Ulysses Patterson for spending money would not be pleasant. "*What would you like to do as a career?*"

She hesitated. "*I have some ideas. I tried to tell my father, years ago. All he could say was, 'deaf people can't do that.' So I stopped trying to tell him.*"

A reasonable decision, in my opinion. "*What are your ideas?*"

"*I'll tell you someday.*" She grimaced. "*My father wants me to be a paralegal. He says he'll get me a job at his firm and arrange it so I just fill out forms, so I won't have to interact with anybody. That sounds like fun. Working for my father, filling out forms all day, hiding in a back office so he won't be embarrassed by people seeing his stupid, deaf daughter.*"

"*I'm sure he didn't mean it that way,*" I signed. He'd probably pretty much put it that way, though. "*Would you like to go to college?*"

"*Someday. But I don't want to sit in school all day, every day. I've had enough of that for a while.*" At last I had something to report to Ulysses Patterson, something that should reassure him about one of his secondary concerns.

But I didn't know how to get information about his primary concern. I couldn't flat-out ask Rosa what she and Sam had done with the money they made by selling her mother's books.

I'd inch closer to the subject. "*Sam's a great martial arts teacher,*" I signed.

She perked up. "*He's wonderful.*" She raised both palms and pushed them forward twice. "*You were wonderful last night, too. You really gave it to poor Charlie.*"

I laughed. "*He had it coming. He tried to stab me.*"

She laughed, too, then paused. "*You seemed really—*

motivated. Was it because of the black eye you had last week? Did someone hit you?"

I bit into my sandwich to give myself time to think. Should I open up a little? Would that encourage her to open up, too? "*Yes. But it wasn't a big deal.*"

"*Was it Hector?*" she pressed. '*Or Jason?*"

"*No.*" I made it emphatic. "*Hector wouldn't hit anyone—he's very nice. It wasn't Jason, either. But Jason isn't so nice.*"

She nodded impatiently. "*You already told me that. And I told you I'm not serious about him. But who hit you?*"

"*It's not important.*" I noticed a man at a nearby table watching us—fifties, flabbily overweight, florid complexion. Well, lots of people stare at people who sign. "*So when did you and Sam meet?*"

She seemed unhappy about the shift in subject but got enthusiastic as she signed about how patient Sam had been during her first class, how they'd started having Cokes afterward, how much they had in common. That last comment made me smile. It's sweet, the way people in love always think they have a lot in common. A deaf African-American teenager from a wealthy family and a significantly older hearing white man from a blue-collar background—what did Rosa think they had in common? I was about to ask when the man who'd been watching us walked over.

"Hi," he said. He waved to Rosa and then turned to me, smiling. "I'm Carl. You're new, aren't you?"

"The center's one big, happy family," Kirsten had said. Maybe it was standard for members to introduce themselves. "Yes," I said, continuing to sign for Rosa. "I'm Jane, and this is Rosa."

He waved to Rosa again then leaned in closer to me, leering. "I'm from Detroit—I've got a Home-Away-from-Home membership. I'm in town through Friday. Maybe we could get together tonight. If tomorrow's better for you, that's fine."

Where did this guy get off? "No, thank you." I made my tone icy. "I have a boyfriend."

The leer dropped away, his face turned redder, and he backed off. "Damn. Sorry. I thought—sorry. Damn. Have a nice day." He snatched his gym bag and hurried off.

I turned to Rosa. "*Can you believe that guy*?" I signed what he'd said for her.

She sat forward. "*You've never met him before*?"

"*Never*." I made the sign emphatic by shaking my head and raising my eyebrows. "*And he's wearing a wedding ring, and he comes up to a stranger, acting like I should jump at the chance to go out with him*! *Where does he get that kind of confidence*?"

"*I don't know*." Rosa looked distracted. '*I should go—I can't be late for work. Thanks for lunch*.'

"*It's just after eleven*."

"*I know, but I have a stop to make. I'll see you at class tomorrow*."

Too bad. The conversation about Sam had started to warm up. I'd hoped she might hint at what was going on. If Sam needed money for a legitimate reason—starting his own martial arts school, say—that might reassure her father and brother. They'd still be unhappy about Rosa's selling books and giving him money, but at least they could stop worrying about drugs.

And Rosa had eaten barely half her sandwich. Well, sprouts before noon are never a good idea. I pushed my own plate away. I didn't have a job lined up until 3:00, and if I went to the apartment, I'd feel obliged to clean it. I'd been putting off my meeting with the nutritionist. Maybe she'd see me now, and maybe after that I'd be up for more exercise, or a better lunch.

An hour later, as I left the nutritionist's office, I ran into Hector. He asked if I'd climbed the rock wall yet and suggested we give it a try. Then, he said, we could have lunch. I'd enjoy that, I said—though if I actually followed all the rules the nutritionist had just given me, I'd never again enjoy lunch, or any meal, for the rest of my life.

The wall was more of a workout than I'd expected. We'd almost made it back to the bottom when we heard a commotion in the hall—someone running, Diana yelling. We rushed out to see her leaning over the railing ringing the mezzanine, pointing down.

"Stop him!" she shouted. "Thief! Thief! Security! Stop him!"

She ran downstairs. We followed, reaching the main level in time to see a tall, broad-shouldered man running for the entrance. The receptionist tried to stop him, and he shoved her aside. Two men tried to jump him, and he knocked them away, sending one sprawling. But a man entering the center saw what was going on and blocked the door with his body, pushing the tall man back. They struggled, and that gave the other two men time to jump the tall man again, gave the center's one security guard time to rush in and join the scuffle. Everyone was shoving, shouting, swearing.

The tall man kept trying to break free, straining to reach the door, but the numbers proved too much for him. The others forced his hands behind his back, the guard cuffed him, and they turned him around and forced him back toward the reception desk.

I saw his face for the first time. My God, I realized. It's Sam.

The noise had drawn people from all parts of the center. Looking around, I saw Rosa, body rigid and face terrified, standing next to Jason.

When I started to walk toward her, she shook her head, pressing her flat right hand against the center of her chest in a circular motion.

"*Please*," she signed. "*Don't say anything*."

Too shocked to think, I stayed where I was. Sam stood immobile now, his shoulders thrown back defiantly, his face expressionless. People shouted questions at him, but he said nothing.

"Jason!" Diana called. "He was going through your desk. He took something—I saw him put it in his pocket, his right front pants pocket."

Instantly, Jason's face filled with rage. He pushed forward, grabbing Sam by the lapels of his jacket. "What were you doing in my office? What did you take?"

Sam turned his face aside. Swearing, Jason grabbed at his pants pocket.

The guard stopped him. "Better wait for the police, Mr. Connolly. Fingerprints."

Jason couldn't back off completely. Until the police arrived, he kept shouting questions at Sam, shoving him in the chest with both hands when he refused to answer, trying to knock him off balance. Hector tried to make him stop, but he wouldn't.

That's right, Jason, I thought. Prove how tough you are. Push a man around when he's handcuffed. Disgusted, I looked away. Rosa stood with tears in her eyes but didn't come forward.

More people crowded into the lobby—talking, staring at Sam, pointing. He didn't throw a single punch, I thought. He didn't kick anyone. If he had, he probably could've gotten away. People would've been afraid to come near him. But he hadn't wanted to hurt anyone. What was going on?

Finally, two uniformed officers arrived. Diana quieted the crowd with a sweep of her arm.

"I'm Diana Connolly," she said. "I'm the chief financial officer, the daughter of the center's owner. Twenty minutes ago, I stepped into my brother Jason's office and saw this man going through the desk. He took something, put it in his pocket, and ran for the door. When I blocked his path, he pushed me aside and ran downstairs. I called down to people to stop him. He tried to fight them off—he knocked Mr. Segal down—but they subdued him. He's refused to say anything, but our receptionist has some information."

Greta stepped forward. She's barely five feet, at least sixty; it must've taken courage for her to step in front of Sam as he barreled toward the door. "His name's Samuel Ryan," she said. "He arrived at 11:47 and bought a one-day pass to the center. He filled out this form. It has his address, phone number, and so on. It should be correct. I checked it against his driver's license."

One officer glanced at the form, then looked at Sam. "Okay, Mr. Ryan. Let's hear your side of the story. If this is a misunderstanding, maybe we can clear it up here."

Finally, Sam spoke. "You have my name and address. I'm not saying anything more."

"Not a smart move," the officer said. "You could face a bunch of charges—illegal entry, burglary, assault. Mr. Connolly, where were you when this incident occurred?"

"In the café," Jason said, "having lunch with one of our members." He gestured toward Rosa.

"Was your office door locked?"

"I don't lock it during the day, but the door to the reception area would've been locked. Ellen always locks it when she goes to lunch."

"That probably adds breaking and entering to the list. Mr. Ryan, wanna change your mind about trying to clear things up here?"

Sam shook his head.

"All right," the officer said. "Then you're under arrest. Ms. Connolly, Mr. Connolly, maybe you could follow us to the station, give your statements there. Where's the guy who got knocked down—Mr. Segal? Do you need medical attention? No? Then if you wanna file charges, please come to the station. If not, give your name to Officer Mikos, and we'll get back to you if we need you. Folks, if you think you witnessed anything we should know about, give your name and phone number to Officer Mikos. Maybe we'll call, maybe we won't—depends on how far this goes. Mr. Ryan, listen carefully." Mechanically, he read Sam his rights.

It was a while before they left. Many people crowded up to Officer Mikos with their names and numbers, probably hoping they'd be called to testify at a dramatic trial. I didn't come forward, and neither did Rosa. The officers didn't seem to be taking the incident seriously. Probably, they figured Sam was a petty thief who'd talk soon, confess to minor charges, spend a few days in jail, and get released to steal again. But that wasn't it. And whatever it really was, Rosa was mixed up in it.

Shortly after 11:00, she'd said she had to leave for work. It was now 1:17, and she was still here. From 1:00 to 2:00 on Wednesdays, she's the only person working at the salon. She'd probably put her job in jeopardy so she could have lunch—a second lunch—with Jason. She must've set this up with Sam, keeping Jason away from his office so Sam could burglarize it.

Hector walked over. "Sorry. Diana wants me to go to the station, in case Jason loses control and demands the death penalty. Rain check on lunch?"

I forced a smile. "Of course." I waited until they were gone, then headed for Rosa. "*What's going on*? *Tell me*."

"*Not here*," she signed. "*I'll text you*."

She rushed out of the center. Damn. I'd have to report

this to Walt, right now, and he'd tell Ulysses Patterson. At this point, I didn't think Mr. Patterson would be terribly comforted by the news that his daughter thought she'd like to go to college someday.

Chapter 23

When I called Walt, he was not happy. "Come in tomorrow," he said.

All day, I waited for Rosa to text me. Nothing. That evening, I texted her three times. No replies.

On Thursday morning, I met with Walt. His shabby little office seemed smaller and shabbier than ever, and his perky pastel posters seemed sarcastic.

"I talked to Mr. Patterson," he said. "The way he sees it—the way I see it, too—you've blown this job. You were supposed to keep an eye on Rosa, and now things are worse than ever. Whatever Sam Ryan was up to, Rosa's involved. I don't know if the cops will bother charging her—it sounds like small-time stuff—but it's an embarrassment to the family. If you'd been doing your job right, it wouldn't have happened."

How, exactly, could I have prevented it? "Do you know Sam's status?"

Walt sat back in his chair. "In jail, refusing to cooperate. Won't talk to the cops, wouldn't say three words to the court-appointed lawyer. He's facing a laundry list of charges, not that they'll all stick. But some will. Sooner or later, he'll tell the cops about Rosa as part of some deal, try to shift the blame onto her, say she was the mastermind or whatever. Nice guy."

No. Sam was protecting Rosa. That's why he wasn't talking. "What should I do now?"

Walt shrugged. "Keep trying to get in touch with Rosa. I'll pay you for any contact hours you put in with her. If you finally get her to open up, make her confess everything to her father and ask for his help. He doesn't want to bring this up. He'd have to admit he hired people to watch her. If you get her to go to him, we'll see. If not, that's it. You tried, I guess, but it didn't work out."

One more botched job—not the ideal way to build a reputation so I could start my own business. But that wasn't what bothered me most. As I drove to Lyndhurst for a residential cleaning job, I thought about Rosa—nineteen, deaf, a father she couldn't communicate with, a brother who wasn't much better, her boyfriend in jail for a crime she'd helped him commit. Did she have close friends in town? She'd gone to school in New England, so maybe not. I'd tried to be a friend to her, but I'd failed. Isolated as she was, scared as she must be, she didn't trust me enough to respond to a text message.

I pulled to the side of the road and tried again: *Please text me. You don't have to tell me anything you don't want to. I just want to know if you're okay. Can I help?*

The response didn't come until five hours later, until I'd finished my cleaning job and gone to the Cleveland State Farmers Market. Rosa kept it short: *I'm okay. I'll tell you someday. You can't help.* That ended that. I didn't think she'd show up for class tonight. I'd rather skip it myself—it'd feel poignant without Sam there.

Even the Cleveland State Market felt poignant. It's perfectly nice, not as big as the Shaker Square market, but plenty of local produce, plenty of homemade baked goods, amazing honey. But Gary Nichols had gone to

Cleveland State. As I wandered through the stalls, making purchases for Abby's dinner with Nate, I couldn't stop thinking about Gary. Only two years older than Rosa, an aspiring journalist, beaten to death two weeks after Walt hired him. Like Sam, Gary had bought a one-day pass to the Reed Center. That felt poignant, too.

No, I realized. It doesn't feel poignant. It feels significant. Last week, when I'd told Walt about the pass I'd found in Gary's apartment, he'd shrugged it off. Obviously, he'd said, Gary had been doing an extra-good job of observing Rosa. She must've gone to the center while he was following her, and he must've bought the pass so he could keep watching. That, Walt declared, was initiative.

I put down the eggplant I'd been considering and called Walt. "Remember that one-day pass to the Reed Center, the one I found in Gary's apartment? Did he tell you he'd followed Rosa to the center? Did he put the pass on his expense account?"

"He must've forgot. So what?"

"So it's odd. If Gary followed Rosa into the center, why wouldn't he tell you? Why wouldn't he want to impress you with his initiative? Why would he follow her into the center at all? He was supposed to watch her sign-language conversations. Nobody else at the Reed Center signs."

"Maybe Gary didn't know that." Walt's voice was heavy with sarcasm. "What are you getting at?"

"I'm not sure, but I bet Gary didn't follow Rosa into the center. He bought a pass for Saturday, October eighth. Rosa works all day on Saturdays. She says it's the busiest day at the salon. I bet Gary didn't charge you for the pass because he wasn't working for you when he bought it. He was investigating something on his own."

Walt sighed. "Or he felt like working out. Look, I know you feel bad about messing up, but coming up with crazy theories won't help. Let it go."

"But maybe—"

"I told you, let it go. I sure don't want you running around, trying to redeem yourself by proving—hell, I don't know what you're trying to prove. Whatever it is, stop. Don't start playing Nancy Drew. Just keep trying to contact Rosa. I'm your employer, and I'm telling you—don't do anything else."

He hung up. But you're my employer only during the hours I put on my timecard, I thought. What I do on my own time is none of your business.

I had to be at Top Skorz by 4:00. That gave me over two hours. Plenty of time for a quick swim at the Reed Center, and a leisurely chat with Greta.

She was alone at the reception desk, looking delicately efficient as always. "How are you doing, Greta?" I asked. "You had quite a scare yesterday."

"Actually," she said, "it happened so quickly I didn't have time to get scared. It *was* a surprise, especially since that young man seemed so nice when he came in."

"Yes, it's hard to tell about people. Maybe it's not good to have one-day memberships, to let people walk in off the street without being screened. Do you often have problems with one-day members?"

"Oh, no. We don't get many, but the ones we do get are fine." She half-smiled. "Though we *did* have a little problem with one, recently."

"Really? How recently?"

"About a month ago. It was on a Saturday. I don't usually work Saturday, but Kelly was sick, and—oh, it doesn't matter. Anyway, this very polite young man bought a membership, early in the morning. He was a college student—Jerry Something, I think. He was full of questions, asked all about the center, the Connollys, everything. He must've stood here an hour, asking away."

Gary Nichols, I thought. Had to be. "But he created a problem?"

"Not that day. He stayed a long time—he was still here when I left. Then he came back, that Friday. He had an appointment to interview Jason for his college newspaper, for an article about fitness options for students. So then I understood about all the questions. He must've been gathering background for his article. I gave him a visitor's badge and sent him to Jason's office. Half an hour later, Duncan, our security guard, came down with him and marched him out of the center, and Jason called and told me never to let him in again. I guess Jason didn't like some of his questions."

I tried to look surprised. "What questions could get Jason upset enough to throw him out?"

"Oh, probably about the price of memberships. That's mostly what people complain about. The special memberships are reasonable—Home-Away-from-Home memberships are *very* reasonable—but it's true, regular memberships are expensive. I couldn't afford one if I didn't work here. Of course, I'm just a receptionist. People don't realize costs are high, too. Liability insurance, lifeguards on duty around the clock—and maintaining equipment! Last week, we had people in four times."

That got her going on stories about equipment breaking down. I listened sympathetically for five minutes before escaping to the pool. I swam slow, easy laps, trying to think things through, trying to get them in sequence.

Late in September, Gary started watching Rosa. On October eighth, he spent a long Saturday at the Reed Center, definitely not watching Rosa. The next week, according to his roommate, he called Jenny Linton repeatedly, leaving messages she didn't return.

That Friday, he came to the center again, met with Jason, and got thrown out. The next night, he got killed.

Just over a week later, Jenny died, too.

Gary must've learned something from watching Rosa. That must be how everything started. Had he seen Rosa and Sam signing about Jenny Linton and Jason Connolly? But Gary wouldn't investigate Jason just because he was having an affair. That, as Walt said, wasn't a headline-grabber.

What had Gary learned during his long day at the center? He must've seen Jenny, since he'd told his roommate she was hot. Had he talked to her, maneuvering her into saying too much? Maybe she'd realized she'd made a mistake, and that's why she wouldn't take his calls.

Professor Morton said Gary sometimes got impatient with research and rushed ahead to confrontation. Maybe he'd done that with Jason. He didn't really have enough information to back up his accusations, but he confronted Jason anyway, hoping to bluff him into revealing more about—what?

I didn't know. I *did* know Jason was hot tempered. If Gary had pretended to have damaging information, Jason might've struck back—breaking into Gary's apartment to destroy any evidence he could find, beating Gary to death when he came home early.

As I got dressed, I thought about whether I had an obligation to tell Walt any of this. No. I wasn't charging him for the time I'd spent speaking to Greta. And he'd get mad at me. But should I tell Detective Diaz?

No, I decided. Gary talked to Jason and got thrown out of the center—that's all I really knew. That wasn't evidence of murder. And if Jason said he'd thrown Gary out for saying memberships cost too much, who could disprove it? I shouldn't call Detective Diaz unless I had something solid.

After putting in my hours at Top Skorz, I debated about skipping martial arts class. It'd been a long day, and Rosa probably wouldn't come. But what if she did? Besides, without Sam, the deaf students would have a hard time understanding the instructors. Sighing, I headed for the community center.

Charlie looked relieved to see me. Great, he said. I could help with the deaf guys. He knew about yesterday—he'd gotten a call from Sam's cousin. Charlie felt stunned. Why, he asked, would Sam pull a stunt like that?

I shrugged, keeping my thoughts to myself.

Rosa didn't show up. As Charlie coached deaf students, I did my best to interpret, struggling to come up with ASL equivalents for martial arts terms. Word about Sam had gotten around. Maybe someone had seen something in the newspaper. I heard hearing students whisper about it, saw deaf students sign about it. Some made jokes.

Not Robert. Since the night he'd tried to bully me and I'd knocked him down, we'd gotten semi-friendly. After class, we talked about Sam.

"I can't believe he'd do that." Robert looked shaken. "He's such a law-and-order type. A few months ago, he caught me sneaking a granola bar—a lousy granola bar!—out of the custodian's office. He made me find the custodian and apologize and spend a whole day cleaning a storage room for him. And now *he* steals! Sam—the one who wanted to be a cop."

"I can't see Sam as a cop."

"Oh, yeah. Last year, he talked about it lots. But he decided he wouldn't like taking orders, and he'd get bored with routine things—traffic tickets, like that. For a while, though, he was all excited, talked about how much fun it'd be to investigate stuff and catch bad guys. Why would he steal?"

Good question. I thought about it on the drive home but couldn't come up with an answer I liked.

An hour or so later, Hector called. "Another crazy day," he said. "You wouldn't believe how upset Jason is about yesterday. I don't see what the big deal is. Some jerk wandered into his office and got caught before he could steal anything. Why get all worked up?"

Another good question. "But he *did* take something, didn't he? What?"

Hector laughed. "Brace yourself. A half-empty box of staples, worth maybe fifty cents. And because he put it in his pocket, he's facing more serious charges. The weirdest part is, he didn't do it until Diana spotted him. She was looking for a file and thought it might be in Jason's office. She opens the door, and there's this guy, going through Jason's desk. She yells at him to stop, and *that's* when he pockets the staples. I think he must be—well, not all there mentally. Or he was high. Don't you think so?"

"It sounds like it." That felt like the safest response.

"It sure does. So I say we drop the charges. He didn't do any real harm. But Jason says no. He called a big meeting this morning to discuss beefing up security. Then he spent hours holed up with Paul Kent, probably trying to figure out how to pay more guards and arm them with Uzis. But enough about Jason. How was your day?"

"Fine." I hesitated. "Hector, have you talked to Kirsten since what happened Monday night?"

"No. I've called and left messages, but she hasn't called back. She's probably steamed at me for suspending her. Fine. Let her take some time to cool down. I still hope you two can be friends. Kirsten can be—extreme. She pushes herself so hard physically, she's always looking for excitement, she gets wildly enthusiastic about things. And when she crashes, she can get really low, or really angry and dark. But it never lasts long. Usually, she's lots of fun."

So far, I hadn't found her all that much fun. "I don't know if she and I can ever be friends. But if she's civil to me, I won't hold a grudge."

"That sounds just like you." I could feel the warmth in his voice. "So, we're still on for tomorrow night?"

"Definitely. Seven o'clock, right?"

"Right. I'll pick you up. We've got reservations at Lola."

"Lola?" It's one of the best restaurants in Cleveland, probably the most famous. I'd looked at the menu online, many times, and drooled. Only on my most optimistic days had I even dreamed of ever going there. "That's too much. It's too expensive."

"It's not that bad. And I whine about money, but I can splurge once in a while. You're a great cook—I want to take you to a restaurant with a great chef. We'll see if Michael Symon can come up with anything to rival your turkey wraps."

That made me smile. "He'd sneer at my turkey wraps. And he won't cook our dinners. He's probably in New York, filming things. Seriously, we shouldn't do anything that fancy. Pizza Hut's fine. You should cancel the reservations."

"Cancel the reservations?" He forced mock horror into his voice. "You wouldn't suggest that—you wouldn't *think* that—if you knew what I went through to get them."

I smiled again. "Sold your soul to the devil, did you?"

"I can't go into details. All I can say is, if we get married, don't get too attached to our first-born son. We can't keep him."

So we were going to Lola. We talked a few more minutes before hanging up. "If we get married," he'd said. He'd been joking, but I liked the sound of the words.

And didn't they suggest his thoughts had strayed in certain directions?

I kept thinking about that as I prepped things for Abby and Nate's Shabbat dinner. But I kept thinking about Rosa, too. Where was she right now? What was she doing? I pictured her sitting alone in her room in her father's house, her door closed, her world dark and silent. She must be missing Sam, worrying about Sam. And she must be afraid that at any moment the police would show up to take her to jail.

I texted her again: *Are you still okay? Can we get together tomorrow? You don't have to tell me anything. I just want to see you. Is there anything I can do?*

This time, I had to wait only two minutes for an answer: *You can't do anything. I can't see you. But it's okay. I have a plan.*

Somehow, that didn't make me feel better.

Chapter 24

Friday morning proved cold and overcast. It's going to rain, I thought as I drove to work, looking at the heavy gray clouds hiding the sky. Or snow—it was cold enough. A light snow would be romantic. Did Lola have a fireplace? I didn't know, but the pictures I'd seen online looked warm, magically both trendy and cozy. I pictured us sitting there, drinking glasses of deep red wine—or, for Hector, deep red grape juice. Dinner would be amazing. And afterward? I hadn't decided. But I was leaning toward yes.

For the next four hours, I cleaned deck furniture at two bars at The Flats, getting it ready to be stored for the winter. Twice, I texted Rosa. No response. Her brother called, though, and left a message. I called back during my break.

"Thanks for calling," he said. "Do you know where Rosa is?"

"No. I assumed she'd be at home, or at work."

"I don't think she's been to work since what happened Wednesday. My father says she's stayed in her room, just coming downstairs for meals. When he got up at six this morning, she was gone. I've texted her, but she hasn't replied. You think she might be at the Reed Center?"

"I'd think that'd be the last place she'd go."

"I'd think so, too, but we don't know where else she might be. She has only a few friends in town, and I've texted them all. Nobody's seen her. Could you stop by the Reed Center and see if she's there? I'd do it, but I can't get away from the office."

"I'll go. I'll be finished with this job in about an hour. Is that soon enough?"

"It'll have to be. Thanks." He paused. "Jane, I've been thinking about the conversation we had when you were cleaning that office. Was I a jerk?"

I smiled. "Maybe a little bit of one."

"I thought so. Sorry. I get like that sometimes. And I'm worried about Rosa, but that's no excuse."

"Actually, it's a good excuse. I'm worried about her, too."

"I'm sure you are. And I'm sure you tried your best. Damn. I'm sounding like a jerk again. Do I still have a shot at that lunch?"

"Definitely," I said, feeling charitable. "But I should get back to work. Then I'll go to the Reed Center."

She wasn't there, not any more. "She left soon after I came in at 8:00." Greta checked her log. "And she came in—goodness!—at 5:00."

I thanked her and called Frederick. "I'd just picked up the phone to call you," he said. "My father's housekeeper called three minutes ago. Rosa came home, made a sandwich, grabbed a Coke, and went to her room. No explanation about where she'd been, naturally. Sorry you went to the Reed Center for no reason."

"Not quite for no reason. I found out she came there at 5:00 this morning and left at 8:15. That's so odd."

"She probably wanted to work out before Jason Connolly got there. Anyhow, she's home now. She's safe. That's all that matters."

Probably. Still, going to the center so early—was that part of the "plan" Rosa mentioned? A plan to do what? Had she completed her plan, or would she do more things to worry everyone to death? Without much hope, I texted her again. No reply.

I went to the Cathy's Cleaning Crew office to turn in my timecard. "Remember," the secretary said, "you get a bonus if you find us a new commercial client. Find anybody this week?"

"No. I don't know anybody who owns a business." Not long ago, I'd dreamed of owning a business myself. That seemed laughable now.

"You probably do. Most people do. If you focus, you'll think of someone."

I started to shrug it off then smiled. Mara Connolly. Hector had said she had a tax accounting business. Wouldn't that be fun—showing up at Mara's office with a brochure, making a sales pitch?

Actually, why not? It was barely 2:00. I could stop by Mara's office and tell her about Cathy's Cleaning Crew. Maybe I'd offer to buy her a drink. Judging by what I'd seen, she'd be receptive. And if, after a drink or two, she unburdened her soul by blurting out evidence proving her husband committed two murders, I had time for that, too.

Connolly Tax Experts has a small but classy suite in an office building in Pepper Pike. Ms. Connolly was free, the receptionist said. I could go right in.

Mara looked up from a stack of forms and took off her reading glasses. "It's Jane," she said. "Hector's Jane. This is a surprise."

"I stopped by on impulse." I held out the brochure. "As Kirsten tactfully pointed out, I'm doing a lot of cleaning these days. We get a bonus if we sign up new clients. It's an excellent service. I could tell you about it."

Mara flipped pages. "Looks good. And our cleaning

service stinks. But it's Friday afternoon. I'm not up to making heavy decisions."

"We could have a drink while we talk," I suggested. "I noticed a nice-looking bar nearby."

"If you want a drink," Mara said, "that changes everything. But why waste time going to a bar?" She opened a drawer, took out a bottle of Bourbon and two plastic glasses, then picked up her phone. "Angie, hold all calls. Ms. Ciardi and I have important business to discuss. And get us some ice." She poured generous drinks for us both, also slopped a generous puddle onto the desk. Probably, this wasn't her first drink of the day.

The sales pitch took two minutes; Mara listened patiently and said she'd think about it. "But that's not the reason you came here," she said. "Is it?"

"It's part of the reason," I said, taken by surprise.

"Let me guess the other part." She drained her glass and refilled it. "You're falling for Hector. You're starting to dream happy little dreams about picket fences and romping puppies and rosy-cheeked toddlers. But at dinner, you got a terrifying preview of what your future might be. You want some frank talk about the downside of marrying into the Connolly family. Right?"

"Right." Thank goodness she'd supplied me with a reason.

"I thought so. And my advice is, don't. Hector's handsome—almost as handsome as Jason—and he's nice. But that's one sick, twisted family. You don't want to be part of it. You don't want your children to be part of it."

"Elise seems—problematic," I admitted. "But Diana seems nice."

"Diana's sick and twisted. She wears herself out trying to please a mother who's never given a damn about her and never will. She's got no life of her own. I don't think she's ever been laid, not once. I used to hope she was a lesbian—all those pantsuits—but I don't think so. I don't think she's anything. I don't think she's ever had anyone, except her mother and brothers. And that means she's done some sick, twisted things."

"Like what?" I asked, and regretted it. Too blunt. Mara would clam up now.

She didn't. She poured herself more Bourbon. I don't think she'd noticed I wasn't keeping up with her. A dreamy haze softened her eyes. "Oh, man. If you'd seen Jason fifteen years ago. He looks good now, but back then! He was beautiful. And the way he played piano, passion pouring out of his fingers—it took your breath away."

"It about took my breath away when he played the other night. Did he ever think about becoming a professional musician?"

"It's all he ever wanted. But his father wouldn't allow it. It embarrassed him that one of his sons loved music, that he had talent. Can you believe that? Jason was a top athlete, too, better than Hector, but he loved music, and that made him a sissy. According to Ray Connolly, real men don't care about anything but sports and making money. And sex, I guess, but even that didn't matter much compared to sports and money. He yelled at Jason for practicing piano too much. He yelled at Jason about everything. Slapped him around about everything, too."

"Slapped him around? Hector told me Jason and his father had conflicts. I didn't realize it got physical."

"Oh, yeah." Mara stared at her glass, fingering a drop of water that had condensed on its side. "Ray beat the shit out of him, all the time. Jason was always showing up at school with bruises and black eyes. He'd say he'd bumped into a door, but everyone knew. The teachers must've known, too, but they never did anything. Nobody wanted to accuse the great Coach Connolly. And it's true,

Jason did lots of stupid stuff. Some people might think Ray was trying to straighten him out. But it was more than that. He hated Jason. Really. He literally hated him. He loved Hector, and he hated Jason. And Elise loved Jason and couldn't stand Hector, and nobody loved Diana. Sometimes I've thought that when Ray hit Jason, it was because he hated Elise."

When Hector had talked about his family, it sounded dysfunctional. Now, it sounded like the fourth act of a tragedy. "It must've been sad for you to see that," I said. "As Jason's girlfriend, I mean."

"I wasn't his girlfriend. When Jason was in high school, we dated a few times. Screwed a few times, to be precise. You couldn't call them 'dates'—half an hour in the backseat of his car, maybe a Coke from a drive-through on the way home. Jason was a senior. He didn't 'date' sophomores. But when he came home from college that summer—well." She started to pick up her glass, then set it down. "I'll tell you a story, Jane. I'll tell you because I like you, and you should know about the shit you'd get into if you get involved with the Connollys. Years from now, I don't want to feel guilty about not warning you. Okay?"

"Okay." I felt filled with dread. I'd come here to learn more about Jason. But I didn't think I wanted to hear this.

"Okay." Now, she did take a drink. "It was the summer after Jason's first year in college. He was nineteen, and I was seventeen. One night, I was hanging out with some girlfriends, playing miniature golf, looking for boys. Then Jason shows up, all alone. We all flirted with him—he was *so* gorgeous. But he was in a foul mood. He'd had a huge fight with his father. He'd worked up the nerve to tell Ray he'd declared a music major, and Ray exploded, said he'd cut off Jason's tuition unless he switched to business or phys ed. So Jason stalked out and ended up hanging out with us. After a while, he asked if I wanted to go for a drive. And I was seventeen, without a brain in my head, and I thought Jason Connolly was a god. I thought I was in love with him. Shit. I *was* in love with him. Love can be stupid and still be love. So I got in his car."

She refilled her glass again. "He had a bottle, of course—a couple of bottles. Even in high school, Jason could always put his hands on a bottle. So we drank and drove around, for a long time. I kept waiting for him to pull over and tell me to get in the backseat, but he didn't. Instead, around midnight, he pulled into his driveway. He wanted to do it in the house, he said, in the den, where his father kept his trophies. I was so drunk I thought it'd be fun. I thought it sounded hilarious. So we sneaked into the house with the bottle that wasn't empty yet, we sneaked into the den, and we did it, right on Ray's couch. We kept doing it until Jason knocked over a lamp. It was an accident, he said."

"But you don't think so."

"It could've been. We were both so drunk—anything could've happened by accident. Or maybe Jason wanted to make a noise, to make sure his father caught us. I don't know. And it doesn't matter."

She sank into silence, staring at the floor, her face growing harder and heavier as she remembered. "What happened then?" I asked.

She roused herself. "Pretty much what you'd expect. Ray stormed in, Jason started to mouth off, and Ray punched him so hard he fell down flat. Diana ran in and tried to calm Ray down, but he slapped her face and told her to shut up. Then he asked me how old I was, and I was too drunk to realize I should lie. I said seventeen, and Ray began shouting about statutory rape, about how Jason could go to prison, about how maybe he'd call the cops himself. Jason started to get up, and Ray kicked him in the groin. I was so scared I threw up, right on the carpet. So Ray told Diana to drive me home. Jason said he'd do it, and Ray said no, he was too drunk, and he had to clean up the vomit. 'And,' he said, 'I'm not done with you yet.'" She shook her head. "That's what he said. 'I'm not done with you yet.'"

"What about the rest of the family?" I asked, thinking I already knew.

"Hector was away, at camp. I didn't see Elise. Maybe she was so drugged up that she didn't hear anything. Even back then, she took lots of pills. Or maybe she was afraid. She loves Jason, but maybe she was afraid to come between him and Ray. I couldn't blame her. Diana was afraid, too. She tried, once more, to reason with Ray. But he gave her this look, and she turned away from him and helped me get dressed. When we left the den, Ray closed the door behind us. I heard him turn the lock." She was silent for a moment. "Then Diana drove me home. That's the end of the story."

It wasn't the end. I hardly needed to have her tell me the rest of it, but I had to hear the words. "Did you see Jason again that summer?"

"Not until after the funeral." She finished her drink. "Did I mention Ray Connolly died that night? He ran his car into a utility pole at about two o'clock in the morning, twenty miles from his home. The gas tank exploded, so apparently there wasn't much left of him. I don't think gas tanks usually explode when people run into utility poles. But this one did. Diana came to see me the next day, and we had a long talk. The police never came to see me. Maybe they never investigated at all, or maybe nobody told them I'd been there. Three weeks later, Jason asked me to dinner and gave me an engagement ring. He looked so handsome that night. A slight limp, but he looked fine. He didn't go back to college in the fall. He went to work for his mother. We got married in November, right after I turned eighteen. My parents tried to talk me out of it, but I was eighteen and still didn't have a brain in my head." She took a deep breath. "And we all lived happily ever after. There. *That's* the end of the story. So. The brochure's vague about costs. Can you give me hard figures?"

When I got back to the apartment, Abby was setting the table in our dining area, covering it with a white cloth, centering the silver candlesticks she'd inherited from her grandmother, fussing about angles of plates and glasses and silverware.

She'd bought some daisies and arranged them expertly in a blue-and-white vase, and she'd bought two intricately braided loaves of challah and placed them under an embroidered cloth. When she saw me, she smiled, spreading her arms out as if gathering the table in an embrace. "*Shabbat, peace*," she signed.

Yes, I decided. Peace. I went into the kitchen and began final preparations for dinner. I wouldn't tell Hector, not tonight. Maybe I'd never tell him. Mara hadn't made me promise not to. Maybe she wanted me to tell him. Maybe he should know. But not tonight. Tonight was for peace. He'd been through so much—interrogated by the police, worried about Jason, upset about Kirsten, probably more than a little unsettled by me.

His week shouldn't end with horrible revelations about his family, with suspicions that, after all this time, could probably never be confirmed but could never, never be quieted.

Yes, I thought as I tied on my apron. Tonight was for peace. Then I smiled. Well. Maybe the night wouldn't be entirely peaceful. At least, I hoped I could inspire some not-entirely-peaceful emotions in Hector. I didn't want him dozing off too soon. But there would be nothing unpleasant. No worry, no suspicion, no conflict of any kind. Not tonight.

Chapter 25

It didn't take me long to finish in the kitchen. I'd cooked almost everything the night before, and Abby had said she didn't want appetizers or soup or anything fancy—just a simple, elegant meal she could serve without using a stopwatch to time the courses. So I'd roasted a chicken stuffed with lemon and shallots and tarragon, with a rich gravy that could simmer indefinitely without needing anything but a last-minute stir. I'd found a recipe for kugel, a kind of pudding made with grated potatoes, sautéed onions, eggs, and matzo meal. To make things easy for Abby, I'd baked mini-kugels in muffin tins until they were crisp and lovely, so she just had to slide them into the oven to warm them. I'd made honey-glazed carrots and the apple-and-pear Waldorf salad Hector had praised at our picnic. For dessert, I'd made spice cake. I frosted the cake, reviewed the reheating timetable with Abby, and went to my room to get dressed.

I didn't have anything new to wear tonight, nothing to rival the dress I'd bought from Jenny Linton's roommate. Fine. It'd feel comforting to put on the faithful dark blue dress that had seen me through so many weddings and confirmations and New Year's Eve parties, with the flattering but subtle square neckline, the wide black belt that emphasized my waistline without making a big deal about it. First, though, I had to do something about my nails.

Rosa had done a good job. The manicure had lasted through two encounters with Kirsten, martial arts classes, cleaning jobs, waitressing shifts, picnic and dinner preparations. But scrubbing down patio furniture this morning had done it in. As I removed the old polish, I thought about how nice it would've been to get another professional manicure. But of course I couldn't afford it. Idly, I wondered how Bethany and Ashley could. They had full-time jobs, but bank tellers and receptionists seldom make huge salaries. They must be better at managing money than I am.

Maybe they made investments, I thought, making cautious swipes with an emery board. It wasn't just the manicures. They dressed well, and they took vacations—actual vacations!—in Cape Cod and Mexico. And they could pay the fees at the Reed Center. They'd started with trial memberships, they'd said, but they'd had regular memberships for years. Those, Greta reminded me yesterday, were expensive. Greta said she couldn't afford one if she didn't work at the center. "Of course," she'd said, "I'm just a receptionist." Bethany was "just a receptionist," too.

I thought of the other women on the volleyball team. Kirsten was a doctor, but there were no other doctors, no lawyers, no stockbrokers. One woman was a daycare teacher, one an administrative assistant. One was a bakery clerk. Good grief—were all these women shrewd investors?

I heard the security door buzzer and listened. Yes—that was the door opening and closing. I'd known Abby would be watching for Nate and wouldn't be likely to miss it when the lights she'd connected to the buzzer flashed. Now I could be sure. Abby's Shabbat dinner had officially begun. Nate had arrived exactly at 6:00. That meant I had exactly one hour to finish getting ready.

I rummaged through my purse for the nail polish I'd bought on my way home. That's right—I'd put it in my tote bag, not my purse. I picked up my red-and-white Try It Out! bag and gazed at it. That's how it started. Rosa noticed Bethany's bag, identical to mine. That's why Rosa joined the center, and because she'd joined, I'd joined. If Rosa hadn't asked about Bethany's bag, I never would've met Hector. And now I had a tote bag of my own. Tonight, that felt like more than coincidence. It felt like fate.

Carefully, I began polishing my nails. Just one coat, or it'd take too long to dry, and I still had to do my hair and makeup. My thoughts drifted back to the women on the volleyball team. Jenny Linton had been on the team, and she'd been a dental hygienist. Of course, Jason probably paid for Jenny's membership fees, and her manicures and clothes. The other women on the team must be finding other ways to manage. They couldn't *all* have rich, married boyfriends. I smiled at the absurdity of the idea. Yes, they were all pretty, probably pretty enough to attract rich, married men. But it was ridiculous to think all those women paid their Reed Center fees by enticing men into adultery.

That made me think of the man who came up to me while I was having lunch with Rosa. What was his name? Oh, yes—Carl, from Detroit. As I put on my makeup, careful not to smudge my nails, I thought about what he'd said: "I'm in town through Friday. Maybe we could get together tonight. If tomorrow's better for you, that's fine." As if he took it for granted I'd want to go out with him—a stranger, a married man! As if the only question were which night I'd choose! Almost twice my age, overweight, red-faced—what made him think no woman could resist him?

As soon as I had the thought, I felt ashamed. It's not right to judge people by appearance. Well, if he hadn't been so arrogant, I wouldn't have given his appearance a second thought. But acting like something he wasn't had made him ridiculous.

And Hector had given him a Home-Away-from-Home membership, the kind of membership Greta had singled out as an especially good bargain. I didn't want to be critical of Hector. Even so, as I put on my mascara, I couldn't help feeling he'd been inconsistent. He hadn't given Emily Davis a trial membership because she was slightly overweight, because she hadn't shown "the right level of commitment to fitness." What "commitment to fitness" had Carl shown? He was far more overweight than Emily. But Hector gave him a membership, even though Carl treated women like whores.

For some reason, that last thought hit me hard. I pushed it aside. Mechanically, not letting myself think, I finished my makeup, slipped into my dress, brushed my hair, put on silver earrings and a silver necklace and my good watch. Only 6:30—half an hour until Hector arrived. I couldn't possibly keep from thinking for that long.

Hopelessly, I sat on my bed, letting the thoughts and images come. The manicures, the clothes, the vacations, the Reed Center memberships. All the pretty women on the volleyball team, all in their twenties and thirties, all with everyday, low-paying jobs. The things Kirsten said to me in the locker room before my first date with Hector. Bethany and Ashley telling me what a great guy Hector was, what a great time I'd have when I went out with him. The way Carl from Detroit leered at me when I sat in the café, my Try It Out! tote bag on the floor next to me. The way he backed off, embarrassed, when I said I had a boyfriend.

And Hector. The questions he'd asked at my interview. The things he'd said when we first got to the Irish pub. The way he'd talked about sex, about ethics. And the way he'd responded when I'd said I'd miss the center if I had to stop coming.

"Who knows?" he'd said. "Maybe things will work out."

No, I thought. Not possible. Then I remembered something else. I looked through my bureau, found Jenny Linton's phone number, and dialed.

"Lisa?" I said when Jenny's roommate answered. "It's Jane Ciardi. I came to your apartment last Sunday, to return a jacket."

"Sure," she said. "You bought that maroon dress. I've sold more of Jenny's clothes, but there's a ton left. You want to take another look?"

"No, thanks. I want to ask you about something, and I hope you'll forgive me if it's sort of tactless. When we talked about the Elise Reed Center, you said you didn't think it was that great. And I—well, I thought you sounded a little bitter."

"Bitter? No, I don't think so. Why would I be bitter?"

I blushed. Thank goodness she couldn't see me. "Maybe bitter isn't the right word. But I couldn't help wondering if you'd applied for a trial membership, too."

She hesitated and then laughed. "Yeah, you're right. And maybe I *did* sound bitter. When Jenny told me about the trial membership, I decided to apply. Hector Connolly interviewed me. He was nice, but then I got a letter saying my application hadn't been accepted. No explanation. It couldn't have been financial. I'm not rich, but I make more than Jenny did. Why do you ask? Did Hector ask you out?"

The question hit me like a shovel to the face. "Yes. We're supposed to go to dinner tonight. Did he ask Jenny to dinner, too?"

"Yep." She seemed to relish the revelation. "He took her to dinner, she didn't come back until morning, and after that she had a regular membership and never complained about the cost. She never mentioned going to dinner with him again. Maybe, after the first time, he doesn't spring for dinner. But once, two of Jenny's friends from the center came here, and it was obvious. Only pretty girls get trial memberships. Only girls Hector wants to sleep with. I guess I didn't qualify."

"Thank you for telling me," I said, and couldn't hold back a sob. Maybe Emily Davis hadn't shown a commitment to fitness. But Lisa's perfectly fit—she looks like an athlete. She just isn't pretty.

"God, Jane," she said. "Are you crying? Did you think Hector really liked you? Do you like him? I'm sorry. Look, maybe he *does* like you. Maybe with the others it's only sex, but with you, it's more. And maybe I'm wrong about everything."

"It's all right," I said. "I have to go now. I have to decide what to do."

"Good luck, Jane," she said, pity strong in her voice.

I sat on the side of my bed and cried, harder than I had in years. Even when I'd finally decided to break off my engagement, I hadn't cried this hard.

The buzzer sounded, and I had to answer it. As I walked through the living room, Abby waved to me. She was serving Nate spice cake, looking deeply happy. I didn't begrudge her that happiness. But the contrast stung.

I opened the door. Hector stood there—smiling, impossibly handsome, holding a single red rose.

"I'm sick," I said. "I can't go." I started to close the door.

Looking stunned, he reached out to stop the door. "Jane, wait. What's wrong?"

"I'm sick." I tried to close the door again. But before I could, he stepped inside.

"You're not sick. You're upset—you've been crying. What is it?"

I shook my head. "I can't talk about it. Not tonight. Maybe in a few days—no. I never want to talk about it. I don't ever want to see you again. I'll stay away from the center from now on. And you have to stay away from me."

He closed the door behind him. "I don't accept that. You don't want to see me again, fine. I'll leave in five minutes, and I won't come back. But you have to tell me why." He looked toward the living room, toward the sound of forks clinking against plates. "Is someone else here?"

"My roommate and her boyfriend. They're both deaf." Maybe it'd feel good to get this out—maybe I had to. "Come to the kitchen."

I walked in ahead of him. The kitchen was still warm with the fragrances of lemon and tarragon, of honey and cinnamon. It all felt unbearably poignant now, like the promise of something I'd wanted so badly but could never have. I leaned my back against the refrigerator and made myself face him. "I feel like an idiot," I said. "It shouldn't have taken me this long to figure it out. The manicures, the clothes, Kirsten, Emily Davis—why didn't I see it sooner?"

"You're not making sense. What didn't you see sooner?"

I shook my head. "You're running a prostitution ring. That's what the trial memberships are all about. Those questions when you interviewed me—how often do I go to church, do I have a boyfriend. You were sizing me up as a potential prostitute."

He set the rose on the counter. I'd expected him to deny it, but he didn't. "It was Carl, wasn't it? He came to me Wednesday and admitted he'd made a mistake. He saw a pretty girl in the café, she had a tote bag, and he assumed too much. When he told me her name was Jane, I swear I literally felt my heart stop. But when I talked to you, everything seemed all right, and I let myself hope you'd shrugged it off."

"I did, at first," I said, "because I'm an idiot. But tonight it finally came together. And I felt so ashamed, so dirty. You thought I'd make a good prostitute because I don't go to church often. And you knew about my 'ethics problem' with the interpreting agencies. That probably made me look like a good candidate, too. A woman with an 'ethics problem' shouldn't mind having sex with strangers for money."

He looked away from me. "When I interviewed you, I thought you were attractive and charming. And yes, I thought you might not have conventional ideas about morality."

"You thought I had no morals at all. And no boyfriend—that's important, too. Is that one reason you rejected Emily? She's slightly overweight, and she's engaged—not a promising prostitute. Maybe she goes to church too often, too. But me—no boyfriend, no morals. As a prostitute, I'm perfect."

"It wasn't like that. And it's not a prostitution ring. Don't be so melodramatic. It's an escort service. I arrange dates for people—that's all. What they do on those dates is up to them. And yes, the men pay me to arrange the dates, and I share the payments with the women. But lots of times, it's just that a lonely man wants to enjoy the company of an attractive woman, take her out for a nice dinner, and have a pleasant conversation. Lots of times, there's no sex involved."

"Don't give me that. If there's no sex involved, you wouldn't need a gynecologist for a partner. But Kirsten *is* your partner, isn't she? She certifies the women are disease-free. Like a veterinarian, clearing horses for a race."

"You make everything sound so crude. Kirsten gives the women checkups, yes, several times a year. They receive excellent health care, and it's free. It's primarily to protect them. And we make sure they exercise and stay fit, they all swear off street drugs and tobacco, and most swear off alcohol. I push hard for that."

"So basically, you're promoting good health." How stupid did he think I was? "And when the men get carried away, when they slap the women around, I bet Kirsten patches them up for free, doesn't she?"

"She's never had to." He looked up almost proudly. "I screen the men carefully. They're all referred by clients I trust. And I make it clear. If there's even one complaint about roughness, if they even urge a woman to do something she doesn't want to do, that's it. They're out. We haven't had a single incident."

"What about Jenny Linton? She was on the volleyball team. She was working for you, wasn't she? Wouldn't you call what happened to her an incident?"

"She wasn't working for me that night. I don't know what happened with Jenny. She'd promised to break off with Jason, but I guess she didn't. Not that I think Jason had anything to do with it. It must've been an accident. Jenny used to drink too much, and she'd promised to stop. Maybe she lied about that, too, and she got drunk and fell in the river. I feel bad about it, but it had nothing to do with me. You've got to believe that."

"How can I ever believe anything you tell me? It's all

been a lie, right from the beginning. Right from the interview—God! When I think about what was really going through your mind, it makes my skin crawl."

"It shouldn't. Look, you're hung up on the word 'prostitute.' If you'd look at it objectively—"

"Objectively! You want me to look at this *objectively*?"

"Yes, I do. Jane, the first woman I ever had sex with was a prostitute. Jason set it up for me, for my fifteenth birthday, and it was the best present anyone ever gave me. She was nice to me, I was nice to her, she taught me a lot—it was fine. As for the escort service, let me tell you how it started. Maybe then you'll understand."

God. I wanted this to be over. "If you want to tell me, go ahead."

"It was about five years ago. We didn't have Home-Away-from-Home memberships then, but some out-of-town businessmen bought one-day passes when they were in Cleveland. One man I'd gotten friendly with told me he'd just broken up with his wife and felt down. He asked if I knew of an escort service. I didn't, but he's a great guy, and Kirsten's always up for anything, so I called her. They had a fantastic time, and afterward he was so happy he wanted to give me some money, to thank me. I said no, but he insisted. So I used the money to take Kirsten out for dinner, we got talking, and that's how the idea began."

"So you started the Home-Away-from-Home program," I said, "and kept the fees low to attract people, and that's how you get your clients."

"At first, yes. Now, most clients are local. People refer their friends, and Kirsten does some recruiting when she goes out. The point is, we never accept clients without checking them out. From the beginning, Kirsten and I agreed everything had to be perfect, or we wouldn't do it—no danger to the women, a fair division of profits, healthful living as a central goal."

"Stop it," I said. "Now I *do* feel sick. Getting women to sell their bodies—that's your idea of healthful living? What does it do to their mental health, Hector? To their spiritual health?"

He shrugged. "Honestly? I think it's great for their self-esteem. Most of these women have lousy jobs. They're underpaid, their bosses don't listen to their ideas, people don't treat them with respect. But two or three nights a week, they dress up, they go to nice restaurants, they spend time with men who think they're exciting and are willing to pay for the privilege of being with them. And they're well compensated. Some use the money for manicures and clothes. That's their choice. One woman's putting herself through law school. One's starting a business. They're making their lives better."

"Oh, *that's* what's going on." I lifted a hand in the air. "Well, I'd like to make my life better, too. So sign me up—tell me who my first client is. Maybe that's what dinner tonight is all about."

"Of course not. The first night we went out, after five minutes I knew that it was wrong for you, that I'd never mention it to you. I had too much respect for you."

I looked at him hard. "And you have no respect for the other women."

He blushed. "I respect them all. But with you, it's different. You—"

"You don't respect them. And the men they have sex with don't respect them, and they don't respect themselves. How could they? How could a woman do that without starting to see herself as a product, something to be bought and sold? How could it not damage her chances of ever having a decent relationship with a man? And the men—how could it not affect the way they see the women they work with, their wives, their daughters, all women? How could it not hurt their marriages? You know it does. But all you care about is the money."

"That's not true." He sounded impatient now. "I don't keep a penny. It all goes to the center—to keep my father's dream alive, to keep my mother in her house."

"And does she know what you're doing to keep her in her house? Do you think she'd approve?"

"No, of course she doesn't know." He paused, looking down at the floor, shaking his head. "Jason found out somehow, a few weeks ago. Ever since, he's been demanding a share of the money—a big share—and pressuring me to expand so I can give him more. He says he'll tell my mother if I don't. Maybe I should let him tell her. Maybe she wouldn't care. Diana and Paul probably suspect already. They know I'm putting extra money into the center, but they're too smart to ask where it comes from. Look, Jane, this isn't what I wanted to do with my life. All I've ever wanted to do is coach. But if I hadn't done this, the center would've gone bankrupt. We're a local business. To compete with the corporate chains, we have to go the extra distance."

"Please," I said, "no sports clichés. And don't get all pious about local businesses. If this was the only way to keep the center alive, you should've let it die."

"I couldn't. I'd made a commitment, and I never back down from a commitment. So if you want to see me as a monster who preys on women, go ahead. But don't tell me I'm doing it for the money."

So far, anger had kept me going. Now, I just felt weak. "I don't think you're a monster. The things you've said—you probably believe them. You probably honestly believe you aren't hurting those women, or those men, or their families. But *I* can't believe that. We're too different."

"I don't think so." He stepped toward me and took both my hands. I didn't pull away, but I couldn't look at his face. "We disagree about some things, but we're not different kinds of people. I feel such a bond with you, Jane. I felt it the first time we had dinner together, and it's gotten stronger. You felt it, too. I could tell you did. I think we both knew something unusual was beginning, something wonderful. This thing—if you convince me I'm wrong, I'll stop. But don't just turn away from me. Come to dinner, and we'll talk."

I felt myself wavering. Maybe I didn't have to absolutely end things, not right now. There was so much good in Hector. Maybe, if I went with him, if we talked, everything could still work out. I felt overwhelmed with longing, with sorrow, with hope.

Abby came into the kitchen with the cake plates, saw Hector holding my hands, and smiled. "*Dinner was amazing*," she signed. "*Nate loved everything. We're leaving for services now. You should leave, too, or you'll miss your reservations.*"

I tried to smile, glad Abby was leaving while she still thought things were fine. I didn't want to spoil her evening with worry about me.

Hector waited until we heard the door close. "Come with me, Jane. We'll figure it out. It's not such a big deal."

Oh, Hector, I thought. I liked you so much. I looked up at him. "No. I can't. And I don't want to see you again."

He let go of my hands. "So you hate me now."

I shook my head. "I don't hate you. Until half an hour ago, I thought I was falling in love with you. I probably was. But I can't be with someone who thinks what you're doing isn't a big deal."

"Then I guess that's that." He stepped away from me.

"And I guess as soon as I leave, you'll call the police. You reported that interpreter. You probably feel you should report me, too."

"I don't know what I'll do," I said, honestly. "I haven't thought about that. I can't even feel anything. I'm just numb."

"Well, when you thaw out," he said, "remember this. If you want to call the police, fine. Maybe you can get them to take me in. One more thing to upset my mother. Or maybe not. Maybe she'd enjoy the drama. You can probably create a scandal, humiliate some women, destroy some families. Maybe you'll close down the center. I'm not sure about that. Maybe a little scandal would bring in more members. But I'll tell you one thing. No one will get convicted of anything, because there's no evidence. I've never kept any records—not one scrap of paper, not a single computer file. It's all in my head, nowhere else. So in the long run, the prosecutor might get frustrated with you."

"Hector, don't talk that way. I don't—"

"Let me finish. There won't be any financial evidence, either—no cancelled checks, no credit card bills—because we've always done everything in cash, and I've found dozens of quiet ways of funneling that cash into the center, bit by bit. And no evidence from surveillance cameras. No shots of johns paying hookers, because the men never give the women money. They pay me, I pay the women, and I make sure all transactions are private. That's why, in five years, nobody's been arrested. And don't count on finding witnesses. The women won't testify, and neither will the men. They'd be incriminating themselves. Maybe you can get some waiters to say they saw married men having dinner with younger women. That won't get you a guilty verdict."

“Stop it.” Another minute, and I’d be crying. “I told you, I don’t know what I’m going to do.”

“And I’m telling you I don’t care what you do.” Turning away, he glanced at the counter. “You can keep the rose,” he said, and left.

I did cry then, hopeless, aching, not able to wait till I got to my room. I leaned my back against the refrigerator and wept, for a long time. I didn’t stop until a thought came to me unasked, more horrible than the other thoughts that had come tonight.

Jenny Linton. She’d worked for Hector. He’d been her pimp—I made myself face the ugliness of the word. And now she was dead, and now I knew Hector had a motive for killing her.

Chapter 26

That thought stopped the tears. If Jenny had turned on Hector, if she'd threatened to expose him, would he kill her to keep her silent? Jason had a strong alibi for the night Jenny died. His mother and Paul Kent and Diana had decent alibis. Hector had nothing.

I started washing dishes. Abby would be upset. She'd made it clear she'd do the dishes. But I had to keep my hands busy.

No, I thought. Hector *didn't* have a motive. He'd said he didn't care if I went to the police. He'd said he'd created no evidence, so nobody could convict him of anything.

But Jenny could have harmed Hector far more than I could. I could give the police theories based on manicures and clothes. Jenny could have given them a confession. She could have given them names of men she'd had sex with, details about restaurants and hotels. The police would probably laugh at me. They would have listened to Jenny.

And even if there hadn't been enough evidence for a conviction, if she'd simply threatened to start a scandal, that'd be motive enough. Hector said a scandal might draw in new members, but he wouldn't want to risk it.

He'd do anything to protect the center. I had plenty of proof of that.

I went to my room to get changed. From now on, I vowed, I'll think twice before dressing up for a date. I'd dressed carefully for two dates with Hector, and both had turned into disasters. It'd been better when I'd worn jeans for our picnic, and when I'd borrowed Rosa's skirt to go to the Irish pub.

As I hung my dress up, I wondered if Hector could be a killer. It seemed impossible. But two hours ago, I wouldn't have believed he could be a pimp. He might have emotional problems I didn't know about. He'd adored his father and lost him at a vulnerable age, and that had hurt him deeply. Rosa understood that. I remembered what she'd said about Elise's birthday dinner, about how Hector would be thinking his father should be there.

I started to reach for a shirt and stopped. How did Rosa know about Hector's father, about his feelings for his father? I hadn't told her, and I didn't think Hector had. He barely knew her. When I'd mentioned her, it took him a moment to remember she was "the deaf girl." Maybe he'd told Jenny about his father, and Jenny told Rosa. But Jenny couldn't sign. She would've had to write Rosa a note about Hector and his father. Why would she do that?

Still puzzling about it, I finished getting changed. Rosa had said another odd thing, during that same conversation. She'd said that I shouldn't have to take cleaning jobs, that it wasn't fair I couldn't get interpreting work. I hadn't told her about my problems with the agencies. I never talk about that if I can avoid it. Rosa's remark had struck me as strange at the time, but I'd brushed it aside. Now, it bothered me.

Don't be stupid, I told myself. Rosa knows I take cleaning jobs, so she naturally assumes I can't get interpreting work, and she thinks that's unfair because she likes me. That's all. Don't try to make some big mystery out of it. What had Walt said yesterday? "Don't start playing Nancy Drew." That was good advice.

But I couldn't follow it. Instead, for the second time that night, I sat down on my bed, letting thoughts and images come.

Nancy Drew—Rosa and her mother had loved Nancy Drew books, all the girl detective books. I pictured them sitting on the couch, reading, laughing, learning to sign.

But Rosa sold some of those books, because she and Sam needed money. For what?

I pictured Sam playing deaf at Nails by Ilana while Rosa gave Bethany and Ashley manicures, while they enjoyed their weekly gossip session, speaking freely because no one could hear them.

I remembered Sam sitting in the bar at The Flats, hair slicked back, glasses, no earrings, nice clothes, expensive watch.

Rosa and Sam—they'd both urged me to apply for a trial membership at the Reed Center.

I remembered how Rosa insisted I borrow her skirt when Hector asked me out, how she hadn't asked for details about my date, how she'd told me not to get the skirt dry-cleaned because she wanted to wear it the next day. I'd seen her the next day, at Nails by Ilana. She'd been wearing slacks.

Other images came back—Rosa looking upset while Detective Diaz questioned her, Frederick saying she'd asked if she'd get in trouble for withholding information, Rosa letting Jason flirt with her even though she knew he was married, even though she knew he was suspected of killing Jenny. I remembered Rosa sitting with me when Carl from Detroit came to our table. I remembered her rushing off—to go to work, she'd said. And I remembered her coming out of the café with Jason almost two hours later, to see Sam get arrested for stealing a half-empty box of staples.

Rosa had said she had "some ideas" about a career. But when she'd tried to discuss them with her father, he'd said, "Deaf people can't do that."

Sam had thought about becoming a policeman. But while he was excited about investigating things and catching bad guys, he didn't want to take orders or hand out traffic tickets.

Rosa told me she and Sam had a lot in common. All the differences in age, hearing, class, race, and she'd said they had a lot in common.

And this morning, Rosa had gone to the Reed Center at 5:00 and stayed three hours.

"Damn," I said, and grabbed my phone and sent a text message: *Rosa—Where are you? PLEASE answer.*

I waited five minutes. Nothing. But Rosa always kept her phone on vibrate, and it was just 8:30. I texted her again: *Tell me where you are. If you don't, in three minutes I will call your father. I will call Ulysses Patterson. I mean it.*

There. Rosa had never told me her father's first name. She probably assumed I didn't know it. Now she knew I did. And I hoped she believed I was serious.

Her answer came promptly: *I'm at the Reed Center. I'm busy. I'll text later.*

I knew it. Back at the center. She'd gone there early, and she'd gone back late. I sent another message: *Get out RIGHT NOW. It's dangerous. Meet me at Ginger's Pantry, and I'll explain.*

Her answer came back: *I can't leave yet. I have to do something. When it's done, I'll text you.*

Damn. Her father had said she was stubborn. He'd been right.

I'm coming to meet you, I texted. *Don't do anything risky.*

Don't come, Rosa texted back, but I snapped my phone shut. Should I ask Walt for help, or Frederick?

No. Despite what I'd texted to Rosa, I didn't really think she was in danger. In danger of being embarrassed, possibly in danger of getting arrested, but nothing worse. At this time on a Friday night, no Connollys would be at the center. If I got there quickly, if I could make Rosa leave, I could protect her dignity. I didn't have to worry about protecting her life. That wasn't an issue. I ran down to my car.

Arriving at the center, I pulled into the parking garage and swiped my membership card through the check-in slot. About a dozen cars in the garage—and one, damn it, looked like Hector's. Had he come here to work off his anger? I couldn't worry about that. With luck, Rosa and I would be gone in five minutes.

I texted her again: *I'm here. Where are you? If I have to get security to help me find you, I will.*

Her answer came back: *I'm upstairs, in the ladies' room. Don't come.*

I didn't answer, just headed for the elevator. Yes, I agreed it made sense to use the stairs in a fitness center. Tonight, I didn't care about anything but speed.

On the second floor, I looked cautiously down the hallway. Damn—the door to the administrative office suite stood ajar, one dim light burning in the reception area. As quickly and quietly as possible, I walked past, casting a glance inside. No one in sight. Someone must be in an inner office, probably Diana. She was most likely to work late on Friday. Anyway, I hoped it was Diana. I didn't want to run into Hector or Jason.

I reached the ladies' room and found Rosa pacing by the sinks. "*You shouldn't have come,*" she signed. "*You don't understand what's going on.*"

"*I think I do.*" I paused. Might as well get down to it.

"*You're here to get the bug, aren't you?*"

She stared, eyes wide. "*What do you mean?*"

"*The bug,*" I signed impatiently. "*The listening device Sam planted in Jason's office. You want to take it away before Jason finds it. You tried to get it this morning but couldn't. Were the janitors cleaning the offices? So you came back tonight.*"

For a moment, Rosa didn't respond. "*How did you know?*" she signed at last.

I couldn't take time to explain. I couldn't even take time to appreciate the irony. Ulysses Patterson hired a private detective to uncover his daughter's big secret. Her big secret, it turned out, was that she wanted to be a private detective. She'd met a man with the same ambition, and they'd stumbled across evidence of a prostitution ring. Eager to get proof, they'd sold books about girl detectives to buy listening devices, disguises for Sam, God knows what else.

They'd concluded, wrongly, that Jason was the pimp. And when Carl from Detroit came to our table, when Rosa realized he was looking for a prostitute, she'd texted Sam, and he'd rushed over to plant a bug in Jason's office, hoping to catch an incriminating conversation between Jason and Carl. And now Sam was in jail, and the only person left to listen to any conversations the bug picked up was a deaf girl.

No, no time to savor the irony now. "*I figured it out,*" I signed. "*Sam played deaf at the salon, and he heard Bethany and Ashley gossiping—is that how it started? You knew someone at the center was running a prostitution ring but didn't know if it was Jason or Hector. So you investigated them both. And Sam followed women from the center to bars, hoping to catch them with clients.*"

She nodded slowly. "*He took pictures with his cell*

phone. But he never got real evidence. He never saw men giving them money."

That was because Hector never let money be exchanged in public. Smart move, Hector. "*And when I went out with Hector, you planted a bug on me, didn't you? On the skirt you lent me? And Sam listened to our conversation and told you about it.*"

She winced. "*I'm sorry. But we thought Hector might try to recruit you.*"

So Hector wasn't the only one who'd thought I had potential as a prostitute. Maybe I should feel flattered. Despite all the terrible things I'd learned tonight, all the terrible thoughts I'd had, I had to smile. I shook my head incredulously.

"*We never thought you'd say yes,*" Rosa signed hastily. "*But if he'd tried to talk you into it, and we got it on tape, we'd have proof. And I'm sorry we suspected Hector. We always thought it was probably Jason, but we wanted to make sure. Now we know. It's Jason, definitely.*"

"*No, it's Hector. I found out tonight. I'll explain later. Now, let's go somewhere and figure out a better way to get the bug back. You can't stay here all night waiting for Diana to leave.*"

Rosa shook her head. "*Jason's the one who's still here, with that man, Paul Kent. Every ten minutes, I walk down the hallway and check. As soon as they leave, I'll get the bug, and then I'll go. Not before.*"

She *was* stubborn. And I wasn't happy to learn Jason was here. "*We don't want to mess with Jason. And if you break into the office, you could get arrested.*"

"*I don't care.*" Rosa's eyes grew sad. "*The prostitution part—that was like a game, like something from a book. We thought we'd expose a big crime, and we'd be famous, and we could start our own detective agency. But then Jenny died, and we think it's our fault.*"

"*What do you mean*?"

Rosa's signs were slow, reluctant. "*After the day Sam played deaf, I started wearing a bug to work, and we found out Jenny was a prostitute, too. So Sam followed her and took pictures of her with men. When he couldn't get real proof, we tried to get her to tell us the truth. The day you and I met, Sam and I showed her the pictures. She was embarrassed, but she kept saying the men were only dates. Then we showed her this one picture.*"

I remembered what I'd seen that first day, in Ginger's Pantry. Rosa's description matched my memories. "*What happened then*?"

Rosa sighed. "*She got really upset and left. That night, she drowned. We think she told Jason about the picture, and he killed her.*"

Dear God. "*Do you have the picture*?"

She took out her phone, found the picture, and held it out. Jenny Linton, pale and lovely, looking wretchedly unhappy, sitting at a table in a restaurant. And the young man next to her—reddish-brown hair brushing against his collar, eyes dark and eager behind his wire rims. Gary Nichols. I looked at the date on the picture. October fifteenth.

I closed the phone. Gary and Jenny together, on the night he was killed. Things came together quickly.

For two weeks, Gary had followed Rosa, watching her conversations with Sam. Even with limited ASL skills, Gary picked up enough to figure out they knew something about a prostitution ring, about the Reed Center, about Jason Connolly and Jenny Linton. Rosa and Sam thought Jason was running the ring, so Gary probably thought so, too.

That'd be a front-page story, all right—not just a married man having an affair, but the son of a local celebrity using his mother's fitness center to lure young women into prostitution.

So Gary snooped around the center, called Jenny, did anything he could to confirm the story. Then, on October fourteenth, he went to Jason's office and confronted him. He had the wrong man, of course, and he wouldn't have mentioned Rosa and Sam—reporters don't reveal their sources, and Gary wouldn't want to share credit for his discoveries. But he must've had some convincing bits of evidence, must've said some things that rang true. Jason realized Gary was right about the prostitution ring, realized Hector must be the one behind it. He also realized that if Gary published his story, the center could be ruined, and Jason's easy paycheck could disappear. But if the story stayed secret, Jason could use it to pressure Hector into giving him more money. He decided to search Gary's apartment to find out exactly what he knew, to destroy any evidence he could find.

And he got Jenny to help. Gary must've mentioned Jenny, must've said he'd been calling her. So Jason pressured Jenny into calling Gary and agreeing to see him Saturday night, into keeping him away from his apartment while Jason searched it. Poor Gary jumped at the chance. And Sam took a picture, thinking Gary was a client, not a foolish, eager kid with dreams of becoming a reporter.

Then something went wrong. Gary came back to the apartment too soon, or Jason decided he knew too much and waited there to kill him. When Jenny found out he was dead, she must've panicked. She could be charged as an accessory to murder now.

But the real panic didn't start until Rosa and Sam showed her that picture. Now she knew there was evidence linking her to Gary, to the night he died. No wonder she ran out of Ginger's Pantry. She probably ran straight to Jason. She couldn't have told him about Rosa—he wouldn't have flirted with Rosa if she had. She probably didn't tell him about the picture. Maybe she'd just said she couldn't take the pressure and wanted to leave town. Maybe she'd demanded money to help her make the move, money Jason didn't have. One way or another, she'd said enough to get herself killed.

But Jason didn't kill her. He had an alibi. Someone did the murder for him.

I couldn't take time to try to figure that out. "*We have to go,*" I signed. "*We have to get out of the building, and we have to get that picture to the police.*"

"*No police,*" Rosa insisted. "*Sam and I want to solve this ourselves. We want to prove—*"

"*You've got two choices,*" I cut in. "*One, leave with me right now. Two, I call your father and tell him everything.*"

"*How do you know about my father?*" she signed.

Before I could answer, the door to the ladies' room opened. Diana looked surprised to see me. "Jane," she said. "You're here, too. Well, that's good. Will you help me talk to Rosa?"

Damn. "We were just leaving," I said, signing as I spoke, scrambling to think quickly. "Rosa's father is expecting her. We'll come back in the morning."

Diana shook her head. "We need to talk now. Please help us."

Too stunned to come up with another response, I turned to Rosa. "Diana wants to talk to you," I said and signed. "She wants me to interpret. Is that okay with you?"

Rosa nodded her fist forward slightly, once. "*Yes.*"

"Good," Diana said. "Rosa, Jason called me a little while ago. He found something in his office, and he thinks a friend of yours put it there. He's upset—he wants to call the police. I think we can avoid that if we talk things through. Will you come to the office with me? Jane can come, too."

Rosa looked at me uncertainly. I didn't know what to think, either. Maybe we should try to knock Diana aside and make a run for it. But Jason and Paul might be right outside—how far would we get? Besides, this didn't feel like a life-or-death situation. They knew about the bug, but not about the picture. They didn't know Rosa had evidence linking Jason to two murders, and neither did Rosa. I didn't see how the situation could turn violent, not with Diana here. Harming Rosa or me would be stupid. Jason might get angry enough to get violent, but not Diana. Turning to Rosa, I raised my eyebrows and lifted my shoulders.

Again, the single, slight nod of her fist. "*Yes.*"

"Good," Diana said, and held the door open for us.

We crossed the hall ahead of her. The door to the administrative suite was wide open now, but there was still only one dim light on. Taking a deep breath, I walked into the reception area.

Chapter 27

Jason stood by the receptionist's desk, fiddling with the letter opener I'd noticed the first time I came here—pressing its point against the desk, flipping it around, pressing the blunt end down, flipping it around again. Paul Kent stood next to him, holding a metallic black box the size of a deck of cards. But they weren't the only people in the room.

Elise Reed sat in one of the narrow chairs against the wall, her face pinched and anxious. Next to her, wearing a tee-shirt and sweat pants, sat Hector.

When he saw me, he drew his head back. "What's *she* doing here?"

Diana closed the door behind her. "She was with Rosa. She can sign for us." She paused. "That's right—you two went to dinner tonight, didn't you?"

"We had a change of plans." He looked at me, anger still cold in his eyes, then stood. "I'm finishing my workout and going home. Whatever you decide is fine."

"No," Diana said. "We need the whole family here. We need to discuss things calmly and make a sensible decision. I want you to stay."

She wants his vote, I realized. Jason wants to have Rosa arrested. Diana thinks it's a bad idea, and she hopes

Hector will be a voice of reason. Well, after what happened tonight, he might vote to have *me* arrested, too. Awkward as it was, though, I felt glad he and his mother were here. How could things get violent with so many witnesses? They couldn't all be killers.

Hector threw himself down in his chair, turning his face aside like a cranky little boy. "Fine. I don't care. Go ahead."

"Good," Diana said. "Rosa, Jane, please sit down."

"Since I'm interpreting, it's better if I stand," I said. That wasn't necessarily true, but I'd feel more in control if I stood, more mobile and ready to respond.

Diana nodded and gestured toward Rosa, inviting her to sit. Cautiously, her eyes on Diana's face, Rosa lowered herself into the chair nearest the door. Diana walked closer to her, and I stationed myself between them.

Diana smiled—a brief, technically pleasant smile. "Rosa, some disturbing things have happened. A man named Samuel Ryan broke into Jason's office two days ago. Jason asked Mr. Kent to find out more about him. Mr. Kent spoke to some people who know him, and several said he has a girlfriend named Rosa. They said she's deaf. Is Samuel Ryan your boyfriend?"

Rosa shrank back in her chair. "*Yes.*"

"Jason says you invited him to have lunch with you that day. Did you do that to get him away from his office? Did you and Samuel Ryan plan the break-in together?" This time, Rosa just nodded.

"I'm glad you're being honest, Rosa," Diana said. "Now, when Mr. Kent told Jason what he'd learned, Jason was very upset. He and Mr. Kent decided to search the office, and they found something attached to the underside of Jason's desk. Is that a surveillance device, Rosa—a bug? Did Samuel Ryan put it there?"

Rosa looked away and nodded her fist forward. "*Yes.*"

"Oh, my God!" Elise Reed exclaimed. "They were spying on Jason! That's terrible! Why would they do that, Diana? Why?"

"I'm about to ask her, Mother," Diana said, not taking her eyes off Rosa. "Rosa, why did Samuel Ryan put that device there? Why did you come here tonight? We know you've been here a long time, keeping an eye on the office. Mr. Kent saw you walking up and down the hallway."

Rosa looked at me desperately. "*I don't know what to say. Help me.*"

Crap. I'd have to violate every ethical principle interpreters are taught. "I don't want to tell you," I said. "I'm embarrassed."

"I'm sure you are, Rosa," Diana said, "but you really need to tell us."

"*Just sign anything*," I signed to Rosa. "*I'll make something up.*"

Obligingly, Rosa began signing the Gettysburg Address.

"My boyfriend gambles," I said, borrowing an idea from Frederick. "He needed money. And Jason flirts so much. We thought if we got a tape of him flirting with someone, Sam could threaten to tell his wife, and Jason would give him money. And tonight, I came here to get the bug, so Sam wouldn't get in more trouble." I brought the side of my right hand down on my left palm, making the gesture as quick and small as possible—*stop.* Rosa stopped signing.

"You bitch." Jason put down the letter opener and started toward Rosa. "After I've been so nice to you! I ought to wring your neck. I—"

"Calm down, Jason," Diana said, sharply. "She can't hear you anyway. And don't come closer—don't scare her. Rosa, is that the truth?"

"Sign yes and apologize," I signed, and Rosa did it.

"Yes. I'm sorry," I said.

"You damn well should be sorry," Jason said. "Diana, that's it. Call the cops. She's an accessory to extortion."

"Attempted extortion," Diana said. "It didn't go very far. And remember who her father is. Do you think she'd spend a single night in jail on a charge like that? And who knows what countersuits he'd come up with? Defamation of character, a dozen other things. We can't afford that. Besides, do you really want this to come to trial? Do you want them testifying they thought they could blackmail you because you run after every woman you meet? Do you want Mara to hear that testimony?"

Jason's face contorted with rage. "So what do we do? Just let her walk out?"

"That's an option, yes," Diana said. "What do you think, Mother?"

"I think it's horrible," Elise said. "Blackmail and gambling—oh, my! I don't want people like that in my center."

"That's a good suggestion," Diana said. "We could cancel Rosa's membership, with no refund. Paul, what do you think?"

He shrugged. "Considering the circumstances, I vote for damage control. Cancel her membership. She won't complain to her father. She won't want him to know the truth. And we'll let Ryan plead guilty to some minor charge. Illegal trespass, maybe."

"And theft," Jason insisted. "He stole from me—he should pay for that."

Hector shook his head. "A box of staples? Get serious. He took that just so we'd think he came to steal, so we wouldn't look for another explanation. This thing's a farce. Let it go."

"Then we're agreed." Diana turned to Rosa again.

"Rosa, what you did was wrong. We don't want you to come to the center anymore, and we're not giving you a refund. But we'll let your boyfriend plead guilty to a minor charge. He'll get out of jail soon. Do you understand?"

This time, I could sign what Diana actually said, and voice Rosa's actual response. "*I understand. I'll leave. I'm sorry.*" She started to stand up.

So it was over. Thank God.

"Not so fast," Jason said, his face still twitching. "We can't just let her leave. How do we know she's telling the truth? How do we know she wasn't up to more?"

"She admitted to attempted blackmail," Diana said. "Why would she say that, if it wasn't true? There's no—"

"Shut up," he shot back. "I've had it with the way you boss me around. And I know there's more to it." He paced, running his hand through his hair, and then turned on me. "Ask her what she knows about Gary Nichols."

Diana's face went white. "For God's sake, Jason! Shut up!"

"No, you shut up. I want to know." He grabbed my wrists. "Sign it. Ask her what she knows about Gary Nichols."

"Shut up!" Diana cried again.

I yanked my wrists free, and Jason pointed at me angrily. "What about *her*? She joins the center right after Jenny dies, she shows up at Mom's house wearing Jenny's dress, and tonight you find her hiding out with Rosa. You think that's all coincidence? Damn it, Diana, you've got more at stake than I do. At least I've got alibis for both nights. Maybe we should ask Jane what *she* knows about Gary Nichols."

"Stop it, Jason," Diana said. "Please, please stop talking."

Grumpily, Jason walked back toward the reception

desk. “We should ask them both what they know about Gary Nichols,” he muttered.

“What’s going on?” Hector asked. “Who’s Gary Nichols?”

“Stop saying that.” Diana pressed her hand against her forehead. “My God, Jason. Do you realize what you’ve done?”

Maybe he didn’t realize. Maybe he was really that stupid. But Diana realized. So did I. Shit, I thought. Diana knows about Gary Nichols.

Now I could nearly finish the story. After Rosa and Sam showed Jenny the picture, she ran to Jason with impossible demands. And Jason ran to Diana. Of course she was the one he’d turn to. Hector was Jason’s competitor, but Diana was his protector. To get her help, Jason must’ve told her Jenny was a threat to more than his marriage. He must’ve said Jenny knew he’d killed Gary. And Diana decided, or they both decided, Jenny had to die.

They knew if the police found out about Jason’s affair with Jenny, he’d be suspected. He needed an alibi. So Diana told him to stay at the singles’ night until it ended. No wonder she’d been upset when she found out he left early. All her careful planning ruined, because he needed a drink.

Diana had an alibi, too, the fundraiser at the Rock and Roll Hall of Fame. But that wasn’t far from The Flats. At a big function like that, she could slip away without being missed, change into the jeans and hooded jacket she’d stowed in her car, kill Jenny, change her clothes again, slip back into the Hall of Fame, and make sure people saw her.

Shit, I thought again. Jason had given so much away. Would Diana still let us leave? I had to try. I turned to Rosa. “Come on,” I said and signed. “We should go.”

“No,” Diana said. It was weak, barely audible. Then

she threw her shoulders back, her face miserable but unflinching. "No," she said again, the word harder this time. "Jane, you and Rosa need to stay. And Mother, you need to go. Paul, take Mother to a restaurant and stay at least two hours. Talk to people, and pay with Mother's credit card."

"Don't be silly, Diana," Elise said. "You know I never eat this late at night—I hardly eat at all."

"I don't care if you eat or not." Diana's voice sounded heavy with resignation. "Just go to a restaurant and stay there, and take Hector with you. Paul, will you make sure that happens?"

"I will. And you can handle things here?"

"We'll have to," Diana said. "Jason and I will have to."

Jason looked at Rosa, looked at me, smirked. "No problem," he said.

How had things turned so bad so quickly? Maybe I could at least get Rosa out of it. "Wait," I said. "Obviously, you didn't want us to hear that name. Rosa *didn't* hear it, and I didn't sign it to her. She has no residual hearing, and she can't read lips. She doesn't know anything. She can't hurt you. You can let her leave."

"I can't." The regret in Diana's voice seemed genuine. "Nice try, Jane, but you know I can't."

Hector stood up. "I don't get any of this. Why can't they leave?"

Diana sighed. "Jason said things they shouldn't have heard. So now we have to take care of things."

Hector looked at her uneasily. "You won't hurt anyone, will you?"

"Of course not. We'll work out an arrangement. It may cost us a little. You may have to help with that." She smiled weakly. "But Jason and I can handle the negotiations. You should go now."

"Yeah, just go," Jason said. "We don't need you. I could handle this alone."

Hector looked at me, and his face hardened. "Fine. I've got no reason to stay."

He turned away. Paul helped Elise stand up, and they all started for the door. Damn, I thought. Jason killed Gary, Diana killed Jenny, and everyone who isn't a murderer is about to leave the room.

"That's right, Hector," I said desperately. "Walk away. You know what they're going to do, but you won't stop them. What'll it be this time, Diana? More tragic drownings at The Flats? Or will my car crash into a utility pole? Will you make sure the gas tank explodes?"

Hector wheeled around. "What the hell are you talking about?"

"Mara told me about the night your father died," I said. "She was at your house. She and Jason were screwing on the couch in the den when he walked in. Come on, Hector. You must've wondered. You were only fifteen, so maybe you didn't question it then. But you're all grown up. Haven't you wondered why your father was driving around at two o'clock in the morning?"

Diana took a step toward me. "That's enough, Jane."

"It's not enough." I had to keep Hector in the room. "Why didn't Jason come to the funeral? Was he sick, or was he so bruised up he was afraid people would guess the truth? Why did he marry Mara a few months later? Does he strike you as the kind who wants to settle down at nineteen?"

Elise had moved away from Paul Kent. There was nothing unsteady about her step now, and her back was straight. "Make her stop, Diana."

"Stay calm, Mother," Diana said. "Hector, wait for me at Mother's house, and I'll explain everything."

Hector was staring at Jason—I saw doubt in his eyes. I

turned to Elise. "You should've called the police, Mrs. Connolly. It started as self-defense. Both Mara and Diana could testify to that. Jason might not have gone to prison at all. Or was your husband still alive when they put him in the car?"

Hector kept his eyes locked on his brother. "Jason," he said. "Is it true?"

Jason stood leaning an elbow on the reception desk. "I thought you'd figured it out long ago. He was a son of a bitch. I'd had enough of his bullshit."

I expected Hector to say something, to swear, to cry out in rage. But he stood silent, immobile. Then he charged across the room, still not making a sound, throwing himself at Jason, getting both hands around his throat. Elise shrieked, and Diana ran forward and tried to pull Hector away.

He wouldn't let go. Not saying anything, his face blank, he pressed his thumbs against his brother's throat. I could see Jason trying to pry Hector's hands away, could hear him gagging. Then Jason reached toward the reception desk, and his hand found the letter opener.

He plunged it into Hector's stomach. Almost immediately, Hector's body went limp, and he staggered backward. Diana caught him and eased him to the floor. Already, his eyes looked vacant, fixed, vaguely puzzled. I could see his chest heaving, could see the blood spreading across his shirt. I grabbed my phone from my pocket.

Elise walked toward me and put her hand over the phone. "No," she said.

I stared at her. "We have to call 911. We have to get an ambulance for your son."

"My son," she said, "will never go to prison. Paul?"

He walked over to us. "We'll get help for him, Jane. Give me your phone."

I glanced at Jason advancing toward me, the letter

opener still in his hand. I couldn't fight them all. I gave Paul my phone. "He could bleed to death," I said.

"We'll get help for him," he said again. "Diana, your mother and I should leave now."

Diana stood staring at Hector, who seemed unconscious. I saw tears start down her face. Elise walked over and put a hand on her arm. "Diana, I'm trusting you to take care of everything. Nothing more can happen here. You understand that, don't you? And there can't be a trace of anything when the janitors arrive. Can you handle that, dear?"

Still gazing at Hector, Diana nodded slightly. "Yes, Mother. I'll take care of it."

"That's my darling girl." Elise touched her cheek lightly, and Diana turned to look at her, eyes soft with yearning.

For one moment, Elise glanced down at Hector. "We should go, Paul," she said, and turned away.

He took her arm, and they left, closing the door behind them. I looked at Rosa. Her eyes were wide with shock, but she was sitting forward, body tensed and alert. "*What's going on*?" she asked.

This is it, I realized, and felt my mouth go dry. But I also felt energy surge through me, felt more awake than I'd ever been before in my life. "*They don't want to let us leave*," I signed. "*Get ready to fight. One encounter, one chance*."

She nodded, and Diana looked at us sharply. "What did you say to her?"

I lifted my hands. "I told her to stay calm and cooperate."

Diana shook her head. "You said more than that. This could be a problem." She paused. "All right. I have something to say to both of you. You can sign it for Rosa. After that, I don't want either of you to sign until I say you can."

Jason came to stand beside her, glaring at Rosa, still holding the letter opener, tapping the side against his palm as if to remind us he had it.

Diana faced us, hands folded primly, as if she were giving a speech. "Jane and Rosa, some upsetting things happened tonight. People said things that might be misunderstood. It's important to our family that these things stay private. If you promise to keep them private, we'll give you a gift to show our appreciation. We'll work that out. But we can't talk here. I'm sure Paul has called 911 by now. Paramedics will arrive soon. We need to go somewhere private. So we'll all go to the parking garage in the elevator, and Jason will drive us to my mother's house. If we all stay calm, no one will get hurt, and we can settle this quickly."

I signed what she said for Rosa, and kept signing as I replied. "Rosa and I both have cars here. We'll take our own cars and meet you at the house."

"That won't work," she said. "You might decide not to come. We'll all stay together. Now, please stop signing. Jason, give me your tie."

He took it off one-handed, not putting the letter opener down, not taking his eyes off me, and handed the tie to his sister.

"I don't want to frighten you, Jane," Diana said, "but we can't have you signing things we can't understand to Rosa. So I'm going to tie your hands, and then we'll all go down to the car. Put your hands behind your back, please."

If someone tells you to get in the car, Charlie had said, don't. Don't let anybody tie you up.

I caught Rosa's eye, and she edged forward in her chair. Slowly, I put my hands behind my back.

Diana smiled—a kind, reassuring smile—and walked toward me, the tie in her hands. I waited for her to get behind me. Then I pivoted toward her sharply, bringing my right elbow back to strike her in the face, hitting her just above the eye. She stumbled backward, holding her hand to her forehead.

Before she could recover, Rosa jumped up and delivered a full-force front kick to her stomach. With a little cry of surprise, Diana doubled over, and Rosa kicked her again, this time in the face. That one knocked her out, and she fell to the floor on her back.

"Bitch!" Jason cried, and ran toward me, the letter opener raised over his head.

Automatically, the moves from class came back. I turned sideways and kicked him in the kneecap, as hard as I could, and he grunted with pain.

But it didn't go as smoothly as it had in class. When I lunged forward to grab his wrist, he swung out wildly with the letter opener, slicing deep into my left arm, just below the shoulder. The pain startled me, and the sight of blood, a lot of blood. *Finish it, finish it*, I thought. Seizing his wrist with both hands, I pulled it up fiercely. He struggled, trying to break free, nicking me in the cheek, but I kept forcing his wrist up, as high as I could. I turned my back to him and yanked his arm down hard, cracking his elbow against my shoulder. He shrieked but still clung to the letter opener. I pulled his broken arm up again, pounded it against my shoulder again. This time, the letter opener fell from his hand. Spinning around, I kicked him in the stomach, and he crumbled to the floor and lay there, writhing and sobbing.

My hands were shaking, and my arm pulsed with pain. I looked down at Jason and thought of Hector—maybe dying, maybe already dead. I thought of Gary Nichols, of Jenny Linton, of Jason's own father.

"I wish I'd hurt you more," I said, and turned away from him.

The safest thing would be to pick up the letter opener. But I didn't want my fingerprints on that thing. I kicked it hard, and it shot across the room, knocking against the reception desk a few inches from Hector.

I turned to Rosa. "*Watch them,*" I signed, and she nodded, standing there bouncing in place lightly, keeping her fists in a fighting stance. Jason had curled up on the floor, pressing a hand against his arm, whimpering. Diana wasn't making a sound, wasn't moving. And Hector—I couldn't see his chest heaving anymore. If he died, it would be my fault, because I'd kept him from leaving.

I ran to the reception desk and reached for the telephone receiver. Just as I picked it up, the door opened, and Walt Sadowski walked in.

"Put the phone down, Jane," he said. "We gotta get Rosa out of here."

What was he doing here? "Hector was stabbed," I said. "He—"

"I know," Walt said. "I called 911. They're on their way. We gotta focus on Rosa. Protect the client. That's priority number one, always."

Rosa watched him warily, still in her fighting stance. She shot me a questioning glance.

"*He's a private detective,*" I signed. But I felt confused, too. "How did you know Rosa was here? How did you get into the center?"

He sighed. "I'm a professional, okay? I can get into places. And I knew she was here because I followed her. After that disappearing act she pulled this morning, her father wanted her under surveillance twenty-four seven. Plus I got my own bugs planted here." He smiled, grimly. "Mine, they didn't find. Look, I'll explain later. We gotta get Rosa out before the cops arrive and start asking a million questions."

Jason looked up at him from the floor. "I knew it. She's working with you. You had her wear that dress. You—"

"Shut up," Walt said. "Things get worse when you talk too much. Haven't you noticed that? Jane, tell Rosa we gotta leave."

This wasn't right. None of it was right. If he had bugs in the room, why hadn't he come in sooner, to help when we were in danger? Why had he planted the bugs in the first place? Jason knew him—how could that be? And why shouldn't we wait for the police? We needed to answer their questions. We couldn't just walk away and pretend we had nothing to do with any of this. I thought of all the times I'd tried to talk to Walt about Gary Nichols and Jenny Linton, all the evidence I'd brought him linking the two deaths to each other, to Rosa, to the Connollys. Every time, he'd shut me down. Now, all that felt very wrong.

"We should wait for the police," I said. "Why should—"

"No more questions," he said. "Grab her, and we'll go to the garage and get in my car."

Don't get in the car.

"No." I signed as I spoke. "We're not going with you. I'm calling 911, and Rosa and I will wait here for the police."

"Fuck this," he said, and reached into his coat pocket, took out a gun, and pointed it at me. "I knew I shouldn't have hired you. Right from day one, I knew. Always too many questions, too many reservations, too much talk, talk, talk. But you looked like a nun—how much trouble could you be? It ends now. We're all going to my car, and that's it. And don't try any judo-karate stuff. I put a bullet in your brain, it won't matter how many fancy kicks you know."

He doesn't want to shoot, I told myself. There are still people in the center—not many, but someone might hear a gunshot and call the police. But if he gets mad enough, if he panics, he can kill us both in seconds.

All things considered, this probably wouldn't be a good time to tell him I'd just realized he was the one who'd killed Gary Nichols.

I raised my hands, palms out, shoulder high. "All right, Walt. We'll come. Let me explain the situation to Rosa."

"No signing," he said. "No saying things I can't understand. Get over here."

It felt terrifying to walk toward a gun—it felt counterintuitive, wrong. But I couldn't fight back unless I shortened the distance between us. He's going to grab me, I thought. Then he can hold the gun to my head and get Rosa to do anything he wants. I have to act first.

Having my hands up might actually help. Keeping them raised, I walked toward him slowly, locking his eyes with mine, trying to keep him focused on my face and not my hands. Get close, I told myself—just six inches away from him. Three more steps, and then do it.

With the last step, I brought my left hand down hard, grabbing the barrel of the gun, forcing it down so it pointed at the floor. Yelling, keeping the gun pointed down, I punched him in the face with my right fist, as hard as I could.

He didn't let go of the gun, kept struggling to pull it back up. My left arm was bleeding, the pain shooting clear down through my fingers. Holding the gun down and pointed away from me left me gasping.

"Bitch!" he shouted and punched me repeatedly in the face—powerful blows, much more powerful than my punches had been. I couldn't block them, couldn't spare any strength for anything but holding onto the gun. I felt myself start to fall back.

Desperate, I grabbed the gun with both hands, pulling Walt forward. I tucked my chin and started to crouch, trying to roll down instead of falling flat. He tried to move back but lost his footing. I went down on my side, pulling him on top of me, still holding onto the gun. I didn't hit my head.

We grappled on the floor, Walt trying to yank the gun back, while I clung to it. Keep it pointed at the floor, I thought, and couldn't think anything else.

And then he cried out, and I looked up to see Rosa standing over us, lifting a chair above her head, bringing it down to strike him in the back again and again.

She knocked him off me, and he landed on his back. Feeling his grip on the gun loosen, I rolled toward him, pulled his hand up, and bit it till he screamed. He let go of the gun, and Rosa kicked it away from him.

I jumped up and kicked him in the head, three times, until I knew he was unconscious. I turned to Rosa.

"*Give me your phone*," I signed. "*Get help*."

She gave me her phone and ran. As I dialed, I looked quickly around the room. No movement from Hector, Jason still moaning, Diana starting to stir. Walt lay flat on his back, hand bleeding, eyes closed.

I called 911 and shouted my information, trying to make my answers coherent as the operator pressed for details. My hands started to shake again as the panic I'd held back spread through me. I looked up.

Diana lay on her side, holding the gun in both hands.

Damn! How could I have been so stupid?

"Do it, Diana." Jason's voice was cold now. He seemed almost calm. "Kill her."

She gazed at him, raised herself up to look at Hector,

then turned her eyes to me. They were wide and hopeless, soft with something like longing, something like regret.

Slowly, she eased the gun into her mouth and pulled the trigger.

Chapter 28

I wish they'd let me go home," I said. "I don't see why I had to go to the hospital at all."

Frederick Patterson tilted his head, pretending to think it over. "Oh, I don't know. That inch-deep gash in your arm? The cut on your cheek? The black eye, the bruises making half your face look like a slab of raw meat? And I'm sure they want to check for a concussion."

"I can't possibly have a concussion. When I fell, I didn't hit my head." I felt proud about that, and pointed it out to anyone who would listen.

He grinned. "As I understand it, one can also get a concussion from being punched in the face five or six times. Or maybe they want to run blood tests, see if you picked up any diseases when you chewed on Sadowski's hand."

Frederick was my third visitor of the day. Rosa had brought a basket of irises and daisies, Abby a vase of lavender roses and pink lilies. Instead of flowers, Frederick brought an arrangement of cactus plants—some round, some tall, some dark green, some light—in a multicolored ceramic pot. The small wheeled table on the left side of my bed looked like a florist's display. Frederick sat on the other side of the bed, in a narrow chair in the narrow, relentlessly white but surprisingly sunny room. Despite my grumbling, it felt comforting to be in a scrubbed-down place drenched with light. Even the antiseptic smells were welcome, like an invisible barrier separating me from the dim, bloody room where Diana Connolly died last night.

I smiled at Frederick's little joke. "I wouldn't be surprised if I *did* catch something from that bastard. I can't imagine how livid your father must've been when he found out about Walt."

"Not a pretty sight." He pretended to shudder. "My father doesn't like being wrong about people. I think the anger helped him, by keeping him from dwelling on what could've happened to Rosa. You really think Sadowski would've killed you both?"

"Definitely. He couldn't have let us talk to the police. If Jason got arrested, if the police asked him about Gary Nichols, he would've told them about Walt. Walt must've planned to kill Hector, too, or to have Diana and Jason do it. I don't know how Walt planned to manage all that—he probably didn't know, either—but he would've had to. Otherwise, he'd be charged with murder."

"As he will be." Frederick looked grim. "And attempted murder. When I think of him holding a gun on my little sister—"

"Your little sister," I said, "did fine. Nineteen years old, only a few months of martial arts classes, and she did everything she had to without flinching. I couldn't have held out against Walt much longer. She saved us both."

"I guess so." He sounded as if he still found it hard to believe. "I've always seen Rosa as fragile, probably partly because she's so much younger, partly because she's deaf. I was wrong about her. My father was, too."

"This time, being wrong probably feels good."

"It does. We were wrong about you, too, Jane. I can't say how sorry we are for misjudging you, or how grateful we feel. If you hadn't risked your life to save Rosa—"

"I didn't choose to risk it, and I was trying to save myself, too. I don't deserve any points for nobility." I paused. "You know who does deserve some points? Sam Ryan. A few weeks ago, Rosa and I couldn't have fought back the way we did. Sam's an excellent martial arts teacher. He's a nice guy, too. Planting the bug in Jason's office was stupid. The whole let's-play-private-eye bit was stupid, and he's old enough to know better. But he meant well."

"I realize that. So does my father. He came close to saying he might've been partly wrong about Ryan. He also said he may have driven Rosa to playing detective, by making her think it was the only way to get him to take her ambitions seriously."

That had occurred to me, too. "Then maybe some good will come out of this mess. I'm sorry about your mother's books, though. I hope you can get them back someday."

Frederick smiled wryly. "They're back. As soon as Sadowski located them in those used book stores, my father bought back every one. He didn't tell me until today. Even now, he won't say how much he paid, which must mean he paid plenty. I don't think he wants anyone to know what a softie he is. But Rosa will find out when she gets home. He's put them back in her bookcase."

"That's wonderful," I started, but broke off when Detective Bridget Diaz appeared in the doorway.

She looked at Frederick and raised an eyebrow. "I could come back."

Frederick stood up. "I should go anyway. Jane, I'm glad you're doing better. My father would like you to join us for Sunday dinner, if you're up to it."

Probably, I'd felt more terrified when Walt Sadowski pointed the gun at me. I'm not sure. "That's nice," I said. "But I'm weak. I may have to spend the next few months in bed. Maybe the next few years."

"You'll recover more quickly than that. Seriously, I hope you can make it. I think my father wants to have a real conversation with Rosa. I think that's one reason he'd like you to come. *I'd* you to come, too, for different reasons. I'd also like to finally have that lunch with you. May I call you tomorrow?"

"Fine," I said, not sure I felt ready for lunch with Frederick, much less dinner with his father. Frederick seemed to like me. Probably, I liked him, too. But I hadn't even begun to get over Hector. I hadn't had time to even think about getting over Hector. Things kept happening too quickly.

Bridget Diaz took Frederick's place in the chair. "You're looking better today. Feeling better, too, I hope?"

"Much better." Now the questions would start—one more thing I didn't feel ready for but had to face.

"Are you up to answering some questions? The information you gave us last night was helpful, but there are some gaps. If you need to rest, we can talk later."

She already had her notebook out. She had no intention of talking later. "We can talk now. May I ask how Hector Connolly's doing?"

"The doctors say he'll recover. So far, they've allowed us only a few minutes with him, and he's refused to say anything. That may change, especially when he finds out we're getting information from other sources." She paused. "May I say something? I know you were involved with him. I can see why. When I questioned him last week, he seemed intelligent. Despite the circumstances, he was likeable, even charming. And of course he's handsome. Frederick Patterson, though—when our people testify in a case he's handling, they prep for days. He's fair, they say, and doesn't take cheap shots. But he never misses anything, spots all the holes in a case at twenty paces. It's none of my business, Ms. Ciardi, but you should say yes to lunch."

Good grief. "If you're going to get that personal," I said, "you might as well call me Jane. So you're getting information from other sources? Kirsten Carlson?"

"No, we haven't located her. She may have left town. But I've spoken to the other women you mentioned, and one is cooperating. When I told her the prostitution ring may be linked to two murders, and one victim was Jenny Linton, she *wanted* to cooperate." Detective Diaz shook her head. "Hector Connolly had quite a system. He'd give these women trial memberships, ask them to dinner, and talk about how healthy sex is. Then he'd make it clear they could get another month at the center by going to bed with him. That was probably an audition, partly, to see how good they were. It was also the first in a series of temptations leading up to the big question: 'If you'll have sex with me to extend your membership, why not have sex with some great guys I know and make real money?' I'm sure the system didn't work every time. I'm sure he learned to spot the ones who wouldn't go for it, and to back off before making the final proposition. But it worked often enough to let him put together a nice-sized stable."

And at first, I thought, Hector wanted me to become part of that stable. I didn't have a concussion—I knew damn well I couldn't have a concussion—but my head began to ache. "You said you had questions."

"I do. I hope you can help me resolve some discrepancies. Both Jason Connolly and Walt Sadowski are cooperating, or claiming to. Unfortunately, they're telling different stories."

"Let me guess," I said. "Walt claims he had nothing to do with Gary Nichols's death. He's shocked, shocked that anyone thinks he did. He never saw or spoke to Jason before last night. And he didn't know Gary had discovered anything damaging about Jason, because Gary's reports were vague. Am I right?"

She struggled against a smile. "I shouldn't say."

"Probably," I said, "you shouldn't have told me how Hector lured women into prostitution, either."

"True." She smiled more freely. "But that part was too juicy not to tell."

She probably also wanted to cure me of any lingering fondness for Hector—obnoxious, but sweet. "If Walt did give you a story like that, it's bullshit. Walt and Jason obviously knew each other. I told you what they said to each other last night, and since then I've remembered something else. The first time I mentioned Jason, Walt acted like he'd never heard of him. But then he talked about how rich Jason is. He even knew Jason drives an Audi. I'm sure he saw Jason as an endless source of cash. He could either work for Jason, or blackmail him."

"Do you have a basis for that statement?"

"Not really. I'm assuming that after confronting Jason, Gary talked to Walt. Gary may have been almost ready to go public—he may have hoped Walt could help him get final confirmation. And Walt saw an opportunity to make money by doing favors for a rich man. What does Jason say? Did Walt call and offer to save him from a scandal?"

"Again, I can't say. But if you have evidence to back that up, I'd like to hear it."

"Well, last night Jason said he had alibis for 'both nights.' He must've meant the night Gary died and the night Jenny died. So I assume Walt said he'd take care of

Gary and told Jason to set up an alibi, just in case. *Does* Jason have an alibi for October fifteenth?"

She thought it over. "I don't think I'd be violating confidences to say he took his family for a spur-of-the-moment vacation at Put-in-Bay that weekend."

He must've shocked the hell out of Mara, I thought. Jason didn't seem like the type to take his family on vacation often. "So Jason couldn't have killed Gary," I said. "I was sure he had. I should've known better. The lock was picked. Jason wouldn't know how to do that, but Walt would. And Walt would know exactly what to take, exactly how to mess things up enough to make it look like a real burglary. Jason would've bungled it. Walt once said something about most murderers making mistakes because they're amateurs. He must've felt smug when he said that. He's a professional. He'd committed a murder that fooled the police."

She arched her eyebrows. "Thank you."

"I didn't mean it as a criticism. Besides, Walt made a mistake, too. He stayed in the apartment too long. Gary walked in on him, so Walt had to kill him. Or maybe, after searching the apartment, Walt decided Gary knew too much and had to die, or maybe he'd planned to kill him all along. Jason might've hired him to do just that."

"Those are all logical possibilities," she acknowledged.

"I'm sure Jason denies the last one. I'm sure he says he never wanted Gary harmed and was shocked, shocked to hear he was dead. He probably says the same thing about Jenny—he asked Diana to negotiate with her but never dreamed she'd hurt her."

Bridget Diaz half-nodded. Was she confirming what I'd said? "And now we'll never know Diana's side of the story," she commented.

"I don't think she wanted to tell her side." I remembered the sorrowful look she'd given me before she pulled the trigger. Maybe she killed herself to escape the indignities of arrest and prison, but I'd guess she did it so she wouldn't be tempted to betray her brother. What a tragic, wasted life.

I shook off the gloom. "You probably can't say, but I assume you're checking bank records to confirm Jason paid Walt—checking for withdrawals in Jason's account, matching deposits in Walt's?"

"Police officers often check such things in such situations, yes. Such procedures often yield strong confirmation. Now, about Mr. Sadowski's reaction to Jenny Linton's death. He seemed interested, you said?"

"Yes, he talked to a police friend about it, and the receptionist in Jenny's office. I thought he did that to make sure Rosa and I weren't in danger. When he asked you about Jenny's death, I thought he wanted to mislead you about our reasons for watching Rosa. But I bet he was looking for more information he could use to blackmail Jason. Jenny's death must've looked like a promising opportunity to Walt. He probably figured Jason had to be involved, had to be nervous."

Had Walt threatened to slip information to the police, implicating Jason in Jenny's murder? "But Jason wasn't as rich as Walt thought. Mara might buy him an Audi in a desperate attempt to win his love, but she was too smart to hand over much cash. So Jason refused to pay, and Walt kept hounding him. Then I came to Elise Reed's house wearing a dress Jason gave Jenny," I said. "He must've figured I wore it to increase the psychological pressure on him. He figured I was working for Walt. I was, but not in the way he thought."

"You hadn't told Mr. Sadowski about the dress?"

"No, not until the day we all met in his office. Before that meeting, when I said we should tell you about Gary

Nichols, Walt forbid it. I thought he was protecting Rosa, but he was protecting himself. He didn't want the police looking into Gary's murder again. Every time I tried to talk to Walt about Gary, he cut me off. I thought he was narrowly focused and not open to new suggestions. But he had other reasons for not wanting to discuss Gary."

She glanced up from her notes. "I'm surprised he hired you—I'm surprised he hired any interpreter. Wouldn't he be afraid you'd discover the same things Mr. Nichols did?"

"Ulysses Patterson insisted he hire an interpreter. Walt mentioned that. And Walt didn't think I'd be much trouble, since I looked like a nun. Besides, if Jason did a convincing job of saying he wasn't running a prostitution ring, Walt might've figured Gary misinterpreted what Rosa and Sam had signed. Maybe Walt thought he'd have better luck with a certified interpreter. He mentioned my certification, during my job interview." I grimaced. "He never mentioned my 'ethics problem,' though. That should've made me suspicious."

"Why?"

"Well, *you* mentioned my ethics problem, the second time we talked. You'd checked me out, to see if I'm a reliable witness. And Hector called my references before interviewing me for the trial membership. Walt never said a word. We talked about ethics during the interview, so it would've been natural for him to bring it up. I thought he hadn't bothered to check, but of course a private detective would check references for someone he was thinking of hiring. I'm sure Walt knew about my ethics problem. He probably thought it made me ideal. A woman who looks like a nun but has shaky ethics—who could be easier to control? Walt probably figured if I stumbled across damaging information, he could keep me quiet by slipping me twenty bucks."

Another half-nod. "There's something else. I can speak openly about this, since it involves statements made about you, and it's only fair to let you respond. Sadowski admits to planting bugs in Jason Connolly's office. He couldn't deny it, since we found them. He says he got alarmed when you told him Connolly was flirting with Rosa Patterson, so he posed as an exercise equipment repairman to get into the center."

"He didn't bug the office to help Rosa," I said. "He wanted more dirt for blackmailing Jason."

She didn't comment. "He also claims last night he realized you and Ms. Patterson were in danger and rushed in to save you. But you panicked and attacked him for no reason."

"That's a lie. Rosa can confirm that. So can Jason—and I bet he will, since now it's in his interest to make Walt look bad. Jason's trying to plea-bargain his way out of as much as he can, isn't he, by testifying against Walt? Or can't you tell me? Fine. I'll read about it in the newspaper. But I assume Walt will get charged with murder, and Jason and Hector will get charged with things, too. What about Elise Reed and Paul Kent? They walked out of that room knowing Diana and Jason would kill Rosa, and Hector, and me. Elise practically told Diana to do it. Are you investigating them?"

She hesitated. "Yes. And since this concerns you, I can say Ms. Reed and Mr. Kent claim they left the center because she became hysterical when her son was stabbed. True, they then went to a restaurant for two hours. That makes the hysteria claim problematic. They also claim they never imagined you and Ms. Patterson were in danger and don't understand why Diana Connolly attacked you. Ms. Reed is under a doctor's care, too heavily medicated to answer more questions. Mr. Kent, on the advice of counsel, is declining to disclose details. Oh, that's right." She reached into her purse and took out my cell phone. "He says he picked this up by mistake, thinking it was his own. Odd mistake, since he uses a BlackBerry. But here it is."

"Thanks. Did he say anything else?"

"Only that he may file assault charges against you, for being so rough on poor Jason Connolly. I wouldn't worry about it."

"I won't," I said, but felt glad I didn't get my fingerprints on the letter opener. Who knew how Paul Kent's lawyers might've twisted that? "I hope they get charged with something. I hope the center goes bankrupt tomorrow, and Elise has to sell her house to pay Jason's lawyers. If you ask me, in lots of ways, she was the guiltiest person in that room last night."

"I can't comment on that." She stood up. "I have more questions, but why don't I get us some coffee first? You look like you could use a break."

"Coffee sounds wonderful. And do cops really like doughnuts?"

"We generally find a way to tolerate them. You want a doughnut?"

"I'd love one. Chocolate, please, or glazed. No powdered sugar—too messy for a hospital bed."

"Got it," she said, and left.

I stretched, plumped my pillow, and picked up my cell phone. Several text messages, including one from Abby. She was making chicken soup, she said, to help me get better. At first, things went fine. Then all this grease started rising to the surface, and then all this scum started floating on the grease. No matter how often she skimmed, it kept coming. What should she do?

Oh, Abby, I thought. Why do you ever try to cook? Sighing, I began texting a list of suggestions. Probably, it wouldn't be tactful to put "open a can" on the list. As I worked on the message, I was dimly aware of a tall, white-coated figure entering my room, wearing one of those flimsy light blue things that look like shower caps. People like that came and went constantly here, checking charts and refilling water pitchers. This person bent over and tucked my blanket in more snugly, pulling it tight over my legs and shoving the ends under the mattress.

That felt cozy. "Thanks," I said, waving in acknowledgment, not looking up.

But there was a sound—an angry sound, a sound that didn't belong. I glanced up in time to see a hammerfist shoot down at the right side of my face, the bruised side. I tried to lift my arm to block it, but there wasn't time. The pain stunned me. Then a powerful hand clamped over my mouth, pushing my head down, and another hand grabbed my right arm, holding it helpless against the mattress.

I looked up into the ice-blue eyes, the blunt-featured face. Kirsten Carlson.

"Did you think I'd just go away, Jane?" she asked, pressing down harder on both my mouth and my arm. "Did you think I'd leave you alone, after what you did to Hector? He might die. Or they'll patch him up and send him to prison. That's just as bad. And it's your fault. Do you think Jason could've touched him, if you hadn't made him weak? You have to pay for that now. For that, and for what you've done to me."

Frantic, I tried to kick free of the blanket. But it was tucked in so tightly I couldn't loosen it. Trying to punch Kirsten with my left hand didn't do much good. The angle was wrong—she held my head down so hard I couldn't turn my body enough to aim a forceful punch, and my arm was sore and weak from the cut below my shoulder. I hit her side a few times, but not hard enough to hurt her. She glanced at my pathetically flailing arm and smiled. Her grip on me didn't loosen.

"These head injuries," she said. "Sometimes, they're much more serious than they seem. A patient can do fine for a while. Then, suddenly, that's it. I hope your doctors don't blame themselves for not initiating a more aggressive treatment plan. Really, there was nothing they could do."

My God, I thought. She's going to do it. I kicked harder and felt the blanket start to give way.

She looked down at me again. "Goodbye, Jane," she said.

She let go of me, grabbing my pillow and pressing it down hard over my face. The sudden darkness terrified me, almost as much as my inability to breathe. Instinctively, I tried to push the pillow away, felt for her hands and tried to pry them off.

But that was wrong. She was stronger, much stronger. I'd never get free this way.

Hurt her, I told myself. Hurt her as much as you can, as long as you have to.

I reached up blindly until my right arm knocked against her head. Pushing the cap off, I grabbed her hair, yanking as hard as I could, pulling her down toward me. I heard her grunt with surprise and pain.

I yanked down again. Now I could reach her face. I went at it with both hands, scratching and clawing. I heard her swear and knew I was hurting her. But she pressed the pillow down more tightly. How long could I keep this up without air? How long until I blacked out?

I spread both hands across her face and found an eye. Then I jammed my index finger into it with all my might.

She cried out. The force holding the pillow down was gone. I ripped it away from my face and sat up, gasping. Kirsten had backed off a step and bent over, holding her hand to her right eye.

Still gasping, not able to call for help, I pulled at the

blanket, freeing my right leg, and kicked her in the ribs—not much of a kick, but it stunned her, giving me time to free my left leg and roll off the other side of the bed.

Already, she was running toward me, fists raised. I shoved the wheeled bedside table at her, hitting her in the hips. She doubled forward, and I grabbed the potted cactus, lifted it in the air, and smashed it down on her head.

That did it. She fell forward over the table and collapsed to the floor.

I leaned against the wall, exhausted, panting, still not able to gather enough breath to shout for help. The call button, I thought—press the call button. But it was on the far side of the bed, I'd have to walk past Kirsten to get to it, and I wasn't sure I could take two steps without passing out. Wearily, I made myself push away from the wall and lift my fists, not taking my eyes off Kirsten.

I was still standing there when Bridget Diaz walked into the room, carrying an orange plastic tray loaded with two mugs of coffee and two doughnuts—one chocolate, one glazed. She looked at me, looked at Kirsten, dropped the tray, and grabbed her gun.

She crouched, holding the gun in both hands, pointing it at Kirsten. "Dr. Kirsten Carlson?" she said.

I nodded, not putting my fists down.

"She's the one who gave you the black eye?"

I nodded again, finally finding my voice. "I told you she's odd."

"You could've put it more strongly than that," Bridget Diaz said.

Chapter 29

For Sunday dinner, Ulysses Patterson's housekeeper had made standing rib roast—a huge, succulent standing rib roast, crusted with garlic and rosemary and cracked pepper, surrounded by fingerling potatoes. She'd roasted green beans with pearl onions, and she'd baked soft, buttery biscuits and apple-and-cranberry pie. Everything looked and smelled delicious. The few bites I managed to sneak tasted delicious, too. Through most of the meal, though, my mouth and hands were too busy for eating—too busy voicing everything Rosa signed, too busy signing everything her father and brother said. Frederick tried to sign, too, but his ASL vocabulary was tiny, his syntax off. Often, he needed help finishing sentences. It was an interpreter's nightmare: scrambling to keep up with all three of them, trying desperately to do justice to family references and inside jokes they understood and I could only dimly grasp.

I didn't mind. I'd been afraid dinner would be tense and awkward, but everyone seemed eager to communicate. We stuck to fairly neutral topics—stories about an aunt's gardening mishaps, about a crotchety senior partner at the law firm, about Rosa's most unreasonable customers. Ulysses Patterson shared his thoughts about a

Thurgood Marshall biography he'd read recently, and Frederick described his plans to look for a new car. Ulysses Patterson wasn't exactly jovial, but he seemed to be in a good mood, and he had opinions about everything and didn't hesitate to share them. Rosa, reserved at first, relaxed as dinner went on. Frederick seemed completely at ease. By the time the housekeeper cleared the dessert plates, I felt hungry but relieved. Really, this hadn't been bad.

Ulysses Patterson stood up. "Frederick, please excuse us. Miss Ciardi, I'd like you to come to my study, please, and to ask Rosa to join us. I'd like to have a conversation with my daughter."

Oh, God. I turned to Rosa. "Is it okay with you if I interpret?" I said and signed, and she nodded, eyes filled with dread.

We followed him to his study—exactly the sort of study I'd expect him to have, with cream-colored walls and dark woods and maroon carpet, with a massive mahogany desk and built-in, floor-to-ceiling shelves heavy with books. He sat behind the desk, turned on his old-fashioned, green-shaded banker's lamp, and pointed us to two wooden armchairs.

"Thank you for helping us, Miss Ciardi," he said. "May I assume you'll keep everything said here—and signed here—confidential?"

"Of course," I said and signed. "That's the most fundamental ethical principle for interpreting."

"Good. Then please tell my daughter I'd like to discuss the subject of higher education."

Here we go again, I thought. During the salad course, he'd been the same way—"Please tell my daughter this," "Please ask my daughter that." As the meal went on, he'd started to talk to Rosa directly, probably without realizing it. Now, we'd regressed.

"Please speak to Rosa," I said, continuing to sign. "I'll sign whatever you say and voice whatever she signs. Pretend I'm not here."

He shook his head. "It makes no sense for me to speak to her. She's deaf. And how can I pretend you're not here, when you clearly are?"

"Please try it that way, Mr. Patterson. It really will work better."

He looked utterly unconvinced. "This is some damned form of political correctness, isn't it?"

"It's not. It's simply the most natural, efficient way for you and Rosa to communicate. Please. Speak to Rosa, and forget I'm here."

"I will *not* forget you're here," he muttered, but resigned himself to it. He folded his hands on his desk and made an elaborate point of looking at Rosa, not me. "Hello, Rosa. I would like to discuss higher education. Have you had further thoughts about college?"

The first five minutes were rough, but it got better. And damn it, he *did* forget I was there. They talked for almost an hour, until Rosa looked at her watch and said she had to go meet Sam. Her father nodded and rose.

"I'm glad we had this talk, Rosa." He caught himself. "Excuse me. I should have said I'm glad we had this conversation."

She scrunched up her face and shook her head. "*You don't have to be careful about that. I say 'talk,' too.*"

"That's good to know. I hope you have a pleasant evening."

He held out his hand. She shook it, paused, and ran around the desk and hugged him. A quick hug—he seemed so surprised he didn't have time to hug back. He lifted his arms awkwardly, as if unsure of what to do with them.

And she was gone. I stood up. "Thank you for dinner,

Mr. Patterson. It was delicious, and it was kind of you to invite me."

"You're welcome." He hardly seemed to hear. Then he motioned for me to sit down again. "No. Stay."

I stayed. If he'd told me to bark and roll over, I might've done that, too. Some people have that air of command. He sat shaking his head, looking down at his folded hands.

"What she said about Samuel Ryan," he said. "Did that surprise you?"

"I'm sorry. I'm not allowed to comment on conversations I interpret, not even to people who—"

"Oh, very well. Don't comment on anything you interpreted. I'm telling you now, in a distinctly separate act of communication, that during a recent conversation with my daughter, I asked her if she loved Samuel Ryan and planned to marry him. You're allowed to comment on things I tell you directly, aren't you? And she said she loves him but doesn't think she'd ever marry him. Not because he's white, not because he's too old for her, not because he's uneducated, not because he seems in many respects to be a complete idiot. No, not for any of those perfectly valid reasons. Because he's not deaf—*that's* why she doesn't think she'd marry him. Did that surprise you?"

"Not really. My roommate's deaf, and she says she'd never marry a hearing man. There *is* a high divorce rate for marriages between deaf people and hearing people, much higher than the rate for interracial marriages."

"I don't understand it," he said. "You'd think she'd want to marry someone who can hear—so he could help her, answer the door when the bell rings, and so forth. But she doesn't want that. That's how she defines herself, isn't it? Not as Black. She doesn't care about that. She defines herself as deaf."

"I'm sure she cares about being Black. But being deaf affects Rosa every minute of every day. It affects every communication she has with another human being. So that may be the primary way she defines herself, yes."

"I don't understand it." He looked up. "I thought, on the whole, our talk about college was satisfactory. So she'll attend Cuyahoga Community College part-time this spring, taking general education courses. And she'll apply to Cleveland State, hoping to enroll full-time next fall as a criminology major. That wouldn't be my first choice of a major for her, but it should allow her some flexibility. In time, she'll realize how foolish this idea of becoming a private detective is and shift to something more suitable. Social services, for example. I believe a criminology major provides adequate preparation for some areas in that field."

"I don't know anything about that, Mr. Patterson."

"I'll look into it. You must agree, at any rate, that private detective work is a particularly perverse career choice for a deaf person. Private detectives listen in on conversations. They question people. How could a deaf person do that?"

I shrugged. "There's a saying, 'Deaf people can do anything except hear.' There are deaf police officers, deaf attorneys, deaf judges. Probably, there are deaf private detectives. If not, Rosa might have what it takes to become the first. I'm sure there would be challenges, but if that's what she wants to do, she'll find ways to overcome them. You once said she's stubborn, Mr. Patterson. She is. But 'stubborn' is almost a synonym for 'determined.' Rosa's a determined young woman. I wouldn't bet against her."

"Nor would I." He smiled. "So my Rosa might be a trailblazer. In some respects, that's an appealing idea. Perhaps I should find a way to give her a taste of what private detective work is really like—not through the sort of stunt she tried to pull with that Samuel Ryan, but through an internship with a reputable private detective. After our experience with Mr. Sadowski, I'll be doubly careful to make sure the private detective is truly reputable. Triply careful."

"An internship would be perfect, Mr. Patterson. I'm sure Rosa would be thrilled—thrilled, and grateful."

He waved his hand. "I don't care about that. But I'd like her to know I *do* listen to her—figuratively speaking, of course. My son lectured me last night, saying in many ways Rosa's a better listener than I am. I'd like to show them both that's not true. Well. I'm sure many private detectives would be reluctant to take on a deaf intern. If I agree to pay an interpreter to assist her, perhaps something could be arranged. Might you be interested in such an assignment?"

An interpreting job—a particularly interesting interpreting job that might help build a reputation, build a business. Visions of letterhead danced before me. "Very interested."

"Good. There's another matter I wish to discuss. I asked you to encourage Rosa to learn to speak and read lips. Is it your opinion she has no interest in ever learning to do either?"

"We never discussed it. I wouldn't rule it out completely. If she had a particular reason for wanting to learn—if she thought it would help her career plans, for example—she might develop an interest."

He smiled. "You're not subtle, Miss Ciardi. You needn't keep pushing. I've already agreed to the criminology major and said I'll arrange an internship. But you've evidently seen nothing to indicate she has an immediate interest in learning to speak and read lips. Neither have I. And it felt good—extremely good—to communicate with her this evening. This was the first real conversation Rosa and I have had since my wife passed away. I'd like to have more conversations with her. So if she won't learn to speak and read lips, perhaps I should learn to sign."

I could hardly believe it. "That's a wonderful idea, Mr. Patterson. There are excellent classes available in the area. Or I could recommend some books and videos."

"At my age," he said, "I am not about to sit in a classroom and let someone lecture at me, to let some youngster correct my homework and write facilely encouraging comments in the margins. Books are fine, but I doubt this subject can be mastered through books alone. And I have yet to be convinced that anything of significance can be learned through watching videos. No, I want private lessons. Two or three one-hour lessons a week, time and place and payment to be determined at a later point. Would you provide me with such lessons, Miss Ciardi?"

More interpreting work—sort of. But Ulysses Patterson wouldn't be a docile pupil. "I'm not qualified to be an ASL instructor. I could recommend some people."

"No, I want you. You've mastered the subject, and you're not an arrogant fool. In my opinion, that's all that's required for instruction. I prefer taking lessons from you to taking my chances with a stranger who's accumulated the prescribed number of credit hours in preparing lesson plans and assessing student progress. Will you do it?"

I scrambled to think of something intelligent to say, failed, and settled on the truth. "I'm not sure I can. Mr. Patterson, you intimidate me."

"That's unfortunate," he said, "not insurmountable. I do want to learn to communicate with Rosa, Miss Ciardi. Two days ago, I nearly lost her. If you hadn't been there, I *would* have lost her. I'm grateful to you, but also frightened. If Rosa had felt she could speak to me—or sign to me—I don't think she would have ended up in that situation. I don't want anything like that to happen again. Will you help me?"

I looked at his face—its stony intelligence so uncompromising, its strength so overwhelming. Yet it was a kind face, a good face, and, at least at this moment, a vulnerable face. I stood up.

"I will." I walked over to him. "I'll give you your first lesson now. This will be a free lesson, a short lesson. I'm going to teach you your first sign. All right?"

"All right," he said uneasily.

I took his right hand in mine. "You fold down your ring finger and your middle finger. See? And you leave your other fingers and your thumb up. It combines the American Sign Language handshapes for 'I,' 'L,' and 'Y.' You can use it to greet Rosa when she comes home tonight."

He looked down at his hand, then up at me. "And what does it mean?"

"It means 'I love you,'" I said. "Thank you again for dinner, Mr. Patterson. Good night."

He nodded, and I walked away from him. When I reached the door to his study, I looked back and saw him sitting at his big desk, circled by soft lamplight, surrounded by his many books, practicing his first sign.

THE END

ACKNOWLEDGEMENTS

This novel is dedicated to the memory of Cathleen Jordan, editor of *Alfred Hitchcock's Mystery Magazine* from 1981 until her untimely death in 2002. In 1987, Cathleen accepted a short story of mine called "True Detective." That was the first piece of fiction I ever published, and it was the beginning of my long, happy association with the magazine. If Cathleen hadn't taken an interest in my work, I would have given up on mystery writing decades ago. I will always be grateful for her encouragement and good advice. Since 2002, editor Linda Landrigan has provided the magazine with strong leadership, insisting on excellence (yes, I still get rejections sometimes) while always treating writers with kindness and respect. I'm greatly indebted to Linda, too, and to Jackie Sherbow and the others who have helped her keep *AHMM* at the top of its field. It strikes me as deeply appropriate that the protagonist of *Interpretation of Murder* was introduced in an *AHMM* story. I can't say how proud I am to be an *Alfred Hitchcock's Mystery Magazine* author.

I'm also proud that I'm now a Black Opal Books author, too. Many people have contributed to this novel, including Lauri Wellington, LP Norris, Faith, Mike, and Jack. I'm grateful to all of them for their hard work and expert guidance, and I'm delighted that *Interpretation of Murder* found a home with Black Opal Books.

I owe special thanks to Sarah Gershone, N.I.C., a nationally certified American Sign Language interpreter who guided the manuscript of *Interpretation of Murder* through several drafts, generously sharing her expertise not only about sign language and deaf culture but also about characters, plot, dialogue, and so much else. Sarah is a gifted fiction writer as well as a dedicated and knowledgeable interpreter. Her contributions to the novel are too many to count.

Many people in the mystery community also helped by reading and critiquing drafts, providing advice on everything from plotting problems to legal issues, and giving me support and encouragement when I needed them most. I don't dare single anyone out by name, since for every person I'd mention, I'd be sure to leave a dozen out. But I owe a great deal to the consistently perceptive and generous Sisters in Crime Guppies, to my good friends at the Mid-Atlantic chapter of Mystery Writers of America, to the sometimes contentious but always lively crew at the Short Mystery Fiction Society, and to the usual suspects at Malice Domestic.

I owe even more to my family. My daughters, Sarah and Rachel, read drafts willingly, making many valuable comments and suggestions. They were a tremendous help, as well as an unfailing source of enthusiasm. Rachel, who worked part-time at an upscale fitness center for several years, also provided insights and information that contributed to the fictional Elise Reed Center. As always, though, my greatest debt is to my husband, Dennis Stevens. We met when we were students at Kenyon College; ever since then, he's been the center of my life, my best advisor and firmest supporter. It seems almost trivial to say that, as a fifth-degree black belt in *sogu ryu bujutsu*, he supplied all the martial arts expertise in the novel. He's done so much more than that, helping to shape *Interpretation of Murder* from the day I started taking notes through the final editing. His insights into human nature have strengthened the novel immeasurably, and his faith in me has kept me going when I felt like giving up. For that, and for so much else, I will always be grateful.

About the Author

B.K. Stevens grew up in Buffalo, New York and met her future husband, Dennis, on her first day of classes at Kenyon College in Ohio. They got married two weeks after graduation and, since then, have lived in seven different states and ten cities and towns. Her favorite was Cleveland, which provides the setting for her debut novel with Black Opal Books, *Interpretation of Murder*.

For many years, Stevens was an English professor, writing mystery stories whenever she could pry a few minutes free. She's published over forty short stories, most in *Alfred Hitchcock's Mystery Magazine*. One story was nominated for Agatha and Macavity awards, and another won a suspense-writing contest judged by Mary Higgins Clark. A 2010 *Hitchcock* story introduced American Sign Language interpreter Jane Ciardi, the protagonist of *Interpretation of Murder*. That story won a Derringer from the Short Mystery Fiction Society.

Currently, Stevens and her husband live in central Virginia. They have two daughters, Sarah and Rachel. When Dennis became a dean and finances got easier, Stevens decided she'd graded all the freshman compositions any human being really needs to grade. She's taking a break from teaching to focus on writing. If all goes well, the shift may become permanent.